Henry Kingsley

Leighton Court

A Country House Story

Henry Kingsley

Leighton Court
A Country House Story

ISBN/EAN: 9783337151355

Printed in Europe, USA, Canada, Australia, Japan

Cover: Foto ©Andreas Hilbeck / pixelio.de

More available books at **www.hansebooks.com**

LEIGHTON COURT

HENRY KINGSLEY'S NOVELS.

Uniform edition.   16mo, price per volume, $1.00.

RAVENSHOE.   Two volumes.

AUSTIN ELLIOT.   One volume.

THE RECOLLECTIONS OF GEOFFRY HAMLYN.
     Two volumes.

LEIGHTON COURT.   One volume.

A COUNTRY HOUSE STORY

BY

HENRY KINGSLEY

NEW YORK

CHARLES SCRIBNER'S SONS

1895

LEIGHTON COURT

Part 1

Chapter I

THE River Wysclith, though one of the shortest in course of the beautiful rivers of Dartmoor, still claims a high place among them. None sooner quits the barren granite, and begins to wander seaward through the lower and richer country which lies between the Moor and the sea. None except Dart sends a larger body of water to the sea, and none forms a smaller or less dangerous estuary.

Indeed, its course is so exceedingly short, that the members of the Wysclith Vale Hunt, whose kennels were within a mile of the sea, were well acquainted, from frequent observation, with the vast melancholy bog in which it took its rise. More than once, more than twenty times, within the memory of old Tom Squire, the lean, little old huntsman, had the fox been run into in the midst of that great waste of turbary, from whence the infant stream issues; on ground which no man, leave alone a horse, dared to face. Laura Seckerton has a clever sketch in her portfolio, of the wild, desolate, elevated swamp as it appeared on one of these occasions. A sweep of yellow grass, interspersed with ling, and black bog pits : in the centre, far away from human help, a confused heap of struggling hounds killing their fox : round the edges, as near as they dared go, red-coated horsemen, most cleverly grouped in twos and threes ; beyond all, a low ugly tor of

I

weather-worn granite. Laura Seckerton could paint as
well as she could ride, which is giving her very high praise
indeed.

On a hot summer's day, if you had crossed the watershed
from the northward, from the head-waters of the Ouse for
instance; and if you found yourself in this desolate lonely
swamp, with no signs of animal life except the cry of the
melancholy peewit, or the quaint dull note of the stone-
chat; you would find it hard to believe that anything so
wild, fierce, and loud as the river Wysclith, could be born
of such solitary silence. But if you hold on your way,
round the bases of the low granite tors, between the tumbled rocks and the quaking bog, for four or five miles, you
will begin, afar off, to hear a tinkling of waters, you will
meet a broad amber-coloured stream, and find that the
many trickling rills from the great swamp have united, and
are quietly preparing for their journey to the sea; are making for that gap in the granite, below which the land drops
away into an unknown depth, and from which you can see
a vista of a gleaming glen miles below, in which the river,
so quiet and so small up here, spouts and raves and roars
like a giant as he is. Right and left, far, far below you,
are crags, tors, castles of granite. Twenty streams from
fifty glens, from a hundred sunny lonely hills, join our
river far below; until tired of fretting and fuming among
the granite crags in the glen of ten thousand voices, he
finds his way out into the champaign country, and you see
him wandering on in wide waving curves towards his estuary. All this you can see even on a blighty easterly day;
with a clear south wind, Laura Seckerton used to say, that
standing within two miles of the river's source, you can
make out the fisher boats on the sands at its mouth, and
the setting sun blazing on the windows of Leighton Court,
which stands on a knoll of new red sandstone at the head
of the tideway. I cannot say that either there or elsewhere
I have ever distinguished drawing-room windows at a distance of eighteen miles as the crow flies: but I confess to

have seen the vast tower and dark long façade of Berry Morecombe, which lies on the other side of the river, blocking the westerly sun and casting a long shadow over the sands towards Leighton Court, when I have stood on a summer's evening at the tip of the lonely marsh in which the Wysclith takes his rise, fifteen hundred feet above the sea. Standing just where he begins to live, and whimper like a new-born babe over his granite rocks.

Chapter II

THERE were only three families in this part of the country: the Downes, the Seckertons, and the Poyntzs. We shall meet them all directly; but it is necessary even here to say that the Downes (represented by Sir Peckwich Downes) were eminently respectable and horribly rich. That the Seckertons (Sir Charles Seckerton) were eminently respectable, very rich, though not so rich as the Downes; but that they had entirely taken the wind out of their, Downes', sails, by Sir Charles marrying Lady Emily Lee, a sister of the Earl of Southmolton, and by taking the hounds nearly at the same time. And lastly, coming to the Poyntzs (represented by Sir Harry Poyntz, younger by a generation than either of the other baronets), we are obliged to say that the family had grown so utterly disreputable, that a respectable Poyntz was considerably rarer than a white crow. The third family, these Poyntzs, were what the Americans call " burst up," and their seat, Berry Morecombe Castle, was now let on a lease to Mr. Huxtable, a Manchester cotton-spinner.

Sir William Poyntz, that very disreputable old gentleman, had been the last master of the hounds, and had handsomely finished his ruin by taking them. He was a sad old fellow, and kept a sad establishment there in the castle. The only signs of decency which the old fellow showed, was that he would not allow any of his sons, legitimate or other, to come near the place. Harry Poyntz, now the baronet, used to come and stay at Leighton Court; Robert, the younger, was only dimly remembered by a few of the older servants, as a petulant, wayward, handsome child. There was a third one yet, whom some remembered, a very beautiful, winning boy; but he had no name, he was not acknowledged.

When Sir Charles Seckerton took the hounds, Mr. Huxtable took the castle, and very shortly after the wife of the latter died, leaving him with a little girl, heir to all his wealth. Sir William Poyntz left Sir Charles Seckerton a legacy also; he left him old Tom Squire, the huntsman. He was a silent, terrier-faced little fellow, who seemed to know more than he chose to tell, as indeed he did. He was a jewel, however; he had hunted that difficult country for many years, and if you had not taken him with the hounds, you might as well have left the hounds alone.

A very difficult hunting country. Why, yes. Irish horses strongly in request, not to mention Irish whips and second horsemen. A stone-wall country in part, and in part intersected by deep lanes and high hedges. Not a safe or promising country by any means. Bad accidents were not unknown; one very severe one had but recently happened, just before my tale begins. The first whip, a young Irishman, O'Ryan by name, had ridden into one of those deep red lanes, which intersect the new red sandstone hereabouts, and had so injured his spine as to be a cripple probably for life. Sir Charles had pensioned him with a pound a week; and being determined to try an Englishman this time, wrote to a friend in Leicestershire for a first-rate man, fit to succeed old Tom Squire, the wiry terrier-faced ex-Poyntz retainer aforesaid, as huntsman, when he should retire to the chimney-corner, and twitter on the legends of the Poyntz family till he twittered no longer.

An answer had come by return of post. There had

never been such a chance as now, wrote Sir George Herage. A young man, possessed of all the cardinal virtues, with several to spare; who was the most consummate rider ever seen, could tell the pedigree of a hound with one moment's glance, of gentle temper with man, horse, and dog. A young man who had hunted not only in Leicestershire and Berwickshire, but at Pau; a young man entirely up to every conceivable sort of country. Such a young man was To Let. And Sir George Herage's advice was, " Snap him up on any price; the more especially as he has expressed to me strongly his intense anxiety to improve his already great experience by hunting in that very county of yours; indeed, has given me warning the instant he heard of your want." On further examination of Sir George's letter, it appeared that this young Crichton, Bayard, Philip Sidney, St. Huberts' price was extremely moderate, considering his amazing virtues and talents. His very name, too, sounded well, Hammersley. Sir George was also anxious to impress on his friend's mind the fact that he was no ordinary person; that he was a deuced presentable fellow, and a fellow who would not stand much talking to, but was perfect at his work. Sir Charles thought himself in luck, and passed the letter over the breakfast table to Lady Emily, his wife, to see what *she* thought of it: by no means an unimportant matter.

Lady Emily was making a somewhat witch-like mess in a china basin, the basis of which was chocolate. Sir Charles had seen her put in sugar, brown bread, baked yam, and cream, and began to wonder when she would begin to eat it. She delayed her pleasure, however, and he grew impatient.

" Emily," said Sir Charles at last, " I wish, when you have gone through your morning ceremonies with your olla podrida, that you would look at that letter."

" My love," she said, " I will do so directly." And she went on with her preparations quite regardless of the impatient exasperated way in which Sir Charles tore the *Times* open, pitched the supplement on the ground, and rattled the other part open.

At last she had done. She read the letter steadily, put it down again, and gazed into space.

" Well," said Sir Charles, testily, " will that man do or no ? "

" I do wonder," she said, with her great, cool, high-bred voice; "now I really do wonder."

" I wonder at our luck in getting such a man at such a time," said Sir Charles.

" I don't mean that," said Lady Emily. " I wonder what on earth this paragon of a creature has been doing which makes Sir George Herage so exceeding anxious to foist him off upon us, and get him three hundred miles out of his own way. That is what I am wondering at."

" You look on it in that light, do you, Emily ? " said Sir Charles.

" I wonder," said Lady Emily, going on in her own line, " whether the fellow is good-looking, and has been making love to one of those red-haired, horse-breaking Herage girls. That is it, depend on it. Not another word, Charles—here comes Laura.

" My dear mother, good morning."

" You think he ought to come, then, Emily ? " said Sir Charles. " You think he will do ? "

" My dear Charles ! Do ! Such a paragon of a creature ! The question is not whether he will do, but what he has been doing. I have the deepest curiosity to see the man. I suppose he will take his meals with us : what rooms shall I get ready for him ? "

" Then he had better come ? "

" It is not in my line at all to say yes or no. If my personal wishes were consulted, I should say let him come. You seem to have collected all the available rogues and fools in the South of Devon about your stable and kennel, and I am getting tired of them. I want to see a rogue from another county for a change. Have the man down."

" My dearest Emily, why are you so disagreeable this morning ? "

" I did not mean to be so to you, Charles," said his wife, kissing him as she passed him. " Since you have taken me out of society, I have no one to whet my tongue on but you, you selfish man. And it *is* rather cool of Sir George Herage to try and foist off a man, who evidently has made the country too hot to hold him, on to us."

" But, Emily dear, I won't have him if you think so."

" Have him down, Charles, by all means have him down."

And so the paragon Hammersley came. And no one having said anything against it, it must be supposed that everyone was perfectly satisfied. But Lady Emily determined to find out the reason of this wonderful recommendation of Sir George Herage, or perish in the attempt. She neither did the one thing or the other at first ; but she was not easily to be beaten.

Her sister, Lady Melton, on being appealed to by letter, at first could find out nothing more about the young man than that Sir George Herage had picked him up at Pau, where he was hunting the hounds during the illness of the huntsman, and had brought him home ; that he certainly understood his business in a masterly way, but was uncivil, loutish, quarrelsome, and rode very little under twelve stone. Lady Melton added that she had never seen the young man, that he had never appeared with the Quorn; and that was all she knew about him.

Chapter III

I HAVE described the lay of the country as you look from the mountain down to the sea, and will describe for you directly the appearance of that country, looking up from the tideway towards the mountain, from the terraces of Leighton Court. But my eye rests on something in the immediate foreground which arrests it.

I find I cannot describe the dark, purple moor, with Wysclith leaping from rock to rock down its side, without first getting rid of two figures in the foreground. From the terraces of Leighton Court, which surround the house east, seaward, and westward, one looks over the sandbars of the river, here beginning to spread into its little estuary, on to the red country, beyond on to the flashing cascades of the river; above all on to the dark, black-blue moor. But there are two figures in the foreground, which seem to impersonate the scenery, and being animate, they must be looked to first.

Lady Emily stands nearest to us. A large, handsome, gipsy-looking woman, whose real age was five-and-forty, but whose constant good humour, and the fact of her having had her own way both in the county and in her family, for some twenty years, caused to look ten years younger. She was a noble, kindly, nay jolly-looking woman, so very like the nearer parts of the landscape; so rich in colour, so bold in rounded outlines.

If Lady Emily stood well as a central figure to the blazing reds and greens of the fertile red sandstone country, her daughter might well represent to our fancy, the dark purple moor which hung aloft in the distance, furrowed by deep rifts which in their darkest depths showed the gleams of the leaping torrent; and yet which, through ten miles of atmosphere, seemed little more than a perpendicular plane, without cape or bay, prominence or depth. She was a little taller than her mother, her face though like her mother's, was more refined, with the refinement of youth; her face might get a trifle coarser by age (who knows?), or might be swept by storms of passion; but at present, she was as placid, as delicately tinted, as lofty, and apparently a thousand times more unapproachable, than the mountain on which she gazed.

People tell one that at the end of the last century there was a school or party among people of rank, whose *specialité* was the extreme care with which they educated their women—a party who hailed Mrs. Hannah More as their leader and example. Very few of us have so little experience of life, as not to have seen and respected one of the old ladies thus trained, and to reflect, one hopes, on the very great deal we owe to them and to their influence. None of us, however, have probably had the luck to see a more perfect specimen of this type of lady than was the old Countess of Southmolton, the bosom friend of Hannah More, grandmother of Laura Seckerton, whose gentle influence was still felt in her daughter's house. She had formed Lady Emily upon the most perfect model, and Lady Emily had fully answered her expectations, but partly from the natural vivacity of her disposition, and partly from her having married a sporting baronet, she had become a trifle corrupted; so that her manners, beside her more sedate mother, appeared almost brusque and jovial. She, however, had vast reverence for her mother, and for her mother's system. And so Laura had been brought up, not so much by her mother as by her grandmother, in the very straightest mode of Queen Charlottism.

And she had taken to the style of thing kindly enough. As a child she was too slow and dreamy, too "good," as her grandmother would have said, to make any flat rebellion, and as she grew up, her grandmother, as having more talent, attracted her perhaps more than her mother; besides the style of thing suited her. She was idle and dreamy, and she liked rules for life ; and such wells of passion as were in her were as yet unruffled by any wind. So it was that her manner was far more staid, and her habits of thought far narrower than those of her mother.

A grand, imperial, graceful-looking girl, with a Greek face, bearing not much colour, and an imperial diadem of dark black hair, dark as the moor after a thunderstorm ; was there a fault in her face ? Only one ; the mouth was rather large.

Chapter IV

THESE two figures were so very prominent, as being perhaps the only two things visible in the landscape I have in my mind's eye, that I could see nothing, or make you see nothing, till they were disposed of. We will soon have done with the rest of the landscape, at which the reader will possibly rejoice.

Leighton Court was what is generally called Tudor, of a sort ; stone-built, mullions and transoms of granite. Length 105 ft., depth 52 ft. It was very like Baliol, uncommonly like Oriel, and a perfect replicat of University. It stood near the extreme end of a promontory of the red country, some 400 acres in extent, and say 100 ft. in extreme height, densely wooded, down to the very shore : which divided the little estuary of the Wysclith from the larger estuary of the Avon.

An old Tudor house, say, standing on a promontory of red rock, feathered with deep green woods, whose base lost itself in an ocean of wide-spreading sea sand. As you looked towards the sea from the hill landward of the house, you saw narrow sandy Wysclith on your right, broad sandy Avon on your left ; the house deep bosomed in feathering woods, which ran down and fringed the sands, in front, and beyond sands and sands bounded by the blue Channel with toiling ships.

Leighton Court

Wysclith, on your right, made but a small estuary, hardly could carry the tide a mile above the house, for he had to make the sea between the rib of sandstone on which Leighton Court stood, and another higher rib, three hundred yards to the westward, on the summit to which stood the great Norman keep of Morecombe Castle, which, at the equinoxes, threw its long shadow across the narrow tideway, and in March and September, at sunset, lay the shade of its tallest battlements on the smooth shorn turf of Leighton Court pleasance. At those two periods of the year when the sun was due west, and began to darken towards his setting, the tower of the keep of Morecombe seemed to hang minatory and darkly over its more peaceful neighbour the hall; but at all other times the castle was a thing of beauty for the inhabitants of the Court. At morn it rose a column of grey, tinged with faint orange; at noon pure pearl grey with purplish shadows; in the evening dark leaden colour, with the blaze of the sunset behind it, and its shadow barring the narrow river, and creeping towards the feet of those who sat on the terrace of the Court.

The river just began to narrow in opposite Leighton Court and Morecombe Castle, and not a quarter of a mile up, left creeping among sandbars and took to chafing among vast shingle beds. There is no town on the river, only the big red village of South Wyston round a turn in the river. So you looked up a reach in the river, feathered with wood and ribbed with reddish purple rocks, up to the cornfields, wooded hedgerows and woodlands of the red country, and above and beyond at the blue brown moor, with young Wysclith raving down in a hundred cascades through a rift in the granite.

Chapter V

PROFOUND as was Sir Charles' respect for his wife, and his reverence for his mother-in-law, there was one point in Laura's education on which, once for all, he had so coolly and calmly opposed them, that they, like sensible women, knew he was in earnest, and gave up the contest there and then.

Laura was to learn to ride; nay, oh Shade of Hannah More! to hunt. He was so very distinct about this, the first point on which he had ever opposed them, that they —knowing that although he was so easy going to them, yet had among men the character of being a resolute, valiant man—gave away at once, and did not even openly protest.

Laura was strong and healthy, and got very fond indeed of the sport. One need hardly say that under Sir Charles' tuition she turned out a first-rate horsewoman. The country was a difficult, nay dangerous country, but then, with its continually recurring copses, it was a very slow country, by no means a bad country for a lady who knew every gap, low stile, and gate, for ten miles round; a better country, for a lady, perhaps, than faster countries nearer London, certainly easier than Leicestershire.

So she got very fond of the sport, and if the pace got too great for her, there was nothing to prevent her riding home alone. Mr. Sponge, not to mention Mr. Jorrocks, don't make hunting tours in the West. There were no strangers for her to meet, except perhaps an officer or so from Plymouth. And very few officers were at Plymouth many weeks without making her father's acquaintance, so that of real strangers there were none. She very much enjoyed the times when she got thrown out among the stone-walls, and had to ride home alone through the deep lanes, dreaming.

Dreaming! What could she do but dream? When she sat on her horse alone, on the hill which lay half-way between the sea and the moor, she looked round on the widest horizon she had ever seen. She had heard of a great world which roared and whirled beyond that horizon; but she had never seen it, or seen a glimpse of it with her own eyes. She heard her grandmother and her mother talking of this world; she had been expressly trained, carefully trained, for moving in this world. She could have gone, with her training and her nerve, into the best drawing-room in London, or more, in Paris, and have found herself perfectly at home. Lady Southmolton confessed that she was perfectly formed; but meanwhile they could not go to London this year, and then they couldn't go next year. Sir Charles was hard to move, and the hounds had cost a deal of money—a great deal too much money, indeed.

So she heard of the world only from without. She heard her grandmother and her mother talking of the great governors of the country, and the great givers of parties, which were reported in the *Times*, most familiarly; heard a great Liberal nobleman talked of as " dear Henry," and came to the conclusion that if dear Henry had taken her grandmother's advice, things would not have come to the present dead-lock. She heard these two women continually living in the past among the great men they had danced with, growing more familiar in the mention of their names as time went on, expanding and developing their legends and recollections about these people, and egging one another on until a doubtful recollection became an article of faith, and a third-hand story became a personal experience. She heard all this, and possibly laughed at it. But she knew well that her mother had known the War God, and sometimes she thought it rather tiresome that she could not know him also.

She heard of the world, too, a very different world from the soldiers and sailors who came over to them from

Plymouth. Her mother startled her one night by telling her, that of all the sailors and soldiers she had ever entertained for the space of twenty years, Captain Fitzgorman was the only one who had ever thoroughly known the great world. She was startled, for she had set him down as the dullest and most unmitigated noodle she had ever had inflicted on her; a man who could talk about lords and ladies, their marryings and intermarryings, and nothing else. She had asked her mother not to ask him again.

" My dear, he knows the world ! "

" He knows the peerage," said Laura peevishly ; " and I don't want to have the peerage talked to me. If I want to know anything out of the peerage, I get it down and refer to it. He seems to have got it up. I listened to him, and you, and grandma to-night, until I was sick. The whole conversation amounted to a competitive examination on those sort of people. And while we are on the subject, allow me to tell you, having listened through curiosity, that you got considerably the worst of it. That noodle was better up in that particular kind of talk than the pair of you put together."

Jovial Lady Emily had to stand on her dignity.

" Because I withdrew myself from the world when I married your dear father, I cannot see that it is becoming for my daughter to cast in my teeth my forgetfulness of the world."

Though her grammar was involved, as it always was when she tried to be grand, Laura did not laugh at it. She only said good-humouredly—

" Well, mother, I may be wrong, but it seems to me ridiculous for a younger son to talk about nothing but his own and other people's connections."

She had a sharper arrow in her quiver than that for young " Fitz ; " but who could snarl or say a bitter thing in the presence of her genial mother, who kissed her, called her a radical, and went to bed.

Laura, you see, did not believe in the *grand monde*. She believed that the real great world was the wide world the sailors and soldiers told her of. West Coast of Africa, India, and all that sort of thing, which the reader may supplement, out of the history of these wonderful thirty millions of islanders who have seized on the strongest and richest parts of the world, according to his fancy. But this world was as much shut out to her as the London world, and she was thrown on to her own, a very small one, more the pity.

The peasantry were all her world. Poor visiting had always been one of the rules of the family, and Laura took to it not unkindly. She got to love the people, she understood their wants, she excused their faults, and got more deeply, than she was aware, imbued with their superstitions.

Chapter VI

LORD HATTERLEIGH was a young man of great promise, aged twenty-two, who wore goloshes, carried a bulgy umbrella, and took dinner pills.

Generally he took them in the hall, getting a confidential glass of water from the butler. But if he had been somewhat late, and had forgot them, he would have no hesitation in taking them after his soup, or even after his fish, before an admiring dinner-table. Lord Hatterleigh's inside was the most wonderful inside ever known. It was a complicated and delicate piece of machinery, which required continual oiling. He was exceedingly proud of it. Two or three doctors had set it right for him, but he found himself somewhat lost if it was not out of order. A subject of conversation was lost to him. He could talk peerage by the yard; he could pipe out feeble wishy-washy politics by the hour; but to the dearest friends of his heart he always led the conversation to his inside.

It was a great joke in the county for some time, that Lord Hatterleigh had appointed Sam Bolton his chaplain, because Bolton had a complication in his liver or somewhere, nearly as fine as the hitch in Lord Hatterleigh's "ilia." It was notorious, and what is very different, perfectly true, that he was very fond of Samuel Bolton, and that they would sit up half the night comparing their symptoms. Sam Bolton was the most intimate friend he had, and it was as plain as the nose on one's face, that as soon as the present rector dropped, Lord Hatterleigh would give him the living of Hatterleigh to keep him near him. Sam Bolton got engaged on the strength of it. The Rector himself, a lean old gentleman, a bishop's man, who preached in his surplice, turned to the east at the Creed, and in spite of it kept his church full, recognised him as his successor.

" When I am gone, my dear Mr. Bolton," he would say, " you will find that the dilapidation money will hardly make the house fit for a family man. You are going to marry, and you will have to build, sir, you will have to build."

The Rector "dropped" suddenly, through attending a typhus case on a fast day without a good dinner and a glass of port, but Sam Bolton never was Rector of Hatterleigh. Lord Hatterleigh wrote off to Dr. Arnold to send him the best available parson he could lay his hands on. Dr. Arnold did so, and the Rector of Hatterleigh was not Sam Bolton.

Sam Bolton sulked, and at last one evening grew pathetic, nay, got near to a state of injured indignation.

" I never promised you the living, Bolton," said his lordship, nursing his big knee. " I like you very much, but I don't think you are fit for it. Besides, your digestion, my dear fellow, your digestion !"

A high-minded man enough, this Lord Hatterleigh, always putting before him, according to his light, a lofty ideal, and fighting up to it with the obstinacy of a mule and the cunning of a fox. The world called him false and untrustworthy, but if you catechised the world, you would find that he had never departed from his pledged word, and had never disappointed hopes which he himself had given.

He had tried Rugby, but his health wouldn't stand it (so said he and his grandmother). He had gone to a great private tutor's and had read continuously and diligently (as for reading *hard*, it was not in the man) and in due time had made his appearance in Peckwater. Here he was recognised at once as a young man of great promise. He could, give him a bottle of water, talk you washy politics by the yard, by the hour. But the union, most patient of assemblées, very soon got impatient of him, and certain square-headed, bright-eyed, young rascals from Balliol and University began to make terrible mince-meat of him. Still he was a young nobleman of promise.

Of great promise but of little performance; he was so very steady and studious that outsiders put him down for all sorts of degrees, treble first, said some, for he had sent a gigantic order to Shrimpton for chemical and geological books, and was evidently going in to win. But after dandering about the University for three years, he got a bad fourth in classics and merely passed in the other schools. After which, he transferred himself and his talents to his paternal acres and the House of Lords. On his own estates he did his duty manfully and well. In the House of Lords he spoke on the Address and none afterwards. He found he was out of his depth, and had the sense to float without trying to swim. Most likely his failure at Oxford had done him good. There he had been measured with a moiety of the talent of the country, and had failed. I think that in his way he understood this.

But with perfect good temper. If he was sly, it was only through a kind of half physical, half nervous cowardice. There was none of the cat-like bitterness of the real coward about him. He hated a scene beyond all things, but he would face a scene, and go through with it to the end if one of his principles was at stake, and *win*. Temper! his temper was angelic, so long as he had not lost his umbrella, mislaid his goloshes, or forgot his dinner pills ; and then his temper only showed itself in a kind of plaintive peevishness. When any one of these three things happened, Laura could always bring him into good temper again. The rules of society prevented her talking over his complaints with him, but she could talk genealogies and marriages with so many mistakes as to rouse him into animation to set her right, and she was fond of the poor creature. She was very tender to the village idiot, too, and had prevented the boys from bullying him into madness many times. Lord Hatterleigh had seen her but from childhood, and Laura had never cared to look for such finer qualities as there might be in him. They used to call him Ursa Major.

Chapter VII

THE little affair of Assewal scarcely deserves to be called a battle, it was merely a prelude ; nay, not even that, only a tuning of fiddles for the " Grand Devil's Opera," which crashed and roared so late into the next day that the last mutter of it was heard as the sinking sun flamed upon the Eastern ghaut ; and night, and silence, only half-broken by the low wails and moans of the wounded, settled down upon another great field, whose name henceforth is one of the landmarks of history.

Yet a remarkable thing happened there. The advance-guard of the enemy, as well as one can understand, were in a strongish position, on the other side of a nullah, and were keeping up an infernal fire of artillery at a native regiment of ours, which was only half sheltered by a roll in the ground. It was absolutely necessary that this regiment should stay in its present position, for it was the extreme of our left flank in that little affair, and our general was engaged in turning their left flank, and forcing them into that disadvantageous position in which they gave us battle the next day, and got so terribly beaten.

Sir Charles had deputed the work to be done on his right to three or four men whose names have since been burnt deep into the memories of their countrymen, and therefore he knew that the work on the right was being as efficiently done as if he had been there himself.

It was necessary, however, for the Eagle's eye to watch this left flank, which was our weakest place. And so the Eagle was there with his great hooked beak stretched towards the enemy, from time to time shaking out his ruffled feathers ready to swoop and strike.

As he was. The 140th Dragoons were behind the tope in which he stood; and if the Sikh artillery did not soon feel the pressure which he was putting on their left, it would become necessary to hurl our cavalry at this artillery, and silence it with the loss of half of one of our best regiments.

No one could doubt that. The plain — more correctly the glacis—which lay between the Sikh artillery and the half-concealed native regiment in the lower ground, was being ripped and torn and riven by their furious cannonade. Life, even for a single individual, seemed to be impossible there. What would be the fate of seven hundred close-packed horsemen—Thermopylæ or Balaclava?

Some of the shot were reaching the native regiment, and they were getting fidgety. If they could be kept there until the pressure on the enemy's left was felt? If the sacrifice of the 140th could be saved? But a good many shot had come ripping in on the flank companies, which were exposed on each side of the roll in the ground, and they were getting unsteady.

"Go and tell him to draw his flank companies behind the ridge," he said, and turning found himself face to face with a cornet of the 140th, a handsome pensive-looking boy, who by some accident had been sent up to him with a message.

The boy, a scarlet-and-gold thing, all over golden fripperies and tags and bobtails, topped with a white pith helmet, a very beautiful and expensive article (receiving one-third the pay of a Staffordshire iron-puddler), went jingling down the hill and passed behind the native regiment till he came to the Colonel. They saw him deliver his message, and thought he was coming back again.

So he was, but by a very queer route. He rode past the left flank of the wavering regiment, and then, mounting the hill, turned, and came coolly jingling back at a sling trot over that terrible plain slope, which was being ripped and torn and sent into the air in all directions by the enemy's shot, and on which human life appeared impossible. Fountains and showers of stones and sand were rising and falling all around him as he rode, but he came coolly clanking on, and while the staff were expecting to see him cut in two every instant, he managed to knock his helmet off.

He stopped, dismounted, picked it up, put it on hindside before, altered it, and prepared to mount. His horse was restive, and he gave it a good-natured little kick in the ribs, got on again, and came jangling slowly up to the tope where the Eagle was posted. The Eagle never liked that sort of thing. He was very angry; he shook his feathers and opened on him.

" Are you a Frenchman, sir, that you play these Tom-fool's games under fire? Do you know, sir, that your life is your country's, sir, and that death is a very solemn thing? Do you know, that if it were not for an extraordinary instance of God's mercy, you would be lying howling and dying in the grass yonder? What did you do it for ; eh, sir ? "

The boy looked at him with his great melancholy eyes, and said—

" The 84th seemed getting unsteady, sir; and I thought I would show them that it was not so bad as it looked."

"Hem! that is another matter. That is a different affair altogether. You have acted with great valour and discretion; you have done a noble deed at the right time. Such actions as yours, sir, elevate the tone of the army, and deserve to live in the mouths of men for ever. What is your name?"

"George Hilton."

"He is Jack's boy," said a general who stood near.

"Why couldn't you have said so before?" snapped out the Eagle.

"Because I didn't want to spoil the fun of hearing you make a set complimentary speech to Jack's boy. Fancy such a torrent of fervid eloquence being poured out on *his* head. It's as good as a play."

The great warrior was very much amused, and held out his hand to the lad.

"You are at your father's tricks, are you, you monkey? Go back to your regiment. I shall write to your mother."

And so he did, and kept his eye on the boy. Young George Hilton soon changed into an infantry regiment, partly because his mother had lost some money, and partly because his patron and his father's friend wished it. In time his patron died; but he fought his way steadily on through the weary nights of 1854, through the dark and terrible hour of 1855, leaving his mark on everything he undertook, and getting his name well known, not only at the Horse Guards, but to the most careless of the general public. Here we find him now on the terrace beside Laura. Colonel Hilton, C.B., V.C., a tall man of remarkable personal beauty, with a dark-brown beard, and large melancholy eyes; and with a low-pitched, but singularly distinct voice. A dangerous man for any girl to listen to, among the lengthening summer twilight shadows, particularly after having had Lord Hatterleigh gobbling and spluttering out insane political twaddle the whole evening.

Chapter VIII

" AND how do you like Cain, my love ? " said Lady Emily, sweeping in full-dressed into Sir Charles' dressing-room, just as he was tying his cravat for dinner.

" Cain, my dear ? "

" The new young man."

" Why do you call him Cain ? "

" Because he must have murdered his brother, or something as bad, to get such a good recommendation. Don't you see, you foolish old man, that if what Sir George Herage says about him is in any way true, he would sooner have pulled out his few remaining teeth than part with him ? I hope we shan't have our throats cut."

" I thought you called yourself a Christian," growled Sir Charles.

" I was under the same impression myself," laughed Lady Emily.

" Then why do you go on comparing an innocent young man to Judas Iscariot ? "

" I did not compare him to Judas Iscariot. I compared him to Cain."

" If Cain was such a splendid-looking fellow as he is, he was a remarkable man."

" Oh ! is he so very grand ? Does he talk well ? "

" He talks very little, and seems a little surly."

" Can he ride ? "

" Don't ask me. I have nearly broken my neck looking after him. Absolutely superb ! "

" Tell me some more about him."

" What makes you so eager ? "

" Never you mind ; are his manners good ? "

" Yes, I should say so. He is perfectly Tom Squire's master, by-the-bye. The fellow's London assurance has completely quelled the old man; he takes orders from his subordinate which he could never take from me."

"Now," said Lady Emily, "comes *my* turn. Suppose I was to tell you that I had found out all about him and refused to tell you."

"You know you couldn't keep it to yourself. I should hear all about it if I waited. Better tell it at once."

"I suppose I had. By-the-bye, this young gentleman's name will be George."

"It is so. How did you guess?"

"My love, I know all about everything. My sister has found it all out. You know that Sir William Poyntz had two sons, Harry and Bob?"

"Of course."

"Did you ever hear of a third, an illegitimate one?"

"I know there was such a son. The old man's favourite. Well?"

"This is the man."

"No! Is it, really? That is very strange."

"Sir Harry Poyntz has been in the neighbourhood and has told my sister everything. This George has been a sadly dissipated fellow."

"That is one of Harry's lies. The fellow's eye is as clear as mine," intercalated Sir Charles.

"Well, that is Sir Harry's account of the matter—very dissipated. He, it seemed, got hold of Robert Poyntz, now in India, and led him into all kinds of dissipation. All this brought on a serious misunderstanding between Sir Harry and his brother, and led to this George Hammersley being utterly ignored by Sir Harry, and sent to live on his wits. And that is your Adonis."

"The best thing about our Adonis seems to be his good looks and good manners, and the fact that Harry Poyntz has taken away his character."

"The last item is the most important," said Lady Emily. "I never knew Harry Poyntz tell the truth yet; did you?"

" Not I.   But Poyntz is coming here soon ; in six months,
I believe.   He refuses to renew Huxtable's lease.   What
will Adonis do then ? "

" That is distinctly his business," said Lady Emily.
" We shall see."

" I wonder why he left Leicestershire, this paragon,"
said Sir Charles, just as they got to the drawing-room
door.

" He admired, or was admired too much by one of the
Herage girls.   Don't say a word about that, it is not fair.
Laura will take uncommon good care that he don't make
love to her."

Chapter IX

" AND who is going to make love to our Laura ? " said
a little voice, very like a tiny chime of silver bells from the
other end of the room, as they entered.

There sat, all alone, a little old lady with a white lace
cap on her head, and a white lace shawl over her shoulders.   She wore her own grey hair, and her complexion
was nearly as delicate now as in her youth, but slightly
paler, and covered with tiny wrinkles, only visible when
one was quite close to her.   A most wonderfully beautiful
old lady (how beautiful old women can be), with a cheerful peaceful light in her face, which made one love her at
once : and yet with a look of complacent, self-possessed,
self-conscious goodness, too, which, after a time became
provoking, and which tempted outsiders and sinners to
contradict her, and to broach heretical opinions for the
mere sake of aggravation.

" And who is going to make love to our Laura ? " she
repeated.

Lady Emily would have done a great deal sooner than
have repeated before her mother the audacious joke she
had just made with her husband ; the old lady would have

been too painfully shocked at it ; she turned it off by a little fib.

" Oh, you can guess whom I mean, mamma. I hate mentioning names."

" Poor Ursa Major is terribly smitten, I fancy," said the old lady, smiling. " I am fond of Ursa Major. He comes of a good stock. All the Hortons are good. He will make the woman he marries very happy if she will only let him."

" Yes, he is a good match for any woman," said Lady Emily, seizing her opportunity with admirable quickness, and speaking in a free off-hand way, as though it was a mere abstract question. " He has sixty thousand a-year. He is very amiable and talented, and young. That is a great point. He is not beyond forming, and Laura would form him."

" Laura ! " shouted Sir Charles.

" My love, we are not deaf," said Lady Emily, with lofty quietness.

These two good ladies never *told* Sir Charles anything important, they always *broke* it to him, administered it in gentle doses, as beef tea is given to starving persons ; sometimes driving him half wild in the process. This seemed a fair occasion, though an accidental one, of " breaking " to Sir Charles the fact that Lord Hatterleigh was most undoubtedly smitten with Laura. They were considerably anxious, and had reason to be. But they did not show it.

" I beg pardon," said Sir Charles, " but you gave me such a start."

" I merely said," remarked Lady Emily, shutting her eyes, pulling the string, and letting off the cannon, bang ! —" that in case Laura married him, the excellent training she had received from her grandmother would——"

" Laura marry *him*, that Guy Fawkes booby ! What monstrous rubbish is this——"

" Would polish him, remove any little uncouthness, and so on," continued Lady Emily, with steady severity.

" She's a clever girl," cried Sir Charles, " but she will never make him anything but what he is, an awkward lop-sided gaby, the butt of every club he belongs to. Besides, the man is not a marrying man. There is something wrong with him. He keeps a doctor; and he has not had a proper education; he can't ride or shoot. He couldn't ride about with her. It would never do—shall never be. How could you dare to think of such a monstrous arrange-ment, Emily? But Laura can take care of herself, that is one comfort. There he comes himself, by all that's awkward ! "

Somebody was heard lumbering downstairs and objur-gating somebody else, in a voice compounded of a gobble and a growl. Some one slipped down the last two stairs. That it was the owner of the gorilla voice was evident from that voice exclaiming aloud, " Bless my soul, I have broken my back ! "

"Sweet youth," said Sir Charles, "I hope he won't cry."

Before Lord Hatterleigh had finished a plaintive wrangle with his valet, as to whether his slipping downstairs was his own or the valet's fault, two other people entered the drawing-room together—Laura and Colonel Hilton; a most splendid pair of people, indeed; they had evidently been saying something kindly wicked about Lord Hatter-leigh's accident, and were both smiling. He was slightly behind her, and being the tallest was bending towards her; she, saying the last word of their little joke, was turning her beautiful head back to him, and showing the soft curves of her splendid throat as though Millais were lying in wait for her. They were a wonderfully beautiful pair of people, and the three folks in the drawing-room were obliged to confess it.

Said Lady Southmolton to herself : " That would do, perhaps, under other circumstances. But he hasn't got any fortune, and she don't care for him, and never will. He flatters her too grossly and too openly, and she hates being flattered ; with all his personal beauty and his gallantry, she despises him. I could tell him how to win that girl, but I won't. He has neither birth nor money. That young man don't understand women of her stamp ; very few soldiers do."

Said Lady Emily : " I wish that could come about; he is so handsome and so good. But it can't. He has got no money, and what I can't understand is, that she don't like him. I wish he had Hatterleigh's money, and that she would fall in love with him." Two things which happened to be impossible.

Said Sir Charles : " Sometimes I wish the hounds were at the devil. If it was not for them I should be beforehand with the world, instead of getting behindhand year after year. I wish this fellow had Hatterleigh's money. But he hasn't. She is evidently in love with this fellow. (Was she, Sir Charles ? The mother and grandmother did not think so, and ladies are generally considered judges of that sort of thing.) I suppose it will end in her marrying that booby, the women seem set on it."

That was the way with Sir Charles and with a great many others ; a furious rebellion against the women, and then a dull sulky acquiescence. Stronger men than Sir Charles have been fairly beaten by female persistency. He gave up the battle, however, the moment he saw that the enemy were going to show fight. He hated the very sound of Lord Hatterleigh's voice. He had thought, half an hour ago, that the sacrifice of such a being as Laura to such a booby as Lord Hatterleigh, was a monstrous thing ; but—but Lord Hatterleigh was rich ; and if Laura, noble, honest Laura, could say she loved him, what had he to say ? It would be a great match, and so on, only there lurked in his heart a strong half-formed desire, that Laura would box his lordship's ears, the first moment he ventured to speak to her.

" Aha, my young lady," he said to himself, " I have no doubt you *would* give the hair off your head to have him talk to you in the tone he does to Laura. But you run after him too openly, my poor Maria."

This remark arose from the entrance of the Huxtables, father and daughter. Mr. Huxtable was a fine-looking North-countryman, and his daughter Maria a very fine specimen of a Lancashire lass, by no means unlike Laura, but coarser. Sir Charles, who was standing close to her, had noticed the shade of vexation which passed over her handsome face, when she saw Colonel Hilton bending over Laura, and made the above remark, which he supplemented by another.

"What fools soldiers are! There is Hilton dangling about after Laura, who don't care for him, and sixty thousand pounds ready to drop into his mouth."

The great mighty master of Tomfoolery, Levassor, blundering on to the stage with his breeches up to his ears, just as Rachel had drooped into one of her sublimest attitudes, could hardly have been a greater foil to her than was Lord Hatterleigh to Colonel Hilton; yet Laura left the Colonel directly, and going to the other, began kindly to laugh at him about his tumbling downstairs.

He was extremely flattered and pleased by her kindness, and held himself as gallantly as he could. He had made his valet take particular pains with his toilette, but as the valet had said to himself, it wasn't the fault of the clothes, but of the man inside them. He remained silent, only smiling radiantly until it became time to take Lady Emily in to dinner.

He sat next Laura, but his silence continued until he had finished his soup and his fish. He did nothing but smile. He had invented something pretty in the retirement of his chamber which he was to say to Laura, but he had forgotten it, and his soul was consumed in spasmodic efforts to remember it. Laura saw this to her intense amusement. At the end of the fish she thought he had got it, for he brightened up and gave a sigh of relief. She was wrong, he had only abandoned the effort. He slopped out a glass of water, looked sweetly at her, and said—

" I take it that the great duration of the Liverpool ministry arose mainly from the absence of anything like decision or force of character in the chief. The whole, too, was a mere coalition as profligate as that between Fox and North. The very possibility of a coalition argues an entire absence of principle in the coalescing parties, and of policy in the coalition itself."

Chapter X

HUNTING was nearly the only irregular pursuit which Laura had, the only one the duration of which could not be calculated. With this single exception her life was as perfectly methodical as her grandmother's. The system on which she had been brought up consisted mainly of perfect regularity of time and uniformity of thought. This hunting was an excentric incalculable comet in the regular planetary system of her mother. It was the only exception ; the rest of her life was perfectly regular, nearly as regular as a religious sister's.

A morning walk from six to seven. Religious reading in her own room till half-past. Breakfast at nine. Poor people from ten to twelve. Solid reading (but very few novels admitted into the house) till one. Lunch. Drive out with grandma in the afternoon. Dinner at seven. Prayers and bed at half-past ten.

So much for a non-hunting day ; one of the days after her grandmother's own heart. Idleness, said her grandma, was the source of all temptation ; days spent like this could lead to no temptation (except that of suicide, perhaps ?), and therefore would help to preserve from sin. But a hunting day was a very different sort of thing. What must the poor old lady have suffered on one of them, with her well-regulated mind lacerated at every point! She had learnt to suffer and smile in far more terrible affairs than this.

On those happy hunting days all the old rules were broken through. Waking from some happy dream to the consciousness of an existence still happier, Laura would find herself in her riding habit, hat in hand, in the dim grey morning passing through the great hall to the breakfast room to meet her father. And oh, what divine feasts were those *tête-à-tête* breakfasts with him, and him alone, before the roaring logs. All her nature seemed changed on these occasions. She felt as some old knight must have felt, when, after being mewed up in his castle for a weary week he found himself on the road. She had a day of adventure, of unknown adventure, before her. On other days she was watching the clock to see when it was time to leave off working and begin reading. On these there was no rule, no law. Liberty—wild, mad liberty!

Then came the ride with her father in the cold wild morning up one of the more secluded lowland valleys through ever rising lanes, which grew more steep until the cottages grew scarcer, and the hedges less cared for, until there were no lanes and no hedges, but tracks among scattered oak and holly, and the trickling trout-stream in the bottom gleaming among his alders. And at last, after the stream had divided into three or four little channels, came opener country, and rising above the highest combe, the gentle roll called Whinny Hill, a hundred acres of gorse, now made brilliant by the redcoats which awaited their arrival. Then the summit with a hundred pleasant greetings, the moor in the distance, dark purple wreathed with silver mist.

And the coming home at night, draggled and happily tired, and, last of all, the sweet confused dreams of all the day's wild adventures. What though to-morrow should be a day of dull routine—there were other hunting days to come!

So she had two lives, as it would seem—the one of respectable not unpleasant routine, the other of glorious abandon. "In case of overwhelming trouble," she often asked herself, "to which of these lives should I fly for comfort, for consolation?" Surely a nature so noble as hers was capable of fighting sorrow with the weapons of quiet, order, and industry with which her grandmother had so perfectly armed her, and of winning a glorious peace, such as her grandmother had won? So she said to herself, until she looked in the glass, and then she found it difficult to believe. Could that imperial diadem of hair ever come to be smoothed down under a white-laced cap? Could those steady-set hawk-like eyes ever get into them the tender hare-like look of Lady Southmolton; and, more than all, could that somewhat large stern mouth ever learn to set itself into the peaceful eternal smile which sat like some gleam of heaven on the beautiful old woman's lips? Mrs. Hannah More was a wise woman, but Laura used to doubt her power of having done that even were she alive. "They will never make a saint of me," she used to say to herself. "I'll be a good woman, but I shall never be a saint. Papa has spoilt me. If anything does happen, I will stay by him. He and his ways suit me best, I fear. I shall always have my horse, and be able to ride myself tired among these long-drawn valleys. I wish I was better, but he has spoilt me!"

Chapter XI

LAURA had a great curiosity to see that personage who was called by her grandmother "the new young man." She had been detained at home by some accident on the day of his first appearance. Her father, however, had so consistently bored every one to death that evening by his account of the run, which would have filled three columns of *Bell*, and by the manifold excellences of his new St. Hubert, that Laura remembered that old Mrs. Squire, the huntsman's aged mother, had not been so well for two or three days, and that she was very much to blame for not having been to see her; and moreover, by-the-bye, that there was a new litter of puppies at the kennels, and she might as well step on from old Mrs. Squire's and see them. It pleased her father that she should sympathise with his favourite pursuits. Since the expedition of St. Ursula and the eleven thousand virgins, there never was a more innocent, more necessary expedition than this of Laura that winter morning. It was plainly her duty. Of course, if the New Young Man happened to be at the kennels, she would be rewarded by seeing that remarkable character. That he couldn't, by the wildest possibility, be anywhere else at that time of day never struck her—of course!

Still the Hannah-More half of her was in the ascendant to-day. It was a non-hunting day. She felt a craving to bolster herself up with formulas and precedents, after the manner of that school. Old Elspie, her Scotch nurse, was a great crony of Mrs. Squire, both being advanced Calvinists. Laura would just step up and ask her what she thought of Mrs. Squire's state, and if it was not necessary for her to go, why of course she would stay at home. She was going to do one of the most simple, natural things possible, to gratify her curiosity by looking at a new servant. And yet——, she would be glad of a false excuse for doing so; she would have been almost disappointed if Mrs. Squire had been better.

She went upstairs into a room, whose long-mullioned window looked upon the distant moor; and there she found an old and, physically speaking, very ugly old Scotchwoman, with a long hooked nose, and gleaming grey eyes. This old woman was dressed for walking, with an awful fantastic bonnet, and a crutched stick like Mother Bunch's. Her father's joke struck her forcibly— Elspie did look very like a witch indeed!

" Elspie, dear," she said, " have you heard how Mrs. Squire is ? "

" She is just deeing," was the answer, " and I'm awa to see her. There'll be manifestations when she is caught up, I'm thinking. Last night, while I sat with her, there came a sough of wind round the house, which would have swelled into music, if that ill-faured auld witch, Mother Carden, hadna been there. I ken of her tickling a paddock wi twa barley straes held crosswise, to change the wind. She should be burnt in bear strae herself, the witch. To depart from the gude honest auld practice of knouting aught thrums of hempen cord, with saxteen knots apiece, and calling twal times on—guide us where's my sneeshin—, which mony a time I've done myself, Gude forgie me, with the best success."

Laura laughed loudly, kissed the old woman, and said she would go with her.

They walked slowly together through the shadows of the park, which comprised all the promontory between the narrow estuary of the Wysclith on the left, and the broad dangerous sands of the Avon on the right. Betwixt the tree-stems on either side they could see gleams of yellow sand and sea-green water. Where the trees broke, Poyntz Castle loomed up grandly on the other side of the river close at hand. There was no regular avenue, but beyond the trees which bordered the carriage - way, the Moor, the mother of waters, was visible, and seemed to gladden old Elspie's Highland eyes.

She tattled on incessantly. It was a beautiful country, she said, to the blinded eyes of those who had never seen solitary Rannoch and lonely majestic Schehallion. God had left the people here to wax fat until they kicked, in proof of which He sent no snow ; and twaddling on uncontradicted with her argument, no whisky and deil a screed of the pipes from ae year's end to the ither. The trout were but poor things, and the blessed salmon themselves were naething to the Scottish salmon, though, with her wonderful honesty, she confessed that she had never seen but one at Rannoch in her life. The Gospel in all its purity was preached here, she allowed, but in holes and corners ; and then she gave Laura a piece of her mind about the High Church rector, and about what would happen to her (Laura) for the prominent part she was taking in the Christmas decorations of the church. But Laura only half-heard her, for she was away on horseback, over a particular line of country, over which she had always hoped the fox would go, but over which he never did. Then Elspie went on to say that the people here were sunk in the grossest superstition, after which she rambled on into describing a never-failing spell of her own for doing something or another, " and then ye pit the thimmle halfway betwixt the twa bannocks, and ye turn to the four airts, and ye say four times to ilka airt—' Hech sirs, see to yon hoodie, she's waur I'm thinking.' "

The last sentence was not Elspie's incantation—it was only a natural exclamation. If she had said, " your twa dizzen hoodies," it would have been equally correct. They had arrived at Mrs. Squire's cottage, the last house in the village, close to the tideway, and there were Royston crows enough about in every direction.

They went in, but there was no one on the ground-floor. A man's voice was audible upstairs, apparently talking to the sick woman. Elspie immediately prepared for going upstairs in extreme wrath. The voice, as far as they could hear it, was the voice of Mr. Parsons, the Tractarian rector. In Elspie's eyes the sin of a Romanising Episcopalian, like the Rector, daring to trouble the death-bed of an elected Calvinist with his miserable soulless formalisms, was a sin too horrible to be tolerated for a moment. She charged the stairs, and Laura shoved her up right willingly, knowing that her Highland respect for rank would prevent her insulting a guest of her father's house in his daughter's presence.

They came silently into the room of death, for it was

so. She saw at once that it was not the Rector who was bending over the dying woman, but a stranger. She heard him say, " Mother, your assurance of salvation is so great that if I were a duke I would change with you. Think of your future, and think of the hell which is before me. Do you think I would not change with you ? "

That was all they heard, for the next instant the stranger turned and saw them. Before he had time to do so, Laura's heart was melted with pity towards him; and when he did so, she looked on the most magnificent young man she had ever seen in her life.

There was more mischief done in the next five minutes than was thoroughly undone in the next five years. It was very wrong, and Mrs. Hannah More would have been very angry; but it *will* happen, you know, and it does. Poor Laura tried hard to undo that five minutes' work, but she never entirely did—circumstances were so fearfully against her.

A wonderfully splendid young fellow, very young, so young as to be beardless, yet well-grown and graceful. In her memory he lived as a perfectly beautiful young man, with large steadfast eyes, and a look of deep sorrow in them and in the whole of his face, which had not yet developed into despair.

As Elspie moved towards the bed, he rose and came towards them. He was singularly well-dressed, and looked the gentleman he was every inch of him; there was no man in that part of the country who could compare with him. Hilton was grand enough in his way, but he wanted the keen vitality which dwelt in every look, every action of this one. Laura had never seen anyone like him at all. She was very plainly dressed, as she generally was when about home. They could scarcely help speaking to one another. They both felt they were in the presence of death, and thought but little of forms or introductions. Each was only conscious' that the other was

wondrously attractive, and they talked like two children.
He began,—

" Death in such a form as he takes here loses all his ter-
rors. The most selfish sybarite would hold out his white
hands, and take him to his bosom, if he came in this form."

The young lady was the very last young lady in England to yield to anyone in a conversation of this kind.
She loved it with her whole soul. She plunged into it at
once, looking frankly into the stranger's eyes.—

" The death is beautiful. Yes ! of course it is. But it
is merely the corollary of the life. How could it be anything but beautiful, after such a life : brutal ingratitude
met with patient love and forgiveness—grinding poverty
endured with saintlike patience—a charity which hoped
all things and believed all things—helpful diligence towards
those in affliction, and genial sympathy for those in pros-
perity ? Of course her death is beautiful."

" So you think that the death will be peaceful according
as the life has been good ? "

" Of course I do."

" Do you believe in the converse of your proposition ?
Do you believe that no man after a life of misused oppor-
tunities, of anger, of frivolity which he despised, of aimless idleness which he loathed, would not take death in
his arms as his dearest friend, just as this old woman is
doing ? "

" No, I do not. Death to him would be the executioner
with the mask and axe, not the angel with the crown of
glory."

" That is not a very comfortable creed for those who
seek death as a rest from misfortune and life-long trouble,
which troubles evermore and will not cease troubling."

" No, it is not," replied Laura. " I did not mean it to
be. If I ever met anyone who was so supremely and sentimentally silly as to say in earnest what you have been
advancing as a speculation, I should have much more to
say on the subject."

For she suddenly had to fall back on Mrs. Hannah More and the straitlaced regularities double-quick; for this tall youth was dropping these sentimental platitudes out of his handsome mouth in such a careless, graceful, melodious manner, that she began to find that she must either get angry or cry.

They passed out of the house together, and parted with a bow. Laura was so trained to habit that she seldom departed from a plan she had laid down. She went on towards the kennels, more because she had started with that intention than because she cared to see much of the puppies. Her deeply - hidden design of seeing the New Young Man was no more; she had forgotten all about him.

The old huntsman, a little weasened lean old man about sixty, son of the woman who was dying; a man with a keen grey eye, which, though half hidden under his eyebrows, was always on yours, received her. They were on the flags together in amicable dispute about some one of the young hounds, which had been brought out for inspection, when the stranger whom she had only just left, and of whom she had not yet ceased thinking, came up and said to the huntsman,—

" I'll go across to Clercombe then, and fetch that puppy home. I shall take Xicotencatl, or he'll be too fresh for you to-morrow. Mind you look at that dog's foot again, do not forget it." And so he went.

Laura had voice to ask Squire who that might be.

" The new gentleman, Miss," said the voice, which came from under the keen grey old eye.

" Do you mean the new whip ? " she asked, in blank astonishment.

" I calls him the new master, Miss. I give way to him at once, and so he's took to ordering Sir Charles about now, and he seems to like it."

" You seem to like it too ? " said Laura; " you take it very easily ? "

" If gentlemen takes the place of whips, such as I must

obey their orders," said Squire. " You weren't out a Tuesday, Miss ? "

" You know I was not."

" Did Sir Charles mention to you or to her ladyship the fact that he wouldn't ride in a frock ? "

" No. You mean the new whip, I suppose ? "

" The new Dook I mean, of course, come out in a swallowtailed pink like a gentleman. I point it out to him very gentle. ' I'm not going to ride in a frock,' he snaps. ' The master himself does,' I urged. ' The devil he does !' says he ; 'then I suppose I must. But I am not going to wear that beastly thing the tailor sent home for me. I will have one built at Plymouth. Is there a decent tailor there ?' And so he picks his horse and goes over. And he has been snapping my nose off because the tailor has not sent his coat in, and he is going to ride in his swallowtail to-morrow, and says he will apologise to Sir Charles if he thinks about it."

" Are all the Leicestershire men such dandies ?" said Laura.

" It's to be hoped not, Miss," said old Squire, looking keenly at her with his grey old eye. " Foxhunting would be expensive if they were."

" Does he understand his business ? "

" Not he. But he thinks he do, which is much ; and he is a capital hand at giving orders, which is more. And he is cool."

" Cool over his fences, you mean ? " said Laura.

" Cool with the field *I* mean," said Squire. " A Tuesday he rode The Elk, and he went over a big thing in front of your father, and waits for him. And Sir Charles comes up and he funks it, for it were a awful big thing, for fegs it were ! And Mr. Hammersley goes round and opens the gate for him ; and I hearn him say, ' We shouldn't have funked that ten years ago, Sir Charles—hey ?' And your father says, ' That is a regular Leicestershire trick, to ride a man's best horse, that could carry his ten pounds extra, and then chaff him for not taking his fences.' But he laughed again, and he said, 'No, Sir Charles, it won't do. It's the ten years, not the ten pounds. Old Time has handicapped us all.' And when we checked the first time, he offered his cigar-case to Tom Downes, who asked to be introduced, and looked mad when he found out who he was. That is what *I* call coolness. But he always were the best of the lot, say what you will."

" Best of what lot ? " asked Laura.

" Of the Leicestershire lot, Miss," replied the old fellow, quickly. " They are a troublesome lot for the most part, Miss, as you will find when you get to know the world as well as I do. Too gentlemanly, for instance. But this young man, he is what I call a model."

" Are they all gentlemen ? " asked Laura.

" Not all on 'em, Miss. This young man is perhaps rather exasperating gentlemanlike. But they all have the same ways, in some degree."

Laura went home again : knowing in the inmost recesses of her soul, in her consciousness, that something had happened to her, which the intelligent and the emotional part of her equally refused to recognise—a something, which those two-thirds of her soul, which lay nearest to the surface, absolutely refused to name. Her intelligence would not, as yet, tell herself, nor would her emotions, as yet, allow her to tell anybody else, that she had fallen in love with this young gentleman. If her intelligence had told this fact to herself, or if her emotions had got so far out of the guidance of Hannah-Moreism as to allow her to tell it to anyone else, she would have been covered with shame and indignation. But she knew it perfectly well ; and was most heartily frightened, as was the German student, when he left his monster in his room, and feared to come back there for fear of meeting it, in all its monstrous horror. There are three ways of *knowing* things ; she had only got to the first as yet. Familiar intercourse was to give her the second, grief the third.

Meanwhile that most unaccountable old trot Mother Nature had been casting her kevels, and had arranged that these two young people should fall in love with one another. What that means exactly we none of us know. But it happened here most unmistakably.

Chapter XII

LAURA passed the rest of that day in the most praiseworthy activity. Her poor people done, she armed herself with a Biographical Dictionary, and settled steadily down to Froude's first volume, which had just arrived, to work at it till lunch-time. What had passed that morning she chose to ignore utterly to herself. She once went so far as to make the admission, " I was very nearly being silly this morning. I was not at all myself. It was that poor woman's approaching death upset me." Nothing more than this. She determined on an expansive course of study of the Tudor times, got out a new manuscript book, in the which to take notes, determined to be utterly sceptical about Mr. Froude's conclusions, and diligently to spy out every· deficiency. She got her pens, ink, MS. book, and blotting-paper all ready, settled herself at the writing-table with the volume before her, and then sat down and began thinking about the incomprehensible impudence of this wonderful Hammersley, until she found it wouldn't do, and went to work in serious sober earnest. Her diligence met with its reward ; for after reading steadily till lunch-time, practising until the carriage came round, making herself agreeable to Lord Hatterleigh and her grandmother during their drive, and writing letters for her father till the dressing-bell rang, she found that the little something which had existed in the morning had ceased to exist, and that she was in a mood of lofty scorn with herself, for having in the deepest, dimmest, seven-fold depths of her soul allowed that anything of that kind had for an instant existed.

A mood of lofty self-scorn is seen probably to better advantage on the stage than in the drawing-room. The drawing-room, I take it, is, to use our modern elegant language, a sphere devoted to the gentler and more elegant emotions. The proper place for tantrums is the library, or, if you have such an apartment, the ancestral hall, with the portraits of your forefathers scowling gloomily down on the petty passions of their ephemeral and degenerate successors. Laura had no business to bring her scorn into the drawing-room and frighten her grandmother, not to mention astonishing (no, he couldn't be astonished, he never got so high as that), surprising Lord Hatterleigh to that extent that he feared there was an insufficient quantity of pepsine in his dinner-pills.

"What have you done to-day, Miss Seckerton?" he asked her, leaning back with his legs stretched out and folded before him.

"Being foolish all the morning, and trying to persuade myself that I had been nothing of the kind all the afternoon," replied Laura. "Do you ever do that?"

"What! make a fool of myself?"

"No; of course you do that; we all do. I mean, do you ever try to persuade yourself that you haven't?"

This being considerable nonsense sounded obscure and difficult, and Lord Hatterleigh brought his mind to bear upon it. He refolded his legs slowly, putting the one lately underneath uppermost, folded his hands on the pit of his stomach, and said, to begin,—

"Say that again, will you, Miss Seckerton?"

"It was hardly worth saying the first time," she answered; "I certainly can't say it twice over."

This was very disconcerting, and he sat perfectly silent for a time, and then made another attempt to talk. But she would not talk to him to-day. She was not in the humour to tolerate his weary platitudes, and she let him see it. She was unkind to him for the first time in her life. She disturbed him so much by her brusquerie and petulance that he felt it necessary to go for a jog-trot ride on one of his three hobbyhorses to forget it. The medical horse was unavailable in the present company; he had been riding his political horse all day, to Sir Charles's intense exasperation. So he mounted the genealogical palfrey, and went out for a ride with old Lady Southmolton. He put her gently in her saddle·when he gave her his arm in to dinner, and with the exception of a blundering gallop on his political cob, when the men were left over their wine, rambled with her through green lanes of pedigrees until bedtime; and even over his wine-and-water at eleven, after she had gone to bed, seemed strongly inclined to penetrate as far as her venerated bedroom, and correct her for some blunder which he averred she had made, were it only through the keyhole.

" Who was that, Lady Mary Saunders, we saw to-day ? " he began, as he was taking her in; " the little yellow woman with the wig, at the red-brick house with the bee-hives on the lawn—a very well-bred woman indeed, husband a Tory,"

" She was a Spettigue."

" Which Spettigues, the Cromer or the Scilly Spettigues ? "

" Neither. She belongs to the halfway house; she is the third daughter of Lord Mapledurham."

" Oh, a Spettigoo" (so he pronounced it). " They have dropped the ' *e*,' my dear Lady Southmolton, in the present generation. Wasn't there something about one of her brothers ? I seem to fancy that there was."

" Nothing very much ; Charles lives away from his wife."

" Aha ! " said Lord Hatterleigh, " and how was that ? "

" I hardly know. There were two sides to the story. She has got her party, and he has got his. Some say that he treated her very badly, and some say she gave him good cause. Sir Harry Poyntz was furious at having his name mixed up in it."

" Oh, *he* was in it, was he ? "

" He says he was not."

" All the more—— Do *you* know Sir Harry Poyntz, my dear Lady Southmolton ? "

" I have known him and his from a boy."

" What do you think of him ? "

" I try to think the best of him."

" I should not like to have his character," said Lord Hatterleigh. " They say he is profligate beyond precedent, false beyond contempt, and avaricious beyond—beyond thingamy ! "

" It is rather hard to accuse him of avarice, I think," said the kind old lady. " He has succeeded in clearing the estate, which was dipped so shamefully by his father."

" No, really ; I thought it would have taken years more to do it."

" So did everyone else. But see, he has done it. He has refused to renew Mr. Huxtable's lease of the Castle, and is to be our next-door neighbour after the end of this year."

" Then, will people call on him ? "

" I should suppose, of course, they will," said Lady Southmolton. " He has done nothing which would give them any excuse for such an extreme measure as not doing so."

" Why, no. But I could like a man more, far more, who had made one grand *fiasco*. For instance, Colonel Ikey has made a mess of it, an awful mess, and he don't show. But I tell you honestly, I would sooner be Ikey behind his cloud, than I would keep my name on my club-books with Sir Harry Poyntz' reputation. He will never step over the line, but if he ever did, no man would be found to say, ' Poor Harry Poyntz ! ' "

" I want to make the best of him," said Lady Southmolton.

" You always want to make the best of everybody ; you Hortons always do, you know. You can't help it ; goodness is in your blood ; you have given yourselves to peace-making for these two centuries. But all the Hortons since the Conquest won't whitewash this fellow; he is too utterly ill-conditioned. He has a brother, has he not?"

" Yes ; just gone to India."

" By the same mother?"

" Oh yes. Robert Poyntz; I remember him as a pretty bright boy, a very nice boy."

" There is another brother, I heard of the other day only —a Falconbridge, a splendid fellow by all descriptions; have you ever heard of him?"

" I have heard of such a person, but I never, never heard of his splendour. I have always understood him to be a sad *mauvais sujet*. A very disreputable person, is he not?"

" No. I have heard no harm of him worse than that he was riding steeplechases, or acting as huntsman or something, in Leicestershire last year. He seemed to be a somewhat remarkable fellow — a youth who seemed to play Count Saxe to old Sir George Poyntz' August der Starke. What do you know about Robert Poyntz, the brother?"

" I am afraid but very little good," said Lady Southmolton. " I fear he is very dissipated. Why?"

" Because he will soon be in possession. Sir Harry Poyntz is a doomed man; he has ruined his constitution by profligacy, and has had one or more attacks of angina pectoris. You will have this Robert Poyntz at the Castle in a couple of years, mark my words!"

So Lord Hatterleigh and Lady Southmolton. Let us see what they were talking about at the other end of the table. Laura was sitting next to Lord Hatterleigh; but he did not speak to her, for she had frightened him. He calmed himself by talking to that well-conducted old Lady Southmolton. As I said before, he did not feel equal to Laura for the rest of the evening. She was very much pleased at not having to amuse him, and most willingly left him to talk with her grandmother. But we shall have to follow the conversation at what may properly be called the noisy end of the table, as distinguished from the quiet end, where Lord Hatterleigh mumbled and spluttered as above to Lady Southmolton. Lady Emily tried not to yawn, and Sir Peckwich Downes, who, from his figure, seemed to have three stomachs, ruminated over his dinner, listening to Lord Hatterleigh, and confined his observations to saying in a deep voice "Sherry!" whenever the butler offered him champagne, or any frivolous drinks of that kind. We will take up the conversation at the noisy end.

THE VICAR.—" I deny your position, Colonel Hilton. The great Bithynian Council was merely assembled for the purpose of condemning Arianism. That was its *spécialité*. I deny that I am bound by it further than that. As regards sumptuary laws for the priesthood, it did absolutely nothing. It left them to be developed by the Western Church——"

COLONEL HILTON.—" The Papists. "

THE VICAR.—" The Western Church, sir. Thus our chasuble is developed from the blanket of the shepherd of the Campagna, our dalmatic from—— "

SIR GEORGE.—" But where are you to stop in your development? We fox-hunters, about the middle of the last century, developed our vestments into breeches and top-boots, and there we have stuck for a hundred years. But lately a number of young fellows have shown signs of moving forward again, and have appeared in grey cords and butchers' boots. One of your boys, Huxtable, rode last week in knickerbockers, and went very well forward indeed. I was very much offended; I could not bear the sight of it. But if you allow that Pu—, I mean that Church vestments, were developed out of something which went before, I cannot see at what point you are to stop that development, any more than I can stop breeches and top-boots from developing into knickerbockers and gaiters."

THE VICAR.—" The development should stop, sir, the instant that the original idea of the vestment is lost."

LAURA.—" I agree with the Vicar. Let us use these Church vestments as long as any idea worth preserving is preserved by them. I believe in symbols. If you are to wear anything at all, let it mean something. A gown and surplice mean nothing at all. Now, Mr. Spurgeon, when he goes into the pulpit with a blue necktie and a white hat, *does* mean something—a something *I* don't like ; but, at all events, he means something, however offensive it may be to me."

COLONEL HILTON.—" I am converted. Miss Seckerton has put it so well. I see that we must either have Bryan King, with his albs and his dalmatiques, or we must have Spurgeon, with his white bowler hat and blue tie."

LAURA.—" You are very easily converted, Colonel Hilton."

COLONEL HILTON.—" Very easily indeed—by you."

LAURA.—" Thank you. That means, that you are never in earnest about anything."

COLONEL HILTON (in his softest voice).—" Only very much in earnest about one thing."

LAURA (looking at him with strong disfavour).—" And what may that be, for instance ? "

The Colonel, reduced to silence for a moment, and feeling that he had somehow done just what he did not want to do, said—" Is it really true, Mr. Huxtable, that we are to lose you, and that Sir Harry Poyntz is coming to the castle ? "

Mr. Huxtable, a jolly Yorkshire giant, said—" Indeed it is. He will neither sell, nor give me another lease. And I have offered him a fancy price, too. It is a sad pity for the Conservative interest. If I had lived in that dear inconvenient old castle a few years more, I should have turned a Tory. Lord bless you ! No one could stand the atmosphere of the dear old place. Lock John Bright up a year or two in a Norman keep, with a deer park, and you would find him walking arm-in-arm with Disraeli into the Carlton."

THE VICAR.—" The atmosphere of—— "

MR. HUXTABLE.—" That is just what I mean. As the atmosphere of Magdalen turned you Tractarian, so the atmosphere of the dear old place would turn me Tory. I shall go back to Bradford, build a red-brick house, and go in for a six-pound suffrage to begin with—only begin with, understand. And I shall also turn dissenter. Ha! ha!"

THE VICAR.—" My good Sir—— "

" I know all about that, Vicar. It's all a matter of atmosphere, you know. Hey? ἐς ἑαυτὸν στομαχόν—hey? But, seriously, it does make a man talk radically and wildly, to find himself turned out of such glorious quarters as these, to make room for a profligate usurer."

THE VICAR.—" I can quite conceive it. I wish to heaven that Sir Harry would sell to you. Since you have been here you have done nothing but good. You have strengthened my hands at every point, although you have often disagreed with me. And now you are to make room for a profligate atheistic usurer."

SIR CHARLES.—" My dear Vicar!"

The Vicar only looked at Sir Charles, and Sir Charles held his tongue and carved the venison.

COLONEL HILTON.—" I am afraid that Mr. Huxtable has been pauperising the labourers hereabouts with his liberality. They have got to depend on him as a *deus ex Machinâ*. Nothing can be more demoralising than that. You are a capital political economist, Miss Seckerton; you will agree with me."

LAURA.—" I don't see how Mr. Huxtable, with all his ingenuity, can have succeeded in pauperising men with eleven shillings a week, three to five children, two shillings a week off for rent, a pound a year to the doctor, which brings them down to little over eight shillings, out of which they have to find boots, clothes, and firing."

COLONEL HILTON (somewhat nettled at having put his foot in it again).—" It's a case of supply and demand, I suppose."

LAURA.—" So I suppose. It is a positive fact that the agricultural population could not get on at all without artificial assistance from the gentry; and I suppose we don't help them from Christian good-will, but only to prevent the ricks from catching fire. Is that what you mean ? "

Laura was behaving very badly. Her father was pained and astonished. What she said might be true, but she had no business to speak in that way. What right had she to talk about rick-burning ? No lady ever did.

Kind Mr. Huxtable saw all this, and came to the rescue with the best intentions—with one of those intentions with which a silly, lying old proverb says that " hell is paved." He made, on the whole, a rather worse mess of it; but his meaning was good, and by no means the sort of thing with which to pave hell. He tried to " change the conversation," a thing I have never yet seen done with the slightest success. If the conversation gets awkward, diligently try to *lead* it into a new channel; but don't change it, and leave the whole of the company in a nervous disconcerted frame of mind, each wondering whether or not he or she has said the Dreadful Thing which made such a terrible remedy necessary.

" That is a splendid young fellow—that new whip of yours—Sir Charles, if I may take the liberty of calling him so."

Sir Charles agreed that he was.

" Thrown away here though," continued Huxtable.— " Goes too straight for this country; won't learn to potter. He will go at something half a size too big for him some day, and come to grief. I saw him go at some terrible things the day before yesterday."

" I wonder if I could enlist him," said Colonel Hilton. " He would make a capital dragoon."

" He is a cut above *that* sort of thing, I fancy," said

Laura, who seemed determined to behave worse as the evening got later.

Colonel Hilton was getting angry with her. She had given him the dor two or three times without the slightest offence on his part, and he was not going to stand it.

" Do you think, then, that a whip to hounds holds a higher position than that of the light cavalry who were at Balaclava ? "

" I say nothing about them," said Laura. " But you must acknowledge, as a general rule, that the army is recruited from the lowest class in the community, and that you never get a man to enlist if he can do anything else with himself."

" That is hardly to the point. I deny it ; but that has nothing to do with the argument. What I asked was, do not you think that the position of a trooper, who may have the Victoria Cross, which I wear myself, pinned on his coat by the most august person in the world, is superior to a menial servant dressed in a private livery, who feeds the hounds, and drowns the blind puppies ? "

" It depends very much on the way you take it," said Laura, who had nothing whatever to say, and so said that.

" I don't think it does," said Colonel Hilton. " To bring the matter to practice. I sit at mess with a man whose father, till last year, was working as a journeyman blacksmith on Finsbury Pavement. He was sergeant-major in the 14th Hussars, and got his commission for service ; and as it is best for a man who rises from the ranks to change his regiment, he came to us. We received him with open arms. That man is a trusted companion of mine, one of the best officers I have. I can make a friend of that man, but I don't think I could stand a menial servant—a mere minister to luxury, a kennel-boy. If there are to be any rules about that sort of thing, I am right ; if not, I am wrong."

These sentiments were far too near the creed of most

present to be contradicted. A short silence ensued, which was more flattering than applause, during which Laura was thinking.

"So you *have* got a temper, and *won't* always stand contradiction, eh, Colonel Hilton? Well, I like you the better for it."

It was broken by Sir Peckwich Downes from the end of the table, who, as he had finished his venison, and had as much sherry as he wanted, got tired of thinking what a queer lopsided young gaby Lord Hatterleigh was, and felt conversational. He put a knife up his sleeve, and said :—

"This winter venison of yours is too fat. Winter venison always is. But it is not bad-flavoured. Give me the old rule: a buck a week till September; neck o' Tuesday week, haunch o' Thursday week. There is the same difference between a Paris chicken and a nice young spring Dorking, in my estimation.* Your fawn, again, is new-fashioned and hasty."

Sir Charles thought that the conversation was changed, and that there were better times before him. He tried to catch Sir Peckwich's eye, and bring him into the talk. But his eye had a long way to travel, and before it got to Sir Peckwich it was arrested by a stony stare from the Vicar.

"I suppose," said the Vicar to the unhappy baronet, in a severe clerical voice, "that when Sir Harry Poyntz comes to the castle, you will find it necessary to dismiss your new master of the buckhounds."

That finished him. When the ladies were gone, he sat down over his wine, saying to himself,—

"Confound these moles of parsons! How the deuce did he find *that* out? And how, in the name of all confusion, did he know that I knew it?"

But he was not to be beat by fifty vicars, when he was

---

* The worthy baronet is possibly obscure to some of our readers, but in these days we cannot edit him.

in an obstinate mood. In spite of the Vicar's deprecation, he insisted on seeing him through the darkest part of the park, and as he left him said,—

" What did you mean, Vicar, by saying that I must discharge my man when Sir Harry Poyntz came ? "

" You know as well as I do," said the Vicar.

" Do you think," asked Sir Charles, " that Harry Poyntz knows the relation in which this young man stands to him ? "

"As well as you or I do," said the Vicar. " Harry is, as you know, my relation. I got the living from his father, and am in constant communication with himself. He knows who this young man is as well as I do."

" I am afraid it won't do to keep him here, then," said Sir Charles.

" It won't do for one instant," said the Vicar. " It is not to be thought of for a moment."

"I suppose not," said Sir Charles, stroking his chin. " Well, I am very sorry, for he is a charming gentleman, and I should have liked such a son."

" You haven't seen much of him yet, have you ? " said the Vicar.

" Why, no," said Sir Charles.

" Ah ! " said the Vicar, " so I thought."

" Is he a very bad fellow, then ? " asked Sir Charles.

" There is a natural depravity in our human nature "— began the Vicar, very slowly.

" I didn't mean that sort of thing," replied Sir Charles, quickly.

" I know you didn't," said the Vicar, looking steadily at him. " I know what you mean, and I answer that the human heart is naturally depraved. You are depraved, you know. As for me, I am a most graceless sinner."

" Well, well ! " said Sir Charles, impatiently. " Is this young gentleman so extra depraved that I must send him about his business ? "

" You want an excuse," said the Vicar.

Leighton Court

"I don't want any excuse," said Sir Charles. "Is he any worse than you or I, then?"

"Not much, but it won't do to have him here after Harry Poyntz comes."

"Does he know who he is?"

"Perfectly."

"Does he know that you know who he is?"

"Not in the least," said the Vicar. ".Pack him off about his business. Do you know the dew is very heavy? Good-night."

Chapter XIII

IT is one thing to go to bed with your brain active from conversation and company, brimful of to-morrow's plans; and quite another to find, after you are in bed, that this tiresome brain of yours will go on grinding, utterly refusing to stop, like Mrs. Crowe's mechanical church organ, and declines to sink into sleep; nay, sooner than do that, will go on playing foolish old psalm-tunes, against your pillow, until you don't know whether the weary measure comes from your head or from the pillow. Under these circumstances, as hour after hour of the weary night goes on, the plans of the morning become hateful; every past sin, every past omission, every future contingency of evil becomes prominent and immediate. Life seems a weary mistake, and that darkest midnight thought of all, that death must and will come sooner or later, is apt to sit and brood upon your pillow.

Laura did not feel all this. It was to come to her. But she had what her mother or her grandmother would have called "a wretched night." There was a little dumb, dull imp abroad this night, which was not to be named, whose existence was not to be allowed under penalties too horrible for contemplation—a fiend unnamed, unrecognised, yet horribly real. For as she lay awake, with all the phantasmagoria of an excited brain passing before her so distinctly that some of the most vivid images were actually reflected on her retina, this little imp contrived at every opportunity, at every pause in the procession of incongruous images, to hold up the face of one man before her, and grin from behind it — the face of the man whom she wished she had never seen, whom she hated, and wished dead.

Why should she hate him and wish him dead? Because she knew she was going to fall in love with him, and did not yet actually realise that she had. And she had teased Colonel Hilton until, quite unconsciously on his part and on hers, he had given her three or four deep stabs in the heart. He had spoken so dreadfully of this man.

At last these brain phantasmagoria grew so exceeding incongruous that she began to hope she was asleep, but only found that she was not by watching the dull silvered light of the moon upon her window-blinds. At last it came like a dim grey cloud. The last feeling of outward sensation was a happy weariness upon her eyelids, which drooped and drooped till they opened no more. Then the images were as incongruous as ever, but their incongruity was no longer felt. She had passed into the land where incongruity becomes logical, nay, commonplace. There was the form of a beautiful woman lying in a bed, with no outward signs of vitality except a gentle heaving at the breast; but where that woman *was* for the next two hours I don't know, and none of the authors I have consulted seem able to tell me.

"Easier to prove the existence of spirit than to prove the existence of matter?" I should rather think it was!

The appearance of a very commonplace maid, very sleepy, and in reality very cross, although making a praiseworthy effort to look good-humoured, with a candle and a jug of warm water at seven o'clock on a cold November morning, acts as a foil for this sort of thing. I deny the charge of bathos, or of an *ad captandum* contrast. If life had not perpetually these commonplace turns, we should wander sentimentally through this life with Shelley, Byron, and Heine, behowing the state of a world which we have never raised a finger to mend. Thank Heaven! we have got out of *that* sort of thing now. From the *Saturday Review* down to the '*Tiser*, every man has got his shoulder honestly to the wheel. Where they are going to shove us to is a question which has all the pleasures of profound uncertainty.

If ever there was a young lady in an unsentimental—not to say cross—frame of mind, it was Laura on that November morning. If ever there was a young lady who wondered why on earth that idiot of a girl couldn't have had the tact to oversleep herself, or to say that she (Laura) was ill, it was Laura. If ever there was a young lady who thought that foxhunting could only yield to the national game of cricket, as a gigantic and intolerable humbug, it was Laura.

It was only duty, or the habit of duty, which made her get up at all. Her father would miss her,—

> " And still her sire the wine would chide,
>   If it was not filled by Rosabel."

It is a good thing to get up early of a morning for the sake of other folks. The kindest and least cynical of men said that getting-up early made you conceited all the morning, and sleepy all the afternoon, but that is scarcely fair. She found her reward quickly. The dark nonsensical waking dreams of the night were gone, and her temper had come back. While her maid was doing her hair, she was so far herself as to ask, " What sort of morning is it, Eliza ? "

" A bittiful scenting morning, Miss. You've only got to put your nose out of doors to see it," said Susan, who was the huntsman's daughter. " They meets to Winkworthy, don't 'em, Miss ? "

" Yes ; and I suppose we shall go straight for the moors and get home about midnight. I don't feel up to a long run. I wish we met nearer home."

Her father was helping himself to tongue at the sideboard when she got into the breakfast-room. " My darling," he said, " I don't want to startle you, but I forgot to speak to you last night, I want you to ride ' The Elk ' to-day. Are you afraid ? "

" Not I," laughed Laura ; " but why ? Has he ever carried a lady ? "

" He has carried a lady. Colonel Seymour warranted him to do so, and Hammersley has been riding him with a cloth, and pronounced him perfect. The reason I want you to ride him is that, as Hammersley pointed out, Witchcraft is not up to your weight in those heavy upland clays. I think he is right."

" That settles the matter," said Laura. " If our new lord and master has issued his orders that I am to ride ' The Elk ' I submit, of course. Have you made any arrangements for getting me on to the top of him ? "

" Yes," said Sir Charles ; " Lord Hatterleigh is going to hoist you on from the top of a pair of steps."

" And if I get thrown ? "

" If you get thrown, you must drive him against an eight-foot stone-wall, and get up on to him from that, in the best way you can."

And so they laughed away over their breakfast, and were happy, and Laura's long night was as though it had never been.

This horse " The Elk " was a character in his way, and in consequence of what happened afterwards, is still remembered well in the family. His height was eighteen hands and a trifle, his colour very light chestnut, his temper that of a Palmerston : not a very handsome horse—no concentration of vast speed, beauty, and mad vitality, like " Lord Cliefden ; " a horse with the forehand of " Fisherman," with Barclay and Perkins' quarters, and the gaskins of "Umpire:" a great deal more like William Pocock than like Robert Coombes—a great deal more like Thomas King than Thomas Sayers; a vast sweet-tempered horse, whose speed and staying qualities were like the military excellence of the British and American armies, requiring time to show them, but when once shown, amazing : an elephantine, clumsy, Teutonic sort of beast, with his shoulders sloped back to his girth, and his ribs back to his flank : nothing Norman about him at all, except a beautiful thin arched neck, and a little nervous head ; out of which, however, gleamed a large, speculative, kindly, and most thoroughly Teutonic eye.

Sir Charles refused five hundred guineas for him. His early history is extremely obscure, merely, I think, legendary. If he was ever in the service of Messrs. Chaplin and Horne, how did he get to Dublin ? — though it is equally certain that he was never bred, and most certainly never broken, in Ireland. Even *his* temper would never have stood an Irish breaking. After what I have said, it will be evident that " The Elk's " pedigree was still more obscure than " The Elk's " education.

He first made his appearance in civilised society at Plymouth. Haskerton, of Bear Down, who stood six-feet-two in his stockings, and weighed nineteen stone, married a Scotch lady, who was six feet in *her* stockings, and weighed, say, twelve. They had a big baby, height and weight unknown, purchased a six-foot groom out of a dragoon regiment, a pair of eighteen-hand horses, of which " The Elk " was one, and had the biggest phaeton built that old Long Acre had ever turned out ; and with this elephantine equipage used to charge up-and-down the roads in the neighbourhood of Plymouth, to the terror of the peaceable inhabitants.

" Talk to me about the decadence of Englishmen ! " said Sir Peckwich Downes to Lady Southmolton on one occasion. " Why, if Haskerton, with those horses, that wife, that phaeton, that groom, and that baby, were to charge full-speed against the whole French army, they would fly like sheep!"

Lady Southmolton was obliged to allow that such a thing was very probable. She herself was possessed of the hereditary courage of an Englishwoman ; yet whenever she, in her pony-carriage, met this terrific engine of war, guided by Haskerton of Bear Down, in a narrow lane, she always (to use yachting slang) put her helm down, took a strong pull on the starboard rein, got into the ditch, and remained there, bowing like a Limoges china figure, until the terrible Squire, baby and all, had raged on past her like a cyclone.

Sir Charles had looked " The Elk " over ; had offered Haskerton another horse of the same size, and ten pounds. Haskerton didn't see his way to the ten pounds—rather thought the ten pounds should go the other way ; thought Sir Charles wrong about the horse ; but still Sir Charles said he was never wrong about a horse, and so the horse was sent home.

And now Laura found herself mounted on his vast carcass, declaring she should roll off, and making the dull misty morning beautiful with her ringing laughter.

It was a very dull morning, with a slow-sucking wind from the southward. There was no fog on the lower country, but after they had risen about 100 feet the trees began to drop, and they were enveloped in the mist. Sometimes it would lift and brighten, and rise to higher elevations as the day went on ; but it was a dull melancholy day to all non-foxhunting mortals, but a bright one enough to Laura and her father. They had one another ; all the world was behind them, and a day's sweet enjoyment before.

As they shogged on comfortably together they came round the turn of a lane, and lo! a gleam of white and a forest of waving tails ; in another moment the hounds had seen their master, had rushed forward to meet him, and were crowding joyously around. A pleasant sight always, as I remember it, was the meeting of hounds and master in the fresh morning.

The approach to Winkworthy was through ground which was not yet reclaimed from its original state, although rich and cultivable; heavy yellow clay, with forest of oak and holly; and passing along through the dim aisles of it, they came at last on the breezy hill of Wink_worthy, and a few faithful ones who faced the dark morning and the distant meet.

Sir Charles was the tallest man there; his very lean spare figure and his broad shoulders looked very well on horseback, not to mention his leg, which he and others thought to be the finest leg in Devonshire, and which was certainly as well-*dressed* a leg as any in that county or any other :—altogether a most gallant-looking gentleman, as straight as a dart.

Dickson, the attorney from Totridge, who had ridden up and looked keenly at him, was speaking to him when the hounds were put in; but Laura called him away, and they took their places, with three or four other hard-goers, at the upper corner of the little patch of gorse. The rest of the field were not in order—were talking, smoking, and so on; but our friends knew what they were about. The hounds were no sooner in than they were out again on the other side, with a long-legged mountain fox before them, and going fifteen miles an hour straight for the moor.

As soon as Laura got used to the elephantine stride of " The Elk," she found that she was away from the others, with only her father and the huntsman alongside of her, and Hammersley, who had kept out of her sight till now, sailing gallantly on in front, showing them the way. He *could* ride, there was no doubt of that; and a man master of his horse, going hard, is one of the most beautiful sights in the world. Hammersley knew that as well as you or I.

Laura went storming along, enjoying herself thoroughly. They were rapidly approaching the moor, when, after leaping some not very difficult timber, she missed her father. He had come to grief, and was chasing his horse into a corner of the stone wall, so there was nothing much the matter with him. And Laura went on, the more particularly as it was doubtful whether she could have pulled Elk with any great success. She had just begun to realise that she was away alone with Hammersley, when they were up and out on the moor, and into a dense mist; and he had drawn back and was riding nearer to her, as was absolutely necessary.

How far they went she did not know then. The ground was tolerably smooth—heather with very little rock—and they went fast, just keeping sight of the hounds. They were going along a ridge, for Laura saw, first on one side and then on the other, a precipitous slope below her, with hanging cliffs festooned by the mist—saw and did not like it.

At last, suddenly, Hammersley held up his hand and shouted to her to stop. She pulled up in time, but he, watching her, was too late. They had come suddenly on a loose broken slope of weatherworn granite boulders among the heather, and he had ridden on to it before he could pull up. There was a fierce struggling clatter for half a minute, and then horse and man came crashing down together among the cruel pitiless rocks.

He was thrown clear of his horse, and fell partly behind a small rock, so that she could only see his leg. At first the knee was raised, but after a moment it fell over on its side and remained still. She began to get frightened. " Are you hurt ? " she cried out ; but there was no answer, he lay quite still. Around in the mist she could only hear the faint cry of the running hounds getting fainter each moment, and the trickling of some hidden runnel beneath the stones hard by. She cried for help—there was but little chance of that. Her voice only echoed among the rocks for an instant—after that silence again, and she began to feel that she was alone with Death !

Dead or alive, she must go to him; the higher law told her that. She had never seen death yet, but she must look on him for the first time, now, here, in the darkened face of that man—of that man of all others! She slipped from her horse, and scrambled towards him.

Was this death, this loose attitude of all the limbs, this quiet resting of the cheek upon the arm? If so it was hardly terrible, nay, somewhat beautiful! But it was not death; for the head shifted, the soul came back, and a sharp cry told that pain had returned with consciousness.

Laura's face flushed up with sheer honest joy. She would have felt the same glad bound at her heart, had he who was lying before her been the merest old lazar which lay by the roadside. Our hatred of death is so ingrained into our nature, as the greatest and most terrible of evils, that we rejoice beyond measure when his threatened darkness passes away from the most worthless face, and leaves the light of life flickering there again, however foul and worthless that light may be. Poor Laura did not know as yet how precious this life was to get to her! It was only in the reaction of her terror that she rejoiced now, and went innocently to his assistance. She was strong, and she raised him into an easier position. She was knowing, to a certain extent, in the way of nursing, and she unloosed his neck. She was curious, and she wondered what was this thick gold chain about his neck, and whether it was his sweetheart's portrait which hung so heavy from it down on his breast; and she was an artist, and she saw that he was very, very handsome. She raised her voice once more, and cried "Help!" three times, and the circumambient mist and the rocky hollows around re-echoed "Help!" Poor child, she wanted it as much as he did; God help her!

It was not long before "The Elk," who had been elephantinely grazing, raised his head and whinnied. He had heard, quicker than could she, swift horses' feet brushing through the heather. When she caught the sound she cried, " Pull up, we have had an accident. Father ! is that you ? " She heard the approaching horse pass into a walk, and then out of the mist came not her father but Tom Squire, the old huntsman.

He saw what had happened directly. He jumped from his horse and came towards them, with his little bright terrier eyes sparkling from one to the other. " Is he dead ? " he said first, and then he took off his cap. " Go and get it full of water, Miss. Your father is close behind. Quick ! "

She went, and as she came back she heard her father pricking on towards them, and called on him to draw rein. What did she see ? The old huntsman bending down over the hurt man, moving his hair from his eyes, and using such endearments towards him as a father uses towards a favourite son ; and the wounded man smiling back into his face with a patronising kindly confidence, which puzzled her exceedingly.

Her father came up, and they took stock of the disaster. The man was only stunned, and his collar-bone put out, and he could ride home with assistance. Colonel Hilton and Sir Charles' second horseman came next. Colonel Hilton cleverly tied him up in pockethandkerchiefs, and he was sent home on the second horse with the little groom. Others came up then, and it was determined to hunt the hounds, who must be a few miles off by this time, and make a day of it.

So they did. A glorious day they had ! Laura rejected with scorn the idea of going home, was hoisted on " The Elk " by Colonel Hilton, and went on. But all that con-cerns us in that day is this.

Sir Charles and the huntsman rode first, Laura and the Colonel behind. The Colonel was in one of his compli-mentary humours again, for his theory was that, although women kicked against that sort of thing, they must like it, and that it told in the long run. So he and Laura (who never could bear him when he did not contradict her) had (if you will let me say so) fallen together by the ears—I mean quarrelled—to that extent that Laura, after a biting sarcasm, not handed down to us in the family archives, and therefore suppliable by the reader's imagination, had, with her riding-whip, banged and thwacked " The Elk " into a canter, and pushed on to join her father and the huntsman, leaving Colonel Hilton to fall back on the society of a talkative horse-doctor with a grievance against Lieutenant James.

As she came up she heard her father and the huntsman talking together.

" Then you knew him and liked him in his youth ? "

" Yes, Sir Charles. The best of the bunch, Sir—the best of the bunch ! "

" He has not been treated fairly, say what you will," replied Sir Charles. " Is there no hope for mercy for him ? "

" There is no mercy there, Sir Charles," said the little old man, looking up at him. " Let those who have to ask mercy remember that."

Her father, she saw, turned sharply on the old man as he said this, but he turned away again, and rode on as stiff and as grand as ever.

" His is a sad story," she heard him say.

" A very, very sad story, Sir !—sadder than you dream of," said the huntsman. And when she came up to them they began talking of where the hounds might be.

Chapter XIV

THE only woman of her own age whom Laura called friend was Maria Huxtable, the tenant of the Castle's daughter ; a tall, beautiful, though somewhat loud daughter of Lancashire : as handsome in person as Laura, as like her as she could manage to be in manners, by unassisted

unguided imitation, and a still more successful replicat of
Laura in her dress, in which particular a reproduction of
ideas is more mechanical, and therefore more easy. The
only particular difference between them seemed at first
sight to be, that Laura had that trained far-gazing look of
eye, the " not speak till you're spoken to " look, which is
mainly got by education from a woman of the world, or
by unconscious imitation of such ; and Maria Huxtable had
not. Laura seldom looked at you, except so far as was
necessary to fix your image on her retina for the purpose
of recognition, until you spoke to her ; then she could look
straight enough at you. Maria Huxtable used actually to
lorgner you and, what is more, everyone else, to that ex-
cruciating degree that you were forced to speak to her.
At a lawn-party there would be half a dozen young country gentlemen round Maria Huxtable, leaning on their
mallets, and neglecting their game, only on account of
those eyes ; while Laura, in solitary imperial state, would
be standing alone, waiting until it should please them to
go on.

Noticeable to Maria the good-natured was this : that the
moment a field-officer, or naval man of any mark, or dandy
lawyer on circuit, or any man who, as those benighted
savages down there would say, had " been in London,"
appeared they made up to Laura immediately, and got
amazingly intimate with her. On the other hand, Maria
was very much amused by noticing that six young Oxford
Christchurch men, down in these parts on a reading-party,
used at these croquet rabbles to sneak past Laura with all
the grace and self-possession which young Englishmen
usually display on similar occasions. The two were
tenderly devoted to one another, and their affection was
of the most ostentatious kind, far surpassing any demon-
strations ever made towards such unimportant people as
lovers. Previous to any temporary separation they used
to spend every precious hour with one another ; during it
they corresponded constantly, and were frantically fever-

ishly eager to rejoin one another at the first possible moment. Now a permanent separation was coming on they
spent most of their time together.

"I will come across to the Castle to-morrow, dearest
Maria," said Laura one evening. "I will come in the
morning; the tide will be low at ten, and James can push
me across in the dingy."

"My sweetest Laura," said Maria, "I shall be out all
day."

"And where are you going then?" asked Laura, surprised at this sudden announcement.

"I do not know. I am at papa's orders for the day;
that is all."

So it was arranged that Laura should stay at home on
that day, but the fates ordained otherwise. The next
morning a box arrived from London, containing a beautiful
parting present for dear Maria. How nice it would be to
go. and put it on her table in her absence, or take the
chance of catching her! She delayed till evening in the
hope that Maria would come home, and then she went.

She called one of the gardeners, who followed her down
over the sands, and put her across the little channel of the
river which was left at low tide. Climbing a steep path,
partly cut into steps, up the low red cliff, she soon came
to the platform above and stood before the Castle, in the
Castle grounds, with the great keep hanging dark aloft.

She paused for an instant, to look back across the river
at the Court embosomed in trees, standing on its promontory among the yellow sea-sands, and to think how
many happy hours she had spent with Maria under the
shadow of this keep where she stood, all of which had
come to an end for ever! The Castle would be closed to
her when Sir Harry Poyntz came.

She let herself in by a postern, and passing through
many long dark pleasant rooms, and meeting no one, began to climb the stairs towards the second storey of the
keep, where Maria had romantically made her bower; her

hand was on the door-handle, when she started and drew back, for she heard Hammersley's voice on the other side of the door.

There was no doubt of it; in another moment his question, put in an easy tone, to Mr. Huxtable apparently, was answered by that gentleman's voice.

She determined to satisfy her curiosity at once without further listening, and went in. The room took up the whole of that floor of the keep, and was furnished with only four narrow windows, calculated to avoid archery more than to give light—one on each side. She saw the old prospects through each of them, partly with her outward eye, and partly in her memory, at one glance round. On the north the purple moor; on the south the grey sea getting greyer, as night settled down; to the east the Court, on its terraces, and the wide sand all around, with the tide crawling up; and to the west the sunset, which threw the shadow of this keep towards her home. And now between her and the sunset was another shadow, the shadow of a man who sat in the window, talking to Huxtable—of a man she had never seen, and yet who had been speaking with Hammersley's voice.

Mr. Huxtable hurriedly said, "Oh, here is Maria! Come in, my love; I will be back directly," and hurried past her without recognition or explanation. Laura saw that he had mistaken her for Maria, and was determined to satisfy her curiosity by a view of this man with the other man's voice. She therefore sat down in the half-darkness, and allowed good Mr. Huxtable to go blundering down the stone stairs in error.

The reader knows more than poor Laura did, and therefore can guess who this man was, left with her here in semi-darkness, and why his voice was so like Hammersley's. Laura was in deep curiosity. There was no mistake about the similarity of the voice, however; for when he spoke to her, she could hardly help starting, and stared keenly into the dusk to see what he was like, without success. He leaned against the western window, and entered into conversation with her.

"Much obliged to you, Miss Huxtable, for letting me come in here. I had an object. I never pay compliments, or I should say that I was sorry I was going to turn you out of this room, whereas I am glad."

Laura's voice was a wonderfully well-trained one. She was more careful than usual with it as she replied out of the gloom—

"I am not Miss Huxtable; I am only Miss Huxtable's friend."

"Has Miss Huxtable made friends with a lady, then? On what false pretences? My ear never deceives me, though my eyes are bad. I beg your pardon for my mistake."

Laura was somewhat indignant for her friend, and thought the compliment coarse, or would have thought so but for her education. But she knew in a moment, from the way in which he spoke, that she was speaking to what her mother and grandmother had taught her to call a gentleman. And she spoke accordingly, "refusing," as Colonel Hilton might have said, the subject of Laura Seckerton, and coming into action with her other wing somewhat spitefully, fancying somehow that this man was some led captain of Sir Harry Poyntz, instead of being the man himself, as of course it was. I have shown you how naughty she could be; on this occasion she was rather naughtier than usual—

"The Huxtables are by far the nicest people about here. The whole county will miss them. It will be a sad change from them to Sir Harry Poyntz!"

"What has he been doing, then?" said the man in the dark.

"Getting his estate right," replied Laura; "more's the pity; a dreadful crime in these parts, where no one wants him. From all accounts it will be an evil day for the poor when these good Huxtables go, and we have an exchange."

" A very bad exchange, you think ? "

" A very bad one indeed, I fear ! "

" Then, you have heard no good of Sir Harry ? "

" No good whatever."

" Much harm ? "

" Oh dear no, not the least. Have you ever seen the view out of these windows before ? "

" Yes, I know it well," said the man in the dark. " If I were Sir Harry Poyntz, I would take this room as my own. He was born in this room, you know. And I would sit here every day, summer and winter, and I would look north, south, east, and west, and I would say,— " Before I die, every acre, from the moor to the sea, from the promontory westward to the sands eastward, shall be mine." I would sit in this old robber-tower, and say to myself, " You are the first of your name for a thousand years who has been forced to lend your castle for a pittance to a Manchester radical, a man who would destroy your order. Make war against his order in return. They have fought for their trade. Buy until there is no room in the land, until the middle class hereabouts are your creatures. The little freeholders are dropping like rotten pears under free-trade. Pick them up, and make yourself a Peer.' "

Laura was amused and interested by this singular confidence from the unknown. She went about with him at once.

" Cursed be they that add house to house, and field to field ! you know," she said.

" Oh, I would risk the curse, if I could get the land ; and so would you, and so would any of us. Let's have none of that now, come ! "

" Perhaps you are right," she said ; " but it would be an awkward thing for some of us—for us in particular—if Sir Harry Poyntz were wicked enough to do such a thing ! "

" Sir Harry Poyntz is wicked enough to do anything," he replied. " I am Sir Harry Poyntz, and so I ought to know."

Leighton Court

"Oh!" said Laura to herself. "Have I made your ears tingle for you, my gentleman?" and began trying to remember what she had said. Sir Harry thought he had "shut her up," but he had done nothing of the kind. She was only longing to look on what should be, by all accounts, the wickedest, meanest, most worthless face that ever troubled this unhappy earth. She sat in the dark, trying to picture it to herself—trying to anticipate the reality, with the same feeling which makes men madly bet—not from avarice, but as a proof of sagacity—on some sporting event which will be decided in the next three minutes. She could see that he was tall, and she pictured him satanic: a dark melancholic man, with sloping eyebrows, wicked little eyes, and an upward curl at the corner of his mouth; the man she knew so well by Cruikshank's art; the swaggering fiendish cavalier who has come home from the Spanish main, and who is no less than the fiend himself; a man with a wicked leer for a woman, and a twopenny-halfpenny, who-are-you, Haymarket scowl for a man. As she looked at him in the darkness, this fanciful image grew on her imagination till it was nearly reflected on her retina.

Huxtable, coming in with a candle, upset all her fine theories. She saw, instead of her corsair, a bland, fat, flabby, lymphatic man, with a flat pale blue eye, with less depth in it than a wafer; who was too fat for his apparent age; a man who had apparently, by some mistake in Nature's cookery, been boiled instead of roasted; a man who would not even *grill* well, but would remain mere flabby meat, with a coating of brown. He was so utterly unlike what she had thought, that she forgot Hannah More and all that sort of thing, and burst out laughing. But the nasty, shallow, light-blue, dangerous eye was steadily on hers, with a look of power too; and she stopped laughing.

I think, if the reader will allow me, that I will leave to her or his imagination, to conceive good Huxtable's fuss when he came back with the candle, and found that he

had left not Maria but Laura alone with Sir Harry Poyntz;
and his explanations, and the grand kootooing, and bowing and scraping, the utter ignoring of all passages of
arms in the dark, which went on after Laura and Sir
Harry were introduced to one another, may be also omit-
ted with advantage, in order to get on to what is more in-
teresting.

Chapter XV

BELOW Laura was pounced upon by Maria, who to her
surprise, late as it was, with a rising tide, insisted on coming home with her.   There was not the slightest possible
danger in crossing the Wysclith at any time of night, so
Laura let her come.

Laura called her a traitor and a storyteller for saying she
was out when she was not, for the sake of preventing a
meeting between her and Sir Harry Poyntz.   Maria said
she had only done exactly what her father had told her,
and had fully believed that she *should* be out; that Sir
Harry Poyntz had come one single day on business, and
did not wish to be recognised.

But when they were alone on the Court side of the
river, Maria changed the conversatton, and became very
serious.

" Laura, I want to ask a question, and I am frightened."

" What are you afraid of ? "

" Your answer.   What do you think of Sir Harry
Poyntz ? "

" Think of him ?   What I always have ever since I
played with him as a child.   And now I have seen him
again, I must say that his face does not belie his character, but is the most false, mean, and cruel one I ever saw ! "

Maria gave a little cry, and laid her hand on Laura's
mouth—

" Oh, Laura, Laura !   No, no !   For my sake, no ! "

" What have you to do with the man ? Why should I not say what I please about him ? "

" Because I am going to marry him, I believe. Oh ! do have mercy on me, and make the best of him."

" Marry him ! Where have you seen him ? "

" In the North, many times."

" Do you love him ? "

" Yes — yes, of course ! It's a family arrangement, and he has been shamefully illused and misrepresented, and—— "

" He has been nothing of the kind, Maria. You know you are ashamed of what you are doing, or you would have told me of it before. Sir Harry Poyntz is a thoroughly worthless person. Men wonder how it is that his name is kept on the books of his clubs—a man whom my father would never allow to darken his doors for one instant. You don't love him, and you know you don't. You have withheld your confidence from me in this manner, not in the most friendly way, and therefore I cannot tell at all what is urging you on to this most miserable folly. If it is that you think it a fine thing to be Lady Poyntz, and live at the Castle, I can assure you that you had ten thousand times better be plain Mrs. Hilton. And you could be Mrs. Hilton to-morrow ; I know that as well as anyone. I have taught him to hate me like poison. He don't suit me, and I have let him see it most unmistakably. But Harry Poyntz—good heavens ! "

The shoe pinched a little tight here, it seemed. Laura soon found what she had done with that tongue of hers. Poor Maria turned upon her immediately. That one name had roused her to anger ; she turned on Laura, and Laura soon found, for the first time too, that Maria had naturally every whit as much determination and strength as she had herself, and that at a battle-royal she was her superior, using weapons which Laura had been taught to believe unchivalrous and unladylike.

At this point Maria Huxtable lost her temper.

" Better be Mrs. Hilton ! " she said furiously. " I have
no doubt you think that I had better take up with him,
and marry the man you encouraged, until you determined
to sell yourself to a titled booby. Laura, you have behaved more wickedly than I thought it possible. I loved
that man, and if you had not come between us I know he
would have loved me. Loved me ! You hear what I say,
and see if you can sleep after it. I love him now ; and I
am going to marry Sir Harry Poyntz, who is all that you
say and perhaps more. What fiend made you mention
him by name, and drive me mad ! I could have gone on
smiling, and lying, and pretending I didn't hate you, if
you had not brought his name up. Nay, I didn't know I
hated you before. You must make me know it, forsooth.
You have stood between that man and me, and now,
when Lord Hatterleigh comes forward, you coolly recommend the man to my attention, when it is too late for ever !
Laura, you have made an enemy of me, and you will live
to wish you were dead before you had done so."

All this was so horribly, ridiculously untrue, that if poor
Laura had kept her temper she might have cleared the
cobwebs from the poor girl's eyes, and saved infinite woe.
She was angry herself, however ; and one angry woman
going about with another is as vinegar poured upon nitre.
She lost her temper now : she turned on the poor girl and
said,—

" What you have been saying about me is so very im-
pertinent, and so ridiculously false, that I shall not con-
descend to any explanation whatever. You have often
taken my advice ; this is the last time I shall ever offer it,
and it is this—that you cross the river, go to your bedroom, and pray to God to forgive you your wickedness."
And since tall talk inexorably leads to taller, and since if
you begin talking big you will say a deal more than you
mean, she continued : " I have done with you. You told
me a lie to-day, in saying that you were out. I thought
till now it was the first ; now I see it is the last of many—

the very last. Go back across the river to your fate. You have made your bed, and must lie on it. Your servant is waiting for you at the steps."

And so they parted. Laura was only in time to dress for dinner, and very soon sailed into the drawing-room, looking very beautiful, only a little tired, as her mother and grandmother, two of the wise women of Gotham, could not help remarking.

Lord Hatterleigh was there, got up carefully, with a twice-round white tie, looking as if he was at the meeting of a Young Men's Christian Association, and was only waiting for the chairman's summons to rise and make the speech of the evening. He looked at her in what he considered an amatory sort of way, and tumbled over a footstool, and kicked her father, before he bowed himself stern-foremost into Lady Emily's stand of camellias. There was also Colonel Hilton, who was dressed like a box-keeper, and might have passed for one—only that his clothes were so perfectly cut, his beard (the Duke of Cambridge not having published his order) was so very long, and his Victoria Cross was peeping out on the left side of his whiskers. There was Papa, tall, grey, elegant—in blue and brass buttons : there was Mamma, stout and respectable, yet with twopennyworth of *espièglerie* to carry it off ; there was Grandma, with her waxen complexion, and her lace cap, looking as if she was sitting there until the angels Respectability and Routine came and carried her to heaven, to join Hannah More ; and here, in the midst of them, stood Laura herself, with a secret gnawing at her heart, which to her was guilty and dreadful. She loved the gallant young Hammersley, and she *knew* it. Though she said to herself loudly that it was a monstrous falsehood, yet she knew it to be true.

Lord Hatterleigh twaddled on about the Whigs, that incomprehensible and undefinable body, who form the staple of all political talk and speculation. Her father dexterously helped the turbot, and turned his graceful high-bred head and face towards the Vicar, now and then making a little mild fun with him about the rest of his dinner —this being a Friday, and the Vicar being a ferocious high-churchman. That *preux chevalier*, Colonel Hilton, flirted solemnly and gracefully with Constance Downes. Sir Peckwich Downes beamed over his white waistcoat at his fish. Mamma and Grandma chirruped and cackled away as usual. Richardson the butler, master of the feast, administered stimulants according to his will and pleasure, getting vexed with Sir Peckwich's perpetual growl of "Sherry!" as showing want of confidence. There were their own three footmen in crimson plush, and Sir Peckwich's man in orange plush. Was there ever a more respectable gathering?

Poor Laura was excited and upset this evening. It came into her head: "What if she should rise up and tell them all the truth, that she was—— ? " She couldn't say it, not to herself; she could not articulate it even to her second consciousness, though she knew it was there, fatally sure enough, in her third and innermost soul. Suppose she was to get up and say, "Ladies and gentlemen, I am in love with ——. That way lies madness." What would Lord Hatterleigh do?—The Fox-and-North coalition was nothing to this. Would her father rise and curse her? Would Colonel Hilton's look of distrust develope into a look of contempt, and how? The footmen would "tehee," to borrow an expression from Mr. Carlyle. As for her mother and grandma, she knew what they would do—order her to her room. What Sir Peckwich Downes would do she couldn't think: whether he would have a fit, or order his carriage, or lose his temper, or get tipsy, she could not settle. But she found herself smiling over that little speculation, and was surprised to find that her smile swelled into a laugh, so loud that everyone asked her what the joke might be, but she would not tell them.

So they sat over their meat and drink, as though there were no tragedy in the world, and never had been: as if, because you buried an ugly thing and didn't talk about it, that there were to be no more ugly things for ever: as if the butler's cousin had not been hung for sheepstealing; as if one of the footmen's sisters had not thrown her baby down a well; as if Sir Peckwich's brother had not fled to happier and more easy-going climes; as if the golden lock of hair which Colonel Hilton wore round his neck were not his sister's, red with the blood of the Khyber Pass! And quite right too.

"And what had she done?" she asked herself in scorn. "The man was a gentleman; there was no one in the room who could compare with him, except Hilton. What had made him commit this fatal folly, put on this degrading masquerade? And yet, if he had not, she could never have seen him." She rebelled against the notion that her love for him was disgraceful one moment, and then the next she denied that it existed; but she sat silent, and let them tattle on.

Chapter XVI

POOR Maria Huxtable! Prowling among the desolate and empty flower-beds, lurking behind the shrubs, she got glimpses of the party through the half-drawn blinds. The man she loved was there, gay and cheerful, little dreaming who was watching him; and the woman who could have saved her, had she been more patient, was beside him, laughing and talking loudly and almost boisterously. "Laura has a bad heart," thought Maria; "can she laugh so soon after my story?"—Alas, yes! she has her own story too, Maria. "And yet I loved that woman once." And so she delayed there in the growing darkness, tormenting her poor heart by looking into the house she never would enter again as a friend, and watching eagerly the man she loved so dearly, to think of whom was a crime. At last she turned to go towards her home and her fate.

Leighton Court

The servant who had rowed them over was asleep in the boat before she came back ; behind her, as she crossed, the wood and the low long façade of the Court were bathed in the dim dull light of a young moon ; but before, the cruel keep of her future home rose black and ominous, with the blurred crescent behind its topmost battlement, and the wooded cliff so dark that you could scarcely tell when the boat touched the shore.

Dinner would not be till half-past eight. There was time before her yet, precious time ! Before she went to bed that night her fate would be sealed. She knew that if she said yes, she could never unsay it ; she felt terribly sure of that. All that Laura had said of Sir Harry was true ; yet wealth and title were great things. The wish not to leave her dear old home, where her sunny life had been passed, and anger against Laura and pique against Colonel Hilton were terrible assistants, and there was none by to help her. The hour of grace went by ; and as she swept into the drawing-room, covered with jewels and lace, her father saw that she was dressed for attraction, and that the deed was done.

It was done indeed. These three were alone in the house, and when Sir Harry and Mr. Huxtable rose from their wine, the host gave Sir Harry ten minutes' law. At the end of that time, coming into the drawing-room, he found Maria sitting calmly on one side of the fire, while Sir Harry warmed his knees, and examined his face in the pier-glass. As Huxtable entered he turned,—

" I have been asking Maria not to leave the Castle with you, but to remain as its mistress. She has said ' yes.' She has had the matter put before her in the most favour-able manner by you, and has, I doubt not, heard every word that those two cackling old idiots Lady Emily Seck-erton and Lady Southmolton, not to mention Miss Laura, have had to say against me. She has had the good sense to say ' yes.' "

Dare a man's eye follow the unhappy girl to her room

that night—dare a man's hand, and no light one, write what she felt and what she said ! Not mine. But she knew full well what she had done; and there was no shadow of turning with her.

Chapter XVII

MARIA departed next day to visit an aunt; and Sir Harry Poyntz, keeping in strict seclusion, stayed over another day to see after some business.

Immediately after lunch that next day, Mr. Huxtable got into his phaeton and drove round, announcing his daughter's engagement to the master of the Castle.

He drove all the short afternoon, from one country-house to another, generally finding some members of the family at home at each house. As he drove he looked more aged, and more worn as he left each neighbour's. These old-fashioned country-folks none of them concealed their opinion about the matter. From house to house up the left bank of the Wysclith, they (some member of each family at all events) let him know their opinion of the business unmistakably. Generally the announcement was received with astonished silence ; but some few spoke. Among the latter was Sir Peckwich Downes, who spoke to the purpose :—

" I am very sorry to lose sight of my dear little sweetheart Maria ; but you see of course, Huxtable, that it is impossible for me to know anything of her husband, or to exchange any more courtesy with him beyond a bow when we meet on the bench."

" He has been wild," said poor Huxtable.

" I never heard of *that*," said Sir Peckwich. " I was wild. I may have fought one Simon Stockfish, a fruiterer, behind Gray's Inn. My eldest son was very unsteady before he married—so unsteady, that I used to go away from home when he proposed a visit, and left him to the care of his mother and sisters. They brought him right, and he is as good a son as ever stepped since he married. But this—this 'man.'"

"He may reform, too," said Huxtable.

"Huxtable! how can you look me in the face and talk like that? Who in the name of confusion has induced you to consent to this shameful arrangement? I can only tell you one thing: if this affair comes off, which I can hardly believe possible, I must take the same measure with you as I did with my son—be out whenever you call."

There was nothing more to be said. They neither spoke again. The next house was the Vicarage—the next person the Vicar.

It happened to be the vigil of St. Thomas of Moorstanton (a saint whom the Vicar had evolved, it was said, out of his own internal consciousness originally, but whom the Vicar had "developed," in spite of three or four sarcastic letters from the Bishop of Exeter), whose body had been brought and buried here at Wysclith, in spite of the strenuous opposition of five hundred thousand ass panier loads of small devils. So the Vicar had got out the school-children, and was doing a wonderful service over the grave of the saint in whom no one ever believed but himself, in the churchyard. Consequently poor Huxtable was received by the Vicaress, a childless and submissive lady of fifty, who wore scarlet gloves, in deference to her husband's orders.

Huxtable had been so very much bullied to-day that he was very humble here. Even to this woman, the fool of the neighbourhood—who had brought the Vicar money, and who never had a say in her own house—who followed blindly all her husband's vagaries, while the sounder heads of his party cried out against him for ruining their cause with his folly: even before this woman (the "Umbrella," as Laura had christened her) he was humble to-day. He broke the news to her apologetically; and as he did so, she by degrees took off her scarlet gloves.

" And now, my dear madam," he said, "what is your opinion ? "

" My opinion," said the " Umbrella," "most decidedly is that you haven't got the feelings of a man about you. If that dear girl's blessed mother had been alive, you never would have had the impudence to propose such a thing."

If one of his own Leicester lambs had, after this, ran at him barking, and bitten him in the calf of his leg, he could not have been surprised. If a mere umbrella of a woman like this gave him such a reception, what could be expected of her husband, coming fresh, in a state of supramundane pietism, in a green chasuble, from the tomb of a saint ? Huxtable fled without confronting the Vicar ; and as he took the reins, and set the horses' heads towards the Court, said aloud,—

" Let us have it over at once ; let us get through with it."

" I beg your pardon, sir," said the groom beside him.

" Let us have a finish and end of it ; I'll stand no more of this after to-day."

The young groom's conscience was troubled somehow, for he said—

" It was all along of the Court servants, sir. And we was in afore twelve after all."

Huxtable laughed, but his laugh did him no good. He felt like a beaten dog in this matter. Everyone had turned against him, and why ? If this Sir Harry Poyntz was outside the pale of all society, why had no one ever told him of it ? Most certainly no one ever had. His fourteen years' lease of the Castle was nearly up, and he had, during that time, heard nothing more against Sir Harry Poyntz than he had heard against the eldest young Downes, or against half-a-dozen others ; and yet, now it came to the pinch, the county, which had submitted to his coming back there, who had talked of the Poyntz as of themselves, burst out on him in furious rage, at the first mention of his marrying an honest man's daughter ! Are class prejudices so strong that they would keep a secret like this from him? And now he had to face the Court, Lady South-molton and Lady Emily, who gave laws hereabouts, and announce it to them. But he would go through with it. He was an honest Manchester man, and would know the truth. He would not have half-statements from Lady Southmolton.

"I shall get the truth *there*," he said to himself, with that noble instinct which makes honesty recognise honest folks. And so he would have—but——

As he came thundering along in his mail-phaeton through the park, he turned round the corner of a plantation, and caught sight of a group before him.

Laura was riding side by side with a very gallant-look-ing young fellow in a black coat, but otherwise dressed as a foxhunter, who was leading a horse; and they were al-most alone, talking together in an animated manner. A hundred yards ahead rode Sir Charles on "The Elk," looking every inch the perfect gentleman and gallant horseman that he was. His long but perfectly-shaped and beautifully-clothed legs seemed made to clip that vast mass of horseflesh, and his upright not too broad back moved gracefully, under the perfectly-cut red coat, with every movement of the horse. A gallant gentleman, yet his close-cropped grey head was rather bent down to-day, and he seemed tired with his hunting.

As the phaeton bore down on them, the talkers parted and rode aside on to the turf. He saw both their faces; Laura's was animated and interested. He looked at the dandy in the black coat, and to his unutterable amazement beheld *Hammersley*, and he was *laughing*. He was very much astonished; but Laura was, in her high-and-mighty way, very familiar with servants and dogs, he thought: still this was going rather far.

"Does this young man hunt in black?" he asked his groom.

"Yes, sir. He says everyone wears pink now. He

would not hunt in a frock at first, and now he has given up red altogether."

" Does Sir Charles allow these airs ? "

" Allow, sir ! He orders Sir Charles about everywhere, and he only laughs."

But it soon went out of his head ; for Sir Charles stopped and waited for him, and trotted along with him gaily when he came up, telling him of the run, some part of which, as a matter of course, was one of the finest things ever seen. When they got to the front-door, and had dismounted, Sir Charles said, of course, " Come in, my dear Huxtable."

Huxtable said, " No, come into the pleasance with me ; " and Sir Charles went, seeing that Huxtable had something to say ; and they walked up and down along the terrace, not six hundred yards from the great keep across the river. It never occurred to either of them that Sir Harry Poyntz was watching them through a field-glass, but he was.

" Seckerton, our intercourse has been a very pleasant one for twenty years."

Sir Charles' hand was on his shoulder in a moment ; he needed to say nothing.

" I fear your hand will be moved directly, Seckerton ; I fear this will be our last interview. I have got it over with Sir Peckwich Downes, and have gone out of his house without waiting to be ordered out. I have given my consent to Maria's marriage with Sir Harry Poyntz ! "

Sir Charles' hand was withdrawn indeed ; he put both his hands suddenly to his head, and cried out, " Oh, good heavens ! "

" It is quite true," said Huxtable, delighting in his own torture in a strange kind of way, " and the match is principally of my seeking. He is desperately in love with her —sixty thousand pounds ; and I have put before her forcibly, as a man of the world, and a prudent and affectionate father, the rank, prestige, and title which she will gain by such a match. I have done everything to forward it in every way. I have got my will, and I wish we were both dead, dead, dead, lying quietly asleep beside her mother in the cemetery at Manchester."

" It would be much better," said Sir Charles, quietly. And Huxtable, turning, saw that he was scared and shocked. He grew frightened himself now, and waited for Sir Charles to go on.

" This has come on me rather suddenly. Are you aware of the character Sir Harry bears in the county ? "

" Something between Judas Iscariot and Beelzebub, apparently," said Huxtable, " though no one has had the friendliness to give me any details until it is too late."

" It is not too late now, is it ? Surely not ; your daughter would listen to you ? "

" Not now. I know Maria better than you. And there is something the matter about someone else ; and there's a good deal of spite in the business, that is the truth. And it is too late ; Maria won't go back now."

" But he, my dear sir—he ? "

" He give up sixty thousand pounds ! " laughed Huxtable ; " he'd sooner prosecute her for breach ! "

" But remove the sixty thousand ; cut her off with a penny ; disin——" and there he stopped like a bullet on the target.

Huxtable began slowly : " There seems to be something that no one dares tell me. And I'd sooner do that than ——. What *is* it ? Is it friendly or manly in you, Sir Charles, to keep me in the dark on such a subject ? Come ! "

Sir Charles remained as dumb as a stone for a minute ; his thin brown handsome face seemed pinched up, as though with a spasm. At last he said,—

" I am taken by surprise. Will you go away now, and come to me again to-morrow morning ? And will you be assured of one thing : that I believe that you have acted in the dark about this matter, and that nothing shall ever alter the relations between us ? Stick by me, Huxtable, and I will stick by you through everything."

Chapter XVIII

THAT night, after dinner, Sir Charles, with his wife, and mother, and Laura, were together in the drawing-room. Sir Charles, standing with his back to the fire, and looking steadily over the tops of the women's heads at a Raeburn of himself sitting on his mother's shoulder, told them about Maria Huxtable's engagement.

Laura was not surprised, of course; Lady Emily bounced—yes, indeed, bounced—off her chair in an acute attack of virtuous indignation; while Lady Southmolton only took off her spectacles, laid down her work, and began rubbing her two waxen withered old hands one over the other.

What Lady Emily said was much the same as what everyone else had said, and so the reader may guess at it. Sir Charles had expected her outbreak, but was more anxious to hear what her mother would say. It was some time before he heard it, for his wife took a long time running down. When she had subsided into a state of occasional indignant interjections, his mother-in-law began, in a style which gave Sir Charles great surprise. That she always made the best of things with the most wonderful tact, and an amount of Christian charity he had never seen elsewhere, he was perfectly aware; but he was not prepared for the way in which the old lady, in her optimism, supplied him with the very arguments he was dying to find for himself—

" Maria might have married anyone," she said; " and I think myself, not that it is any business of ours in any way whatever, that she is throwing herself away. Still, we must remember that Harry Poyntz has been much steadier lately—nay, seems to be growing into a model young man altogether. He had a bad start in life. His morals were corrupted by the example of his father, and his estate dipped, I thought beyond all hope, by his father's and latterly by his brother's extravagance. He has brought the estate right, or nearly so, and is going to put it right entirely by a most prudent match with a most estimable girl. I have every wish for their happiness. And I should say—you know how used I am to giving advice, my dears, and you must forgive me—that our duty is not to stand in the way, by any means whatever, of the repentance and the reception into a higher atmosphere of a misguided and unfortunate young man, who seems to be trying to retrieve himself, financially and morally."

They heard a measured beat of oars, coming across the river towards the Court.

Lady Emily, as she heard her mother's infallible saint-like voice putting the case in this form, grew awestruck, and began to get thoroughly ashamed of her late outbreak. Sir Charles was very uneasy, but allowed that the old lady had put it marvellously well. But Laura — the gentle, highly-trained, perfectly-formed, submissive Laura —rose suddenly up in flat furious rebellion, and frightened them all three (though they were too cunning to show it) out of their wits.

" I say," she burst out, " that it is a wicked and shameful business from beginning to end, and I'll stop it! Grandma, how can you use your tact to find excuses ? No, ma, I am not in the schoolroom ! Father, you seem tame and acquiescent over the matter; am I to distrust *you ?* But if we talk about it any more we shall quarrel, for the first time in our lives ; and I can only say one thing, that it can't be and sha'n't be, and that I'll stop it ! Colonel Hilton's little finger is worth Sir Harry's whole body, and I will put things right, and put a stop to it."

If she had been an older campaigner, after having charged the enemy, she would have held the ground won, and waited for her supports, which were close at hand, for her mother was rallying and forming fast. Instead of this she committed the error of retiring, being contented with

the astonishment inflicted, leaving the enemy only tem-
porarily paralysed—in other words, flounced out of the
room, and gave them time to re-form.

Not in the most dignified fashion though, for she came
full-tilt against a footman, unobserved by the whole party,
who was holding the door open ; and having nearly knocked
him down, found herself immediately after cast against a
fierce and severe-looking gentleman, in evening dress, with
two orders on his coat; who on seeing her bowed a great
deal too low, leered a great deal too much, backed against
a table like dear Lord Hatterleigh himself, and in dashing
to hold the next door open for her, trod on her gown, and
tore it out of the gathers. She gave him that particular
woman's bow which means " There is some one in the
neighbourhood somewhere," and wrathfully disappeared.

Before the capsized footman was discovered by the three
left behind, Lady Southmolton had looked across her son-
in-law to her daughter, and said quietly :—

" This is your foxhunting ; this is your galloping about
alone at all hours." The grievance was ten years old, and
had not been turned up before. The retort was not less
precious to the old lady for that.

" Captain Southcot, sir, wishes to speak to you in the
anteroom."

" And who on earth is Captain Southcot ? And what
on earth prevents Captain Southcot from coming at a decent hour in the day ? " snapped out poor irritated Sir
Charles in a loud voice, and at the same moment caught
sight of that gentleman standing within ten feet of him,
and recognised him—one of the very men in this world he
was least anxious to offend. He was very much taken
aback, but perfectly up to the emergency. He burst out
into a laugh, and advanced towards Captain Southcot with
his hand extended, repeating,—

" And who on earth is Captain Southcot ? And why
the deuce has he dared to come into the neighbourhood
without knocking his father's old friend up before this ? "

Poor Sir Charles! Baden would be better than this sort of thing—to be driven to lying for the first time in a life, and old age fast creeping on. He felt this—it came on him like a shock; he tried to sustain the effort, but it was too much for him; he began to get forgetful, and talk nonsense.

With the greatest *empressement* he had Captain Southcot in, and introduced him. The two ladies saw in one moment that he was what our late lamented friend Major Pendennis would have called a "tiger." He was a man with a complexion, a nose, and a moustache which didn't cover his teeth. He had eyes too somewhere, arguing by analogy, or he couldn't have got there without a dog or a boy; but if anyone had told you so, you would almost have felt inclined to deny it. His face was too small and too short, and his hair was parted in the middle—the sort of man one has a morbid desire to contradict flatly, if not to go further.

"Your father was an old friend of mine at school," said Sir Charles, "and I remember your mother Lady Joanna Southcot well."

"Lady Mary Southcot," said the captain, grinning.

"Lady Mary, of course; what am I thinking of? Poor dear Joanna Southcot! I ought to remember her, too, well enough; she was your aunt."

Lady Emily rapped the table two or three times, and said impatiently, "My dear Charles, you are wool-gathering!"

Conversation is generally hopeless when three people are wondering what on earth the fourth one has come for; but it was more hopeless still after Sir Charles' dreadful blunder. It had not become quite monosyllabic, when Lady Southmolton came to their assistance by making preparations for bed, by moving from the chair she occupied all day to the bed she occupied all night—a transition which had something of solemnity in it to these good devoted people; for she was so feeble now, that none of them knew but that the next morning the chair might be empty.

As soon as her work was put in the bag, and her little books of devotion which lay around her all day were gathered up, and she had gone away on her daughter's arm, Sir Charles shut the door behind them, and turning round on Captain Southcot, said quietly—

" Now, sir ? "

He looked so big, so grand, and so melancholy, as he looked down on the miserable little ape before him, that that gentleman was abashed, and only handed him a note. For the fulfilment of the rest of his commission, to report how Sir Charles looked on reading it, he had recourse to his imagination, and lied horribly, but so clumsily that he got himself sworn at.

Sir Charles read the note carefully, folded it up again, put it in his waistcoat-pocket, and began staring at Captain Southcot with his great hazel eyes, which looked awfully prominent under his grey eyebrows. After an interval, longer than was quite polite, he said—

" Do you know the contents of this letter ? "

" Yes."

" And now won't you take something before you go ? "

" Nothing at all, thank you."

" Quite sure ? "

" Quite sure."

" Will nothing tempt you," said Sir Charles, ringing the bell : " sherry and seltzer, brandy and soda-water, noyeau and lemonade ? "

" Nothing, thank you," said Captain Southcot, who didn't like the look of the old gentleman, and was bowing himself out. " There is no answer to the letter, then ? "

" None whatever. You may tell your master not to send you here again if you like. But are you quite sure you won't take anything ? It is to be had in one moment : gingerbeer and bitters, brimstone and treacle— anything ! They are going to supper in the servants'. hall ; won't you join them ? Good-night. Don't let me catch you here again."

Chapter XIX

POOR Sir Charles was in very sad trouble indeed—in a fearful dilemma ; but he would not face it out, and took the consequences.   It becomes necessary to see what these troubles arose from, and how they had accumulated.

About the best way for a gentleman of easy disposition with four thousand a-year to ruin himself, is for him to take the hounds and keep open house. If these two things will not do it, let him farm five or six hundred acres of his own land ; if that does not finish him he must have the most astonishing good fortune.   Now Sir Charles had done all these three things, and his fortune had been bad.

When Sir George Downes died, and his son, the present baronet, declined to keep the hounds on, Sir Charles " nobly came forward," as the county paper had it, and offered to take them if the county would give him a thousand a-year.   An enthusiastic meeting of the hunt and the farmers was called, who voted that sum by acclamation, and, what is more, paid it—for the first year ; after that the subscriptions had got rapidly less and less, so that, for the last ten years, Sir Charles had had little to depend on beyond the regularly-paid fifty guineas of Sir Peckwich Downes, and his own pocket.

He had everything perfectly though not extravagantly done ; and he found that the hounds cost him just about 2,000*l.* a-year.   Devonshire is a cheap county, and Lady Emily was a most thrifty and excellent manager, so she managed to keep house with 4,000*l.* a-year, whereas Lady Downes could not do nearly as much for five ; put another thousand on for sundries, and you will get a very pretty yearly deficit, which had been going on for twelve years.   But this was not the worst.   Sir Charles could calculate all this ; but he never knew, never could dare to think, even to this day, what he lost upon the home-farm.

Leighton Court

I have known 30,000*l*. lost on 1,200 acres, and the muddle in that case was certainly not worse than in that of the home-farm at Leighton Court. He may have lost anything. Meanwhile he had not been over-anxious, for the whole of the Shropshire property came to him at the death of Miss Seckerton of Brignal, who, however, was only six-and-forty.

Of course his estate was deeply mortgaged, but no one knew of it, and many would not have believed it. Sir Charles had such a character in the neighbourhood for foresight and prudence, that he was resorted to for advice by all his neighbours, on subjects varying from the choosing of a gun to the marrying of a daughter ; and, indeed, he deserved this confidence, for a clearer head for other folks' business never was on human shoulders. It would have been an inexpressibly sad thing for Sir Charles to have confessed himself a poor and unthrifty man before these simple people ; but a greater evil than that had threatened him for this year past, and had made him wish sometimes that he could say, once for all, " Neighbours, I have been deceiving you all; I am but the most foolish and the poorest among you. I only ask to die with your faces around me." He thought that he would retrench and get his estate right before the Shropshire money fell in, but he began to think so when it was too late !

His man of business had come to him one day, and informed him that he had discovered that every mortgage on the estate was in the hands of Sir Harry Poyntz. When Sir Charles, aghast, asked how he had discovered it, he replied that that was the strangest part of the business ; that Sir Harry Poyntz, whom he had never spoken to, had stopped him in the street and informed him of the fact in a very few words, had then laughed and ridden off.

From that day Sir Charles' head had begun to bow. Nearly a year passed, and Sir Harry Poyntz made no sign. The latter had improved his acquaintance with his tenant Mr. Huxtable and his charming daughter in the North, and had clinched that matter by coming down to the Castle and proposing to Maria. Until the day after that, no communication had passed between him and Sir Charles. But he had watched Huxtable and him through a glass, and had noticed the attitude of disgust and horror with which Sir Charles received the intelligence, and he saw that he must act.

That evening he sent across his toady, henchman, or what you call that sort of man, a particularly worthless young fellow, with the note of which we have seen the arrival and reception.

There was no actual threat in it. He merely pointed out Sir Charles' great influence over Huxtable, and that if it was used to prevent his marriage with Maria, he (Sir Harry) would miss sixty thousand pounds, for which he should indemnify himself (so he said) if his own father stood in the way.

That was all, and enough too for poor Sir Charles! Forced as it were to lie — he who had always been so acutely proud of his honour and straightforwardness, to be driven to this!

Laura, coming in late into his dressing-room, found him with his head buried in his hands, and the letter lying before him. She came in softly. She was accustomed to coming in softly on these occasions, and to passing a few golden happy minutes in loving talk with the man she loved best in all the world. There was once perfect confidence between those two; their hearts had been so drawn, as it were, to one another, that their friendship had become greater than that between two men who had tried and who trusted one another—greater than the mere instinctive love of father and daughter.

But all this was past. One thing Sir Charles had unhappily concealed from his daughter—his difficulties. One thing Laura would fain have concealed even from herself, but could not. Something had disturbed their confidence, and each thought they were the guilty one.

As she came behind him to-night, she saw the letter lying open before him, and, before she knew what she was doing, she had read, " Yours very truly, Harry Poyntz." The look of wonder was still on her face when he turned, and saw that she had read it. He angrily crumpled it up in his hand and turned towards her.

" Laura," he said, coldly, " I see by your eyes that you have read the signature of this letter."

" Accidentally."

" Of course I mean accidentally, my love ! Laura, when you left the room this evening you said that you could and would put a stop to the match between him (touching the letter) and poor Maria."

" I did, and I will."

" Now, my child, I charge you, on your duty, to remain absolutely neutral in the matter."

" Oh, father—father ! "

" Absolutely neutral ! It is not your business to inter- fere in any way. Older and wiser heads than yours are at work upon it."

" You surely are not going to let it take place ? "

" You talk like a perfect child. In the first place, I have not decided what course to pursue ; and in the sec- ond, what right have I to dictate to Huxtable who his daughter may or may not marry ? I meanwhile insist that the influence of this family shall be used through me, and through me only."

Poor Laura saw that her father was sold to the enemy, but would not acknowledge it to himself. She was too sick at heart to say anything more. For the first time he had spoken harshly to her. She would wait for better times ; she turned away and left him.

When Mr. Huxtable called at eleven o'clock the next day, he was shown into the breakfast-room, where he found only Sir Charles and Lady Southmolton, who had evidently waited there for him, before taking up her usual seat by the little drawing-room fire. Sir Charles merely gave him " good-morning :" he left Lady Southmolton to speak.

She soon began. " We heard a piece of news last night," she said, " and it is my turn to congratulate you on it. The more I have thought of this match between your daughter and Sir Harry Poyntz, the better I think of it. It is an eminently good match ; he has family, a large and increasing fortune, youth, and health. He is not worthy of her—no man is, you say—but she would wait a long time before she did better. Sir Harry might marry nearly anyone he chose in London. It is a good match."

And so she honestly believed. She had been so very much used to see very happy marriages made on mere worldly grounds, that she had got to regard the thing rather as a matter of course. She would not have thought that she was doing her duty had she stood between Maria and such a match—so she spoke as above.

Her word was law to Mr. Huxtable, and the thing was done : Sir Charles sitting by silent, and trying to believe that what his mother-in-law said was true, but not in the least degree succeeding.

Chapter XX

THIS year, on Christmas Eve, the gout, which had for some years been twitching at the long fingers and tugging at the small, well-formed feet of long Jim Pollifex of Fernworthy, flew to his stomach in a kind of pet, killed him, and went off to seek another victim.

" He was a great loss to the county," said the bucolic interest ; " a great loss to county society," said everyone who had ever been in it ; " a great loss to the bucolic interest," said both Tory and Whig. The Whigs determined on a fight for that division of the county, and spent 155*l.*

10s. 9d. on a patriotic address, setting forth the claims of
Colonel Hilton.

Pollifex had been a somewhat remarkable man—a longer, leaner, shrewder, wittier edition of his younger brother
and heir Abiram, the great Australian statesman. He
made his last joke to the doctor when he was told things
were getting serious, and nominated Sir Peckwich Downes
as his successor. The Liberals withdrew the instant his
name appeared in print, and their 155l. 10s. 9d. worth of
stationery was pelted with mud by children scarce out of
arms. The Tories had played too big a card for them.
Sir Peckwich Downes had done so much work for the
Tories in Parliament before—was so very big, so very
good, so very rich, so perfectly convinced of the infallibility
of his opinions—such a model landlord, such a model husband, such a capital horseman, such a thoroughly kind-
hearted gentleman, that the Liberals felt they could not
play even such a card as Colonel Hilton, V.C., C.B., against
him. They retired, and called Sir Peckwich Downes an ass,
in which they were mistaken. There was no opposition.

So the Downes's went off to London early in February,
and Lady Downes gave herself such airs before she went,
that our people were not very sorry when she was gone.
She knew—everyone knew—that Sir Peckwich's peerage
was certain, should the Tories come into power, as they
were sure to do with this reaction going on ; and she took
to patronising Lady Southmolton, until that old lady fur-
bished up her old arms, and did a little mild fighting.
However, she was gone, and Hoxworthy was empty, and
the servants gave a ball in the gallery.

It turned out also that the Liberal agent had been a little too quick in using Colonel Hilton's name. With a
laudable effort to be first in the field, he had started that
gentleman without any attempt at consultation with him
or others. That gentleman, his enemies said, as soon as
ever he saw that his chance was hopeless, resented the liberty which had been taken with his name, by writing a

letter to the county paper, indignantly denying any complicity in the matter, and showing that he had, contemporaneously with the Liberal manifesto, accepted an official mission to Châlons.

It was perfectly true. He had been appointed by the Horse Guards to go and look at the great French camp, and he went away and out of the way. "What he ever came *in* the way for," said Lady Southmolton, "is a question which, with our limited knowledge of the ways of Providence, it will be impossible for us to solve on this side of the grave:" in saying which Lady Southmolton spoke too fast.

Lord Hatterleigh, with his hat on the very back of his head—with his respirator, umbrella, and goloshes, keeping both windows up all the way—had likewise departed for London, to attend to his Parliamentary duties. Maria Huxtable had gone the day after her quarrel with Laura, and had never come back. She and her father were in London, where they were joined, very soon after the beginning of the season, by Sir Harry Poyntz and innumerable north-country friends, while preparations for the wedding were going on most briskly. No one, in short, was left in the neighbourhood but our people and the Vicar, who, after a long wrangle with a dissenting granite-splitter on the moor, had wrought himself into a Torquemada vein and excommunicated him.

All else was very still and peaceful; and as the spring went on day after day, even the Vicar and the stone-splitter ceased to wrangle, and were out trout-fishing together before April was over. Nature felt spring in every vein. Even on the solitary mountain-top of Fern Tor quaint little plants came forth and sunned themselves; the great bog got himself a fringe of gold, and in the deep granite glen of the "hundred voices," down which Wysclith hurried night and day, his roar was dulled and softened by the overarching bowers of greenery.

But down in the slate and red-sandstone country spring

showed brightest. There the greens were more vivid, the shadows deeper, the water in the streams clear as crystal, untinged by peat. The beautiful half-cultivated valleys, which stretched in all directions, deeply wooded, had each one a sleepy brook which murmured on from shallow to pool, crowned with new yellow shoots of king-fern and lady-fern, hazel and alder. Bright and rare butterflies and insects shot to and fro across the surface of the water, and trout, hardly less gaudy than the butterflies, poised themselves below in the crystal, above the pale-blue gravel. It was a beautiful season, a foolish romantic season; everywhere too was the jubilant flute-voice blackbird, filling the air with song.

As for Lady Emily and her mother, they had nothing whatever to trouble them, and were happy enough; but to Laura and her father, with their two wearing secrets, it was a season of rest which they were glad of. They both pursued the same plan, the foolish old plan we have all pursued in turn : making believe because our trouble does not make itself heard, that it is getting distant, while we know well all the time that it is creeping steadily nearer. They both succeeded pretty well, and were gay enough, riding together along the sands, or up aloft on the moor; but their old confidence in one another was gone, and they knew it.

Neither of them chose to know the exact day of Maria's marriage. No one ever talked of it except Lady South-molton, who did so occasionally on principle, to show that a thing to which she had given her approval was of neces-sity a perfectly eligible subject of conversation : however, she did not know the day, and no one else cared to en-quire. Sir Charles had heard so little about it that he be-gan to hope it was all over and done. One day Laura followed him into his justice-room or study after breakfast, and said—

"I have heard from Constance Downes, father. She has been to the Queen's ball."

"Oho! indeed!" said Sir Charles. "And is there any other news from the gay folks, eh?"

"Not much," said Laura, looking out of the window. "Lady Poyntz and her husband are at Ems."

"Hem!" said Sir Charles. "And when — when did the—— ?"

"Wedding take place? Last week."

"There was no bell-ringing; why were the bells not rung?"

"The Vicar found the young men in the belfry getting ready, and he turned them all out, locked it up, and took the keys away. He said that if one of them liked to be locked in by himself he might toll, but that there should be no chiming."

"The man is mad!"

"Quite mad!"

So it was all over. "And a good job too," *said* (not *thought*) Sir Charles to himself. "They'll be able to pay their way, which is a great thing in these times. She hasn't done badly." Alas! Alexander in debt and Alexander out of debt talk very differently.

At the end of July all the old set were back again, with the addition of the Poyntz, who came back last of all. But before that a great deal that was very mischievous and sad had occurred, as we must show you. "It is very hard for idle hands to keep out of mischief," says old Watts. Certainly Miss Laura, that opinionated and self-sufficient young lady, was exceedingly idle this spring; all the more solid of her new books from Exeter lay unread on the table; while she, as Edie Ochiltrie would say, went "daundering" by burnsides with "Maude" and "Aurora Leigh." Idle she was, certainly, and contrived to get into a labyrinth of mischief such as is inconceivable by folks who try to fight against circumstances in any way, and do not altogether give up and believe that "the nice" is co-existent, conterminous, and scientifically identical with "the commonsensible."

Chapter XXI

LAURA had better, for some reasons, have been in pension in a third-class boarding-house at Boulogne, than have stayed "daundering" there in Devonshire that spring. Her father and she had lost confidence in one another. There was just one little matter—the Hammersley matter, to wit—which prevented her telling all things to the Vicar as heretofore : a mere twopenny-halfpenny little business, but one which she was afraid to tell him, and which, after all, was no earthly business of his. Her mother was—her mother—a perfectly commonplace woman ; and as for her grandmother, good as she was, and sensible according to her lights, Laura had seen her little store of experience exhibited so often, that she, had she lived among betting-people, might have kept herself in gloves, by betting on what her grandmother would say on any given subject. The only woman who seemed to have any originality in her whatever was old Elspie, her nurse, the most romantic and superstitious old trot in the three kingdoms.

And I must, sooner or later, come *en visage* with my reader about another matter. Let us get it over, and let the reader make the worst of it, or the best of it, as he chooses. Laura was thinking a great deal too much about this Hammersley — this incomprehensible young *preux chevalier*—a great deal too much.

It is hard to blame her much. Of course she was very indiscreet in ever thinking of him for a moment, but her father was more indiscreet still ; knowing what he knew about the man's quasi-position, he should not have allowed her so much intercourse with this splendid Falconbridge. But debt and anxiety had clouded his mind ; and, moreover, this young fellow was getting very dear to him. He had wished for a son, but had never had one. His daughter was not to him what she had been, and in this young man the old gentleman seemed to see the son of his imagination. Hammersley's continual affectionate attention to him was very pleasant; there was such grace about the young fellow that, even when Hammersley bullied him and ordered him about, he, on the whole, liked it, and did not rebel. It was so well and so kindly done, so well and so gently, that Sir Charles, who thought he had but few years' happiness before him, delighted in this young man's presence, and, forgetting the unhappy circumstances of his birth, treated him as an equal, contrasting him favourably with his half-brother, "Harry the Wicked," with his sallow ruthless face, and his cold blue eye; and Robert (now in India), whom he remembered a fierce, savage, but beautiful boy—a boy more disagreeable for the contrast of his wondrous beauty and his uncontrollable temper. "I am in the hands of Harry Poyntz," he used to think; "and if Harry dies before my ruin, I am in the hands of that young fiend Robert. I wish this fellow were other than he is. I could plead to *him*."

Not one word of what was passing did Laura's mother or grandmother know. They had not given Hammersley two thoughts since he had first come; and even if they had done so, the possibility of Laura's being indiscreet enough to interchange words with him never entered into their heads. But they noticed that Laura was always with her father now; that she had given up all her old orderly habits, and came and went like a wild sea-bird on the shore. All this gave her mother great uneasiness.

"I have lost all power over her. I dare not say anything to her. I wonder if she means to have Hatterleigh. This don't look much like it."

"My dear," said the elder lady, "in my opinion she has made up her mind to have him, and is enjoying her freedom before going into harness. That is it, depend upon it. There is not a more sensible girl in England; she is far too wise to refuse such an establishment as Grimwood."

Lady Emily could only hope so. She knew Laura a

great deal better than her mother. Many a furious out-
burst of childish temper had been concealed from the old
lady, and remained a secret between mother and daughter.
Laura could be headstrong when she chose, and she chose
now.

Meanwhile she looked on herself as a model of discretion, and indeed never, first or last, did she take any step
unworthy of a lady. She kept Hammersley carefully at
bay, and very rarely spoke to him; on one or two occasions she had so far forgotten who he was as to enter into
conversation with him, as when Huxtable overtook them in
the park; at these times she found him to be, just what he
looked, one of the most charming fellows she had ever met.
Of course she saw he was a gentleman. She would have
given a great deal to know his history, but her father and
mother kept that (at least all they knew of it) to themselves.

Her father, during these months, was as restless and as
reticent as herself. The passion almost the pursuit of his
life had been horse-riding. Save that he had done his
duty as landlord and magistrate, he had done nothing else.
Now, with a prospect of Baden or Wiesbaden before him—
now that he saw that it only rested with an utter scoundrel
to ruin him, and to make him walk afoot till he was too old
to ride—he took to his horses and his dogs more diligently
than ever; his grooms and his dog-feeders acquired new
importance in his eyes. The poor gentleman saw that his
power over them was ephemeral—that the time would soon
come when they would call him master no longer. He had
always been a kind and indulgent master—now he grew
kinder and more indulgent than ever. Anxiety acts on
some souls like that. Poor Sir Charles knew that his reign
was coming to an end, and wished that his subjects should
have none but kindly recollections of the banished prince.
Laura had got hold of a foolish negro song, " So Early in
the Morning !" a very pretty little song too—

> Master's dead and gone to rest,
> Of all the masters he was best.

She sang it once, but he asked her not to sing it again. He gave every reason but the right one; it was silly—the lilt was a mere vulgar jingle, and so on. Poor fellow! the truth was that the silly pretty song touched him too nearly.

Ah! poor fellow; if he would only have told the truth to Laura! He could not tell it to his wife or Lady Southmolton—he *dared* not! They, had they taken any pains to calculate matters, might have found it out for themselves; but no. Sometimes he asked himself, now and afterwards, did they ever guess or care to guess the truth? They certainly never gave any sign. The household, so utterly bankrupt, was kept up in the same respectable manner: prayers at nine—lunch at two; service in the hall on wet Sunday mornings—sermon every Sunday evening, wet or dry, in the dining-room at nine; the whole dead-and-alive old routine kept up as though there was no merciless creditor, as though ruin were not knocking at the door. It would have been better if he had told Laura first than last.

But he could not. The dark nameless secret in Laura's heart showed itself in her eyes, and Sir Charles saw that there was a cloud between them. He knew he had sinned, and sinned deeply, in the matter of Maria Huxtable; and he thought that the indecision in Laura's eye, the unwillingness with which she met his look arose from contempt — that she could not forgive him about that matter. He knew that he was guilty, but he never dreamt that she could have anything to conceal too. He was so unused to having anything to conceal, that now, when he had erred, and found himself, through circumstances, left without a friend, he got cowardly and reckless.

But though Sir Charles had no more confidence with his daughter, still he had *her*. Though his position was a fiction, an air-raised castle which might tumble down any moment, still he had Laura. She was his daughter, the beauty of Devon, the best horsewoman and the best-trained lady in the county. And she loved him still, in spite of this cloud between them. It would all vanish soon, into thin air; and after that the dreary hot white streets of Baden. Meanwhile he had his daughter, his dogs, his grooms, and his horses, and no one knew anything; he need not yet walk afoot and see other folks on horseback,

He never was out of the saddle now. He would ride as long as he could. As for Laura, she would ride you from cock-crow to curfew, and she rode with him, loving him as he loved her, while neither dared say the few words which would have restored confidence. In either case it would have been too terrible.

So these two reprobates went about on horseback—away before prayers, home too late for dinner—committing every sin of omission conceivable. The Vicar came down on Laura for missing church on Easter Eve, pathetically noticed her entire neglect of the Easter decorations, and plaintively rebuked her for her backslidings. Laura gave a little laugh, which puzzled the Vicar, and promised amendment. After he was gone she laughed again, louder. How quaint his language seemed to her! His rebuke, earnest though it was, seemed taken out of some book; not a word in it seemed wrong. Yet all that had had a meaning for her three months ago. How far off seemed Christmas — how long she had lived since then! Was the rapt worshipper of Christmas the same being as the wild gipsy-like Laura of Easter? She laughed again; there was nothing irreverent or mocking in her laugh; it was merely a laugh of wonder, such as a savage gives when he sees a new toy.

But her riding habit was on, and her father was waiting for her in the stableyard,

Chapter XXII

So Laura — still laughing, still vaguely puzzled about the change in herself, still vaguely wondering where it would lead—went into the stableyard, with the skirts of her habit gathered in her hand. Her father had mounted "The Elk," and was at the farther end of the yard. Hammersley was leaning against his leg, and talking to him, with the bridle of the horse he was evidently going to ride, over his arm. Laura looked, and saw that the horse he had appropriated was the very horse she had ordered for herself. The grooms meanwhile were bringing out for her another horse, a horse she did not like particularly. She rebelled.

"I ordered Avoca," she said. "I shall not go out to-day, on this horse."

One of the grooms said that "Mr. Hammersley had countermanded the order, and had said that Miss was to ride the chestnut."

And at the same moment Hammersley said to her father: "I want to ride that horse to-day. His mouth has been pulled 'about sadly lately; I want to ride him myself."

This was going too far. Sir Charles was very angry. He said, in Hammersley's hearing alone,—

"You are taking liberties. I will allow no liberties. Do you think, because—because—that I will allow you to speak in that way? I know the secret of your birth, Hammersley, and I have treated you as if you were the first-born. But I will not stand this."

"I am a fool," said Hammersley; and he went quietly forward, and told the grooms to change the saddles, without looking at Laura. They obeyed him in a moment; they knew who was practically master. When the arrangement was accomplished he went back to Sir Charles, without once offering to put Laura on her horse. One of the grooms did that.

Sir Charles and he had time for a minute's private conversation, away from the others. Sir Charles was still angry, but his anger was passing away. He said to Hammersley: " You forced me to speak to you. And there is another thing I wish to say. From your manner, you seem to assert an equality with us, which, under the circumstances, you are scarcely warranted in assuming. Do you know anything which others do not? Is there any chance of your assuming the place in the world to which you are fitted? If so, I will serve you with purse and with influence to the utmost of my power."

Hammersley pressed his hand. " Let it be as it is for the present." They had time to say no more.

To-day Sir Charles and his daughter were bent on an aimless expedition to the wildest and farthest of their farms, on the very moor itself — Fernworthy : a solitary stone house, in the centre of about eighty acres of poor arable land, reclaimed from the moor, lying at the edge of the great Wysclith bog, at the sources of the river, in the heart of the mountains. There were some puppies at walk there, and he made believe he wanted to see them, so as to get a day's riding with his daughter. By a similar kind of self-deception, he persuaded himself that his new favourite, Hammersley, had better come too and see them. The pad-groom was ordered back, and Hammersley followed.

So they rode away from the sound of the sea, through the deep red lanes, through the rich overarching boscage of the first band of country ; and then through a long-drawn valley of yellow clay, through which the blue slate peeped here and there, among world-old oaks, thickly clustered, underlaid with holly—the home of the woodcock. Then, facing on to the culminating height of the slate hills, they drove across the desolate scratch-and-scramble-farmed, infanticide-producing twenty-acre freehold, ten-bushel country, which lies between the thirty-bushel civilisation of the red lands, and the vast barbarous granite desert beyond ; lastly they came to the country of heather and bleating peewits—to the hot silence of the moor ; Wysclith, five hundred feet below them, hungrily gnawing at the ribs of the earth to win his passage to the sea.

But as they rose to this height, great clouds—which un-poetical folks call " cabbage-headed," but which more sen-timental folks call either " blue piled thunder-loft," or else " Alp-formed cirrocumuli "—kept rising also from the south-east, and now hovered so closely overhead that Sir Charles remarked, as if there were the least necessity for doing so, that they were going to have a thunderstorm.

Wysclith only makes one great bound or waterfall in his passage from the hills to the sea, and that is in his very youth, shortly after he leaves the bog, and before he gets into that great grey glen—the " glen of the hundred voices " as we have called it—which stills his roaring by degrees till he comes into the softer strata below. The ford across to Fernworthy crosses the infant stream about one hundred yards above the waterfall ; and as they splashed through it, they saw the little trout scouring away in all directions over the yellow gravel, and heard the first thun-der-crash over Fern Tor.

There is no *need* to describe Fernworthy, because we shall not want it again. Yet we will give three lines to a genuine moor-farm. A low grey stone house, with a wall enclosing what our Scotch brothers call " policies " (and why ?) ; low granite hills, breaking sometimes into low weathered tors, blocking the horizon ; a dozen ill-grown fir-trees, dogs which bark all day, and, for want of any-thing to do, hunt the cats (with a distinct understanding, however, on the part of the cats). Besides this, muck, mess, mad mismanagement, cider and brandy, immorality and ignorance : you must go to the backwoods to match some moor-farms.

The farmer, a vast, untidy, good-humoured, slab-sided

giant, held the gate open for them. "You'm just in time, Sir Charles," he said. "Listen to mun ; and how she stinketh ! mussy."

The "she" referred to the air, which certainly deserved to be so spoken of, for a sulphurous electrical smell penetrated their nostrils most disagreeably. Hammersley took their horses to the stables, and he had hardly come into the kitchen when the rain began to roar upon the roof, and the first red blink of lightning was visible in the room.

It was a very fearful storm, such as the livers in the lowlands seldom remembered, but which were frequent enough, said the farmer, among the hills. Laura sat beside her father in the middle of the room, away from the chimney ; and though she to a certain extent disliked the glare of the lightning, which was almost perpetual, she could not help looking at the window ; for Hammersley stood there, looking coolly out into the livid blaze perfectly unconcerned. At each variety in the lightning his face assumed a different colour—now green, now purple, now flushed with red ; and as she watched, she began to fancy that his face was changing rapidly from one fierce passion to another with a grotesque diablerie exceedingly terrifying. At last, during a flash of lightning more white, brighter, and more prolonged than the rest, which was accompanied by three or four sharp snaps, and then a roar which shook the house, she saw his face take the colour and the rigidity of death.

Her nerve gave way, and she screamed out, "Oh, he's killed !" and sprang towards him. She had seized his arm before she was aware of it ; and he turned very coolly towards her, saying, in his usual voice, looking very steadily at her,—

" It was the effect of the lightning on my face, I dare say, Miss. I will come away from the window."

Laura felt a trifle silly at the exhibition of a self-possession greater than her own, and began wondering whether or no she hadn't made a fool of herself. She thought more of this question on finding that her father had suddenly tuned his fiddle up a full octave higher, and had become afflicted with a somewhat offensively polite silence. Laura was terribly frightened.

If her father's eyes had been for one moment opened, they were very soon shut again. I believe that in the terror of what happened instantly after, he forgot the little circumstance altogether, or, if not, that it dwindled into insignificance. The storm was soon over, and they rode away.

The ford before mentioned, where they had seen the trout scudding over the yellow quartz gravel, was now a whirling porter-coloured torrent of uncertain depth. Sir Charles pulled up at it. When they passed before they could hear the noise of the waters in the glen below; now every sound, even that of the thunder, which was still growling in the N.E., was swallowed up in the roar of the waterfall, which was a bare hundred yards to the right; he could see the water shelve away smooth and glassy and disappear, while from the chasm the spray rose and floated among the rocks, telling of the hell of waters below.

This was all uncommonly pretty. He had an eye for scenery, and admired it, but as a master of hounds he was obliged to call it a very ugly thing. He wondered aloud how deep it was.

" I'll see, sir," said Hammersley, and went clattering and splashing into it then and there. His big Irish horse went at it in true Irish fashion. It looked dangerous, and there was a chance of being killed, and so " at it you go; " and he got through. It wasn't half so bad as it looked. The water had barely reached to his feet — they were only splashed. Sir Charles and Laura instantly followed, " The Elk " striding through it like an elephant, and Laura's smaller horse seeming to make as little of it as the elephantine Elk himself.

The Australians are probably the most reckless riders in the world, and the younger of them think nothing so fine as swimming a flooded river. But you find that the older they get the less they like it. After they have had a horse "capsize" under them a few times they get rid of their superfluous vitality by dangerous forms of steeplechasing, and "funk" the water.

Who can tell at what particular moment what we call an "accident" begins? Something suddenly happens, and while people are wondering what is the matter, limbs are broken and lives lost. The train begins to jump, and you have not time to look up from your *Saturday Review* before you find yourself amidst a ruin of wood and iron, with a lady screaming herself to death before you, and the last piece of fun in the small-print article in full possession of your brain. You watch a dipping sail in the Solent, and think it is dipping too deep; and before you can realise that anything has happened, the boatmen bring you ashore a trembling idiot who, an hour ago, was a gallant young man, and tell you that he was to have been married to the young lady who was just drowned, and that he held her up until his arm gave way, and he was obliged to let her go. This is too terribly true!

Sir Charles saw Laura go safely on before him till she was almost at the other side, when her horse seemed to stumble and feel the pressure of the current; for he rolled on his side, and threw Laura beneath him. When he saw the horse's near hoofs rising to the surface, and Laura's arms only appearing above the water, and her little white gloves clutching about at anything and everything, then he realised the fact that there was an accident, and a terrible one; and tried to spur "The Elk" towards her, and towards the destruction which awaited them both in the seething cataract below.

But the good horse only floundered through the ford, and, getting on land, burst into one of his pachydermatous gallops; by the time Sir Charles, half-mad with terror, had turned him and had got back to the bank, he only saw this—

Laura's horse landing himself about ten yards above the

waterfall; Hammersley's horse grazing, and Hammersley himself in the water, with his feet still off the ground holding on to an oak-root, with his arm round Laura's waist. Their faces were close together, and they were within five seconds of death, and he was encouraging her to hold on. She held on. Sir Charles shouted wildly to them : to her to save herself for his sake—to Hammersley to save her, giving wild promises, which were luckily wasted, as they neither of them heard him. Before he had time to think of what he had said, they got their feet upon a shelf of granite, and came on land safe.

Laura was dripping from head to foot ; she was trembling too, but she was also in " a mood," as her father saw in a moment. He who had watched her so long and so well saw that she was agitated by something more than sheer physical fright at her terrible danger. He saw that she was in a mood, and guessed the cause, sagacious creature !

" Laura, dear, you can't blame me. How could I guess that your horse would have stumbled ? I tried to ride down and help you, but this old brute of a horse wouldn't turn."

" I don't blame you at all, father ; I have no one but myself to blame. Bring me my horse, if you please, as quick as you can. Father, I am frightened ; take me home to my mother."

Hammersley had caught her horse and brought it up, holding the reins of his own horse by his arm, and standing by her horse's head ; he spoke first,—

" Would you be kind enough to put Miss Seckerton on her horse, sir ? I have frightened her a little pulling her out of the water."

Sir Charles did so, appreciating the high-bred instinct of the young man. The moment they were all mounted, the young gentleman, looking as sulky as a thunderstorm, said :—

" I think I had better ride home, sir, and tell them that Miss Seckerton is wet and frightened." And without any more words away he went, as if he was a gentleman, without waiting for leave.

" Laura, dear," said Sir Charles, who had got very much afraid of her since the cessation of their confidence, " let us go to the Downes ; you are wet through, and the housekeeper will rig you out in Constance's things in a quarter of an hour."

" I asked you to take me to my mother, father ! "

" But your chest, dear ? "

" Take me to my mother ; I want to go to my mother ! "

Chapter XXIII

BUT now came a crisis in matters which led to strange results. Poor Laura will remember the 17th of June as long as she lives; and there are more still who will remember the next day quite as well.

What encouragement poor Hammersley had ever received, which induced him to commit the most fatal act of folly he did, we shall never know. From Laura certainly none ; she had scarcely thanked him for saving her life. For the present we must suppose that Sir Charles had so far spoilt him, as to make him so utterly forget his position, and what was due to Laura, as to speak to her in the way he did.

It was very late in the June evening, and the few workmen who had been employed in doing a few stingy repairs in preparation for Sir Harry and Lady Poyntz were gone, and the Castle grounds were left in seclusion. Laura went over to walk there.

We know now that Hammersley had watched her and crossed by the bridge higher up, for another watched and followed him, impelled by an overwhelming curiosity.

He met her in a dark walk, and, going to her, spoke to her more familiarly than he had ever done before. He did

not go far—she did not give him time. She stopped him the
very instant he had gone far enough to make it necessary,
but did not let him go a step too far. She had not been
well-formed for nothing ; no one could do it better than she.

She was very quiet indeed with him. She first pointed
out the extreme act of folly of which he had been guilty,
and then dwelt on the extreme degradation and aimless-
ness of his present way of life.

" If you are what you seem," she said " (I mean a gentleman), throw off this miserable disguise and way of life,
and do something worthy of yourself—something which
will make your fellow-men respect you. Take the advice
of one who wishes you sincerely well, and go from here
at once. Now go ; and, believe me, I shall be always
glad to hear of your welfare. Good-bye ! "

He went quickly, without a word. When she turned
round to see if he was gone she was alone in the gathering gloom, and saw him no more.

" Could her grandmother have been more discreet ? "
was the first thing she asked herself. The answer her conscience gave her was, " Certainly not ! " The very echoes
of the summer's evening seemed to tell of " Cœlebs in
Search of a Wife" and other high-toned books of that
kind. She recalled every word she had said. It was in
her grandmother's best style — nothing could be more
eminently satisfactory. And then she began to cry.

As soon as she had moved away to a safe distance, no
other person than old Tom Squire crept cautiously out, and
looked after her round the corner. He was very nearly
caught, for Laura turned and looked back suddenly ; and
he saw that she was crying bitterly.

" What ! looking back to see if he'd come again, eh ? "
the old fellow chuckled. " There'd be a fine to-do if the
lad had brains to follow you now, my young lady. Well,
if gentlefolks don't know their own minds it's no business
of mine ; but he shall know of this, though he breaks my
head for watching ! "

Chapter XXIV

THOSE dreadfully inexorable people the chemists insist that there is just as much oxygen in the atmosphere on one day as there is on another, but it is very hard to believe. They make up their account with ozone, which is a very nasty thing. It is hard that one may not believe, in this age of toleration, that there is not more oxygen in the air on a brilliant crystalline morning, than on a dim, wild, murky autumn evening. However, they are right, one supposes, and air cannot be oxygenated like water; otherwise the atmosphere round Leighton Court must have been represented by a fresh formula, on the morning after Laura's adventure in the Castle shrubbery.

There was something in the air that morning, however, ozone or barometric pressure or something else, which got into the lungs of Sir Charles Seckerton, as he lay in bed, with his window open as usual, and made him get up and shave at seven, and moreover caused him to ring up Lady Emily's maid, and send her to Laura's room to challenge her to a gallop on the sands before breakfast.

The lady's-maid — a most superior woman, who "messed" alone with old Elspie the nurse, since a great quarrel in the housekeeper's room, which has nothing to do with this story—answered the bell with wonderful alacrity, and before Sir Charles had time to deliver his message, delivered her own: to wit, that the huntsman and the stud-groom had been waiting in the servants'-hall for him since six, and that she believed there had been an accident.

"An accident! To whom?"

One of the grooms, or helpers, or some one of the stable-people was drowned, she believed—young Hammersley, she thought. She belonged to the female side of the house, and shared in the opposition to horse-riding in any form, which was their creed, and which had led to the secession of her and Elspie from the housekeeper's and steward's room.

"Go and fetch them up instantly," said Sir Charles. "And don't wake Miss Seckerton on any account whatever."

On ordinary occasions Madam would have as soon had her dinner in the servants'-hall as show up any of the "stable-people." This time, however, she made no further objection than gathering her petticoats round her and sniffing; she wanted to hear the news.

"Good heavens! what has happened, Dickson?" said Sir Charles to the stud-groom, who stood forwardest.

"Mr. Squire will explain, Sir Charles," he said; "I am only here to make my story good about the horse."

Sir Charles glanced impatiently at the terrier-faced little huntsman, and said, "Go on."

He still kept in the back, with his grey eyes fixed keenly on Sir Charles. He began at once,—

. "Last night I went to bed at ten o'clock. I had been in bed about ten minutes, when he came in in a hurry."

"He! Who? Hammersley?

The old man nodded. Sir Charles looked for a moment from him to Dickson, and then back again, as though he would ask, "Does he know anything?" And Squire shook his head "No," and went on,—

"He came straight to my room with a light, and said at once, 'Get up. I must go far and fast to-night. I want "The Elk," and I want you to get him for me, for,' he said, 'that infernal cross-grained old pig Dickson,' meaning him you know (pointing at him with his hat), 'would never let me have the horse at this time of night.' I immediately did as he required."

"And I, Sir Charles," said Dickson, pompously, "following the routine of the establishment, complied with Mr. Squire's astounding request, and sent out the horse."

. "You did perfectly right, my good Dickson. You may go now."

Dickson the astonished retired, and the old man re sumed :—

"He got on 'The Elk.' I asked no questions, I durnst. He is a Poyntz, you know, or as good as one I should say, and he was in one of his moods; but knowing Sir Harry was nearly due home, I thought it was a case of good-bye. I waited to hear him say it, but he did not till the very last; and then he said, ' I'm off. I can't stand this. Good-bye ! You shall hear of the horse.' And I said nothing. Then he said, 'Good-bye, and God bless you! Come here.' And I came to him, and he bent down and kissed my fore-head."

A pause. Sir Charles turned away, and went on with his dressing. The old terrier took up his story as soon as he found his voice; not a moment before,—

"He turned to the left out of the Bell Yard, and broke into a gallop. Then I saw that he was going to try the sands that night, and I cried out, like a man in the falling sickness, 'The tide's making! the tide's making!' Per-haps he did not hear, at all events he did not heed. I ran, but what was the good of that? I heard him only a few minutes, but I ran on, guessing which way he had gone; and all I could find of him was the way that the deer still stood gazing as he had startled them. I heard him open the gate, and rattle down the lane; and when I got to the cliff above the Avon Sands, I saw that he was lost. He was three hundred yards out on them going like mad, and the breakers were not a quarter of a mile to his right, growling up fast before a strongish south wind. That's the last I saw of him, and the last any man ever will."

"Good God!" said Sir Charles; "you don't actually mean to say that Mr. Poyntz is drowned? I wouldn't have had this happen for a thousand pounds. He was worth the two other brothers put together. What makes you think he is drowned?"

"What makes me think he is drowned, Sir Charles? You have me there. I am afraid there is no hope at all."

"But hang it, man, it can't be true; it is too horrible! An author wouldn't dare to put such a horrid thing in a novel, except Scott, of course, who has some devilish horrid things in his novels. Such things don't happen in real life. I won't believe it. Pish! I don't choose to believe it. I don't want to be shocked just now; we were going on so nicely, as if we weren't all walking blindfold among venetian-glass; and now this comes. Poyntz was no fool; he would have turned from the tide and headed landward. That horse would beat any tide that ever flowed. You are talking folly!"

"He is drowned and dead. You say he was no fool. He was a madman last night; and I know they as drove him so. He got on the Musselbank and was surrounded. Why do *you* talk nonsense, Sir Charles, about his heading up the bay? Don't you know he is dead? Ride his darndest, and suppose the sands were sound, where could he possibly make in time?"

"Barcombe."

"I was in a boat as soon as there was water to carry one, and I have been all along the other shore, to Barcombe and to Seamouth, higher up, but they've heard nought of him. When the sea gives up her dead, Sir Charles, you will meet the best of all the Poyntzes, not before. Oh, my noble boy—oh, my noble, noble lad!"

Poor Sir Charles! He tried to fight against the probability of its being true, but facts were too strong for him. He had got very fond of this unhappy young man, and had more than a dozen times thought how well he would have liked such a son. Since he had known that his own ruin was only a matter of time, he had relieved the ghastly, sleepless watches of the night by picturing in the dark, when he was afraid to turn and toss for fear of arousing and making anxious the innocent unconscious wife at his side, what sort of a graceful home he could make himself at Wiesbaden or Paris; and this young Hammersley, Poyntz, or what you choose to call him, had always made part of the home-group. And now he was dead, and in this dreadful manner!

Although he felt certain that it was true, yet he refused to believe it. For twenty-four hours he was able to say to neighbours that he did not believe it; that the young man had gone off with the horse, and all that sort of thing; but on the next morning there was no doubt about the fate of Poyntz-Hammersley, the nameless man, and they searched no more.

Riding under the red cliffs, Sir Charles and old Squire came upon a little cove or bay of golden sand, which ran up among seaweed-grown rocks; and here, with his head resting on a pillow of purple sea-tang, they found " The Elk " drowned and dead.

It was as well. The cruel quicksands had done their work thoroughly. The carcass of a drowned horse may pose itself artistically, and look grand and noble for a little while, but nothing can make the loose wet lips of a drowned man look otherwise than horrible. The mermaidens had kept their ghastly toy to themselves; or, to put it otherwise, the horse had had strength to struggle from the shifting quicksand, while the weaker man had been sucked down and buried for ever.

Chapter XXV

THE wild July weather set in for a few days now. Nature generally gives us a reminder just about the middle of summer, that there is something to think of in this English climate besides deep green forest boscage, and calm cloudless summer days. Generally about this time she comes tearing back in her strength, to toss the boughs wildly to and fro, to flood the streams and beat down the ripening corn, and to say plainly, " You English, you nation of pirates, you and I are always at war! I am not beaten, but will beat you yet. Here are some wrecks for you; I will come again at the equinox, and fight with you all through your long dreary winter." And then up goes the drum and cone from Peterhead to Penzance, and the telegraph clicks out from one end of Britain to another—" Here she comes; look out!" And those of the small fry who abide her coming are hurled on leeshores, or tossed, terrified and storm-beaten, into holes and corners to hide themselves; while the larger ships and steamers toil grandly on, defiant.

Laura was looking from her window, and watched the dark weather booming and rushing from the south-west across the sands. The evening was darkening so much, and night was so near, that the few toiling ships passing up and down the Channel were getting too dim to distinguish through the haze.

The news of the accident had found its way early that morning from the servants'-hall to the steward's room, and from thence upwards into that sacred eyrie, which those two eagles of respectability—Elspie the Scottish nurse, and Lady Emily's maid—had got built for themselves alone above the base scolding of the shorter-winged birds below, and where they sat all day with their long beaks together over the table, turning over the bones of dead scandals, and scenting new ones. A little wide-eyed dove of a stillroom maid got bold enough, under the general excitement, to fly into their Golgotha, and tell them the news without having heard their bell: after which she wisely fluttered out again.

As soon as she was gone, old Elspie rose up and said to the Englishwoman, " I'll just gang up at once, and break it to her myself."

" I think you are wise, my dear soul," said Mistress Bridget. " Break it to her gently, my dear soul. That it should come to this! Break it to her gently. How very, very dreadful! But it is all for the best. Be gentle with it, my dear soul, whatever you do. Poor young man!

But I didn't see my way out of the mess till this happened. We have a deal to be thankful for in this, Mistress Campbell. Mercies are showered down on us every day. Break it to her gently, my dear soul ; but I fear she will break her heart over it, anyhow."

Elspie, as the saying goes, looked her through and through. Mistress Bridget had before made some feeble skirmishing attempts on Elspie of this kind—attempts to make Elspie acknowledge that there was some kind of mild flirtation between Poyntz-Hammersley and Laura, and Elspie had always stopped her advance with a dead-wall of Scotch caution. Her own darling Laura should never be talked about, by *that* woman at any rate ! She considered Mistress Bridget's last speech as a treacherous attack on her works at a moment of sentimental confidence, and she was very angry.

" Ye'll no sell stinking herrings in Kirkcaldy, woman," she said. " And why should Miss Laura break her heart because one of her father's retainers is drowned in the sand, if ye please ? "

Mistress Bridget " caved in." It was very horrible— such a fine young man !—and so on ; she had not meant anything.

" Ye'd better not mean anything, woman," replied Elspie, leaving the room, " because I ain't just in the temper to stand it."

" So she, who knew how matters stood as well as you or I, went upstairs and broke it to Laura in the fashion which her keen intellect told her was the best.

Laura was in her combing - jacket, combing her hair, when she came in. She stood at the door, and knocked her stick on the floor.

" A bonnie morn, lassie ! "

" A beautiful morning, nurse."

" Ye ken young Hammersley, yer father's favourite man ? "

" Very well."

" He's drowned, drowned, drowned ; buried sax feet in the wicked treacherous sand, and his ain mither will never wail over his bonny corpse! Sirs, he was a bonny lad! I've a tear or twa left for him in my dry eye yet. The horse fought out of the quicksand and got drowned fairly —they found him just now in the cove below the Castle cliff—but your bonnie Hammersley is deid, smoored in the sand, halfway between this and Barcombe ! "

And so she shut the door on Laura, and went downstairs to see if Mistress Bridget was inclined for a fight, which she felt would do her good, saying as she went,—

" There, she has got it a'! Poor dear, poor darling, she loved him ; and he was a bonny boy, a bonny boy, worth sax hundred of your fushionless, doited potato-bogle Hatterleighs? She shall stay alone to-day. I'll tell that round-about whisky-barrel woman Lady Emily, and that feckless auld dolly Lady Southmolton, that she is ill. They lang nebbit hawk-eyed women are best left alone in their grief. I mind me of a red-haired seceder lass taking the jocktaleg to her ain mither, but that's no exactly to the purpose. Laura is too lang in the neb, and too keen in the eye, to be meddled with this day.

" But," groaned out the old woman, " the Papister! If that man get hold of her, now in her trouble, she'll be a Papist in three months; and she'll fly to him now, and he'll pass her on to the abomination, the villain, before I am dead. I shall have to see it. I'll go in and see if Mistress Bridget will have a turn of words with me, and help me to put poor Laura out of my mind. They lang nebbit women—it's either Calvinism or Romanism with them. They must have it hot either way."

Poor Laura had been devising fifty plans to avoid seeing Hammersley again, supposing he had not done as she had asked him, and gone. One plan was to ask to go to her aunt's in London; another to fall ill, and get taken to Bournemouth ; another to tell her father just enough to make him send Hammersley away. But now her difficulty had been solved in this horrible way. She spent all the day by herself in a state of stupefied terror, sending excuses downstairs to say that she was shocked by the accident, and that it had made her ill. All day she stayed in her room, looking over the desolate sands until day began to decline. She felt alternately terror at his death, and terror at what she had escaped; tenderness, too, tried to make itself heard, but she resolutely beat it. " Not to-day, at all events—not to-day," she said resolutely.

As the day went on a resolution grew into a settled purpose, and at evening she rose to put it into practice. In her terror and her grief she fled back to those old rules of life in which she had been brought up. She would appeal to them for protection against herself; they had seemed to do much for her grandmother — let her see what they would do for her, now they were wanted.

She dressed herself very carefully, and went down to dinner. As she shut the door of her room, she said— " There! the discipline is begun; the last six months are shut in that room for ever! "

When she got down Lady Southmolton and her mother were laughing together, but they left off as she came in.

" My dearest girl," said the older lady, " you have had a sad shock."

" Why, yes—rather," said Laura, in her dryest, hardest voice; " it actually made me ill for a little, Elspie announced it so suddenly. It seemed to me so particularly horrible, that a fellow-creature was struggling for life within sight of our windows, while we were comfortably laughing and joking. At what time was he drowned? "

" At about a quarter to eleven."

" Singular! There was a light in my room just at the time, probably the only one on that side of the house. That must have been the last object his eyes rested on before he sank. Of course it is not so shocking in this case, as it was only a servant, but it is very sad! "

This I give as an instance of the mental torture she began to inflict on herself. Not an idle hour in the day was allowed now. The next day she walked up to the Vicar in the morning, confessed to him, and received absolution. He imposed a few penances upon her, which seemed to make her much happier, but they were very light ones indeed ; for the Vicar was not only glad to have her back, having missed her sadly, but he thought, on the whole, that she had behaved uncommonly well. The principal thing he insisted on was, that there should be no more fox-hunting ; all the mischief had come from that, and there should be an end to it.

And Sir Charles put up a tablet on the church-wall to poor Poyntz-Hammersley, and " The Elk " sleeps beneath the immemorial elms in the corner of the Park.

END OF PART I

Part II

Chapter XXVI

By the end of July, before the cub-hunting began, all the neighbours came cackling back again, with new ideas, new dresses, new people to talk about, new combinations to discuss ; and poured into the Court first of all, as being the most popular house thereabouts, to give the folks there —Laura especially—the results of their experience : as if there had been no change down here—as if there had not something happened here which made their mere cacklings ridiculously unimportant—as if she had not lived a life longer than any of theirs since they had gone ambling away into the world!

There was a dinner-party, with some of the first arrivals, on a Friday—a haunch-day, as Sir Peckwith Downes called it. Laura appeared in grey silk, with no ornament but a crucifix ; and, as it was a fast-day, mortified the flesh by taking nothing for dinner but turbot and lobster-sauce, oyster-patties, some omelette, a little cream, and some peaches and grapes. Her conversation, also, was purely theological. In short, with the highest and noblest intentions, she was overdoing the thing altogether ; and when it was over, and Laura had gone upstairs, her father followed her into her room, and said :

" My sweetest Laura, I am not going to argue, to dictate, to command, or even to advise. I merely want to put this before you. Does not your admirable good sense point out to you that your suddenly-changed dress and manner are calculated to make people talk ? "

" Dear me, father—let them talk ! "

" After what has happened ? " said Sir Charles, and thought wistfully.

" It shall be as you wish," said Laura. " I quite see what you mean, dear; and don't be impatient. The old confidence will come back in happier times. There—go ! "

" It will come back in ruin and disaster," thought Sir Charles. But his heart was lighter. " It will come back, at all events," said he.

After this, Laura never made any public—not to say offensive—renegation of the vanities of this world, but let her own common-sense have full play. She was thoroughly in earnest though, and worked away like a carthorse at her good resolutions. I suppose most of us have done what she was doing at one period of our lives, and have found, or have thought we found, peace in factitious activity about small things; and have ended by finding out that, like opium or brandy, the remedy destroys itself, and that " peace of mind " is not the greatest object in this world. But with this we have little to do; we must attend to more trivial matters. We have more to do with the succession of arrivals, which came on the Court people like a deluge of cold water; and had the effect, among others, of making Sir Charles quite forget that he was a bankrupt.

Constance Downes was about the very first of the arrivals. She was a fine, roundabout, bounceable, two-to-a-pew young lady before she went; but now she had sewed pillows to all her armholes, and was two breadths more round the skirt than she had ever been before. She embraced Laura, and, as she said, brought the news herself. She was engaged: to Count Ozoni Galvani, an Italian nobleman, it appeared; who, if his brother, the Duke of Pozzo di Argento, a most dissipated and unhealthy man, died, would become golden pump himself; but who at all events, even if that miserable little creature married, would have his mother's money. She was Miss Butts, it appeared, the banker's daughter, at Whitby. Laura congratulated her, but wondered how it was that Constance, with her beauty and her fifteen thousand pounds,

had not picked up something better : moreover, wondered
how much Constance Downes' dress had cost ; and
whether " his mother's money " would stand such a
tug-of-war as a dozen of such dresses a year : got entirely
worldly, in fact, as she confessed to the Vicar next day,
who was very impatient with her, though from a cause
quite different to what she supposed.

With Constance, of course, came Sir Peckwich and
Lady Downes, vastly deteriorated in everything which
made them worthy, by their visit to London. They had
both developed, or, more properly speaking, thought they
had developed. Sir Peckwich, from an honest county
baronet, had developed into a two-penny-halfpenny poli-
tician, and, what is worse in a story about mere social relations, an absolute bore. Lady Downes, an honest,
roundabout, country-squire's wife, was now by way of
being a fine lady, with about the same capabilities for being one, or of understanding what one is, as a donkey has
of winning the Derby. A fine lady is a very rare and
peculiar article, like certain wines. Any wine-merchant
can *charge* you for them, but it takes three generations—
three bottlings off, and a voyage to India say, to supply
the article. What it is worth when you get it is another
matter. But your real fine lady is a thing of time and
tradition ; you can't, to take the very lowest qualification
of all, get at that unutterably graceful impudence in one
generation. Mere Becky Sharp genius won't do it ; it
wants tradition. The art is, they say, rapidly becoming
extinct in England ; but there are a few fine ladies left
still. We have lost utterly the art of designing decent
buildings and statues, and of making bells ; but those who
ought to know tell one, we have a few fine ladies left,
though none coming in. One would say that fine ladies
would, in the coming bouleversement, be found last in
Prussia. Bismarck, though of the other sex, is, as far as
we have been taught to understand the fine lady, the finest
instance of the fine lady to be found out of England.

Leighton Court

It is humiliating to confess that poor dear Lady Downes tried to be the fine lady before Lady Southmolton: but she did. She sat, and fall-lalled, and patronised, and talked about the Court, and cross-examined Lady South-molton on the peerage, and on people. And Lady South-molton sat and looked at her.

Colonel Hilton appeared next. He had been to Châlons, but not, as was proposed to him, to America. He looked handsomer than ever. He had found so much to do at Châlons, in studying the new military movements, that he had got another man sent to America. It had been very pleasant there and at Paris. The Poyntz people, Sir Harry and his bride, had been there. " At Châlons or at Paris ? " —" At both." — " How was Lady Poyntz ? " — " Lady Poyntz was quite well," he believed.

Next the Poyntz themselves came. Everyone at one time had declared they would not call on them, but now, somehow, everybody did. Lady Southmolton went with singular promptitude, in the most public manner; thundering through Winkworthy ostentatiously, in the family Ark. It is supposed that Sir P. Bownes would have refused to call, but his women-folks were too many for him. It was understood that Sir Harry would keep up the house much as the Huxtables had done, and Constance had a hundred pounds' worth of finery which she must wear out before the fashions changed; and she, as bully of the establishment, had no idea of having a house closed to her down here, where there were so few. So they went, and everybody went. And Sir Harry received them with the most high-headed nonchalance, and showed them all, as plainly as possible, that he did not care whether they came or stayed away.

So the land became peopled again ; and before they had well heard and communicated all the news, Laura, one afternoon coming out of her room, heard Lord Hatter-leigh cackling and screeching in the hall.

Chapter XXVII

ABOUT a fortnight after their arrival at the Castle, Lady
Poyntz was sitting at breakfast, in her own old room in
the keep, the quaint four-windowed room in which Laura
once met Sir Harry Poyntz.

Poor woman ! She had got back to the dear old Castle
as its mistress—she had got title and position, such as it
was ; but she had made a sad blunder, and she had found
it out three days after she had married.

Sir Harry puzzled and shocked her. He was unutterably false, but he was never in the very least ashamed of
it ; and as for physical cowardice, he boasted of it. With
all this he had shown hitherto such a perfectly equable
temper, and such an unmovable persistency in gaining
his end, that, on the two or three occasions in which their
wills had crossed already, she had yielded, although a person of considerable strength of character. Once she had
made him a scene, but it was no use : the more she stormed
the more he laughed, in such an exasperating way that he
left her pale with rage. She vowed to herself that he
should never see her tears again.

Still it was his interest to treat her well, for only half her
money was in his power, and he did so whenever she did
not come between him and his object : when that was the
case, his gigantic selfishness would have made him use
cruelty towards her, had it been necessary.

" Lady Poyntz, I wish you would tell your women to
get the blue room ready for to-morrow," he said on this
particular morning.

" Certainly, dear : who is coming ? "

" Captain Wheaton."

"Sir Harry Poyntz," she said, indignantly, "you promised that you would not let that man enter the house ! "

" I did not promise."

" You did, and, what is more, you know you did."

" Well, that was before we were married, when I wasn't sure of you."

" Or my money ? "

" Or your money : exactly, and I can't keep my promise now—lovers' oaths, you know. I must have the fellow. He is an awful blackguard, but he is necessary to me. I will keep him in order for you. He is afraid of me—physically afraid I mean—as great a hound as that."

Lady Poyntz remained silent, considering how she should act, and, while doing so, fixed her fine dark eye steadily on her husband's. What a curious, shallow, cold, dangerous eye it was—the lightest blue she had ever seen with a kind of moonlight gleam about it ! She would have died sooner than have turned her own eye away, and yet she would have been glad to do so. She made as though she were brushing flies away from her forehead, and at last said—

" Well, I have made up my mind ; I suppose he *will* come."

" Most assuredly ! "

" Then I shall not speak to him, and not allow him in the drawing-room. I must sit at dinner with him, I suppose ? "

" Well, I think so. I am glad you are not going to speak to him ; it will teach him his place. So that is settled ; I thank you very much."

" Harry," said Lady Poyntz, " do you ever hear from your brother in India ? "

" My brother in India is an extravagant and dissipated rascal," said Sir Harry; " I wish he was at Jericho! He has been costing me more money."

" Is there any chance of his coming home soon ? " she asked.

" I should like to catch him at it," said Sir Harry. " Oh, I should so very much like to catch him at it ! "

Maria had asked him this in good-natured curiosity, to see how he was disposed towards his brother, and to try

and find out something of his character. She had been
set on to this by her old friend, Sir Charles Seckerton. It
was an important question to him, for *he* knew the state
of Sir Harry Poyntz's health. She left the result here, as
being somewhat unsatisfactory. There was another matter on which she wished to satisfy herself, and thought it a
good opportunity. She, as nonchalantly as she could, said—

" What a sad accident the Seckertons have had with
their new huntsman ! "

The light-blue eyes were on her in a moment. She
thought that the fowl sat, and she stalked on.

He said, " Yes, I heard of it."

" Did you know anything of the young man ? "

" I suppose you do, from your manner, my pretty fen-
cer. I guess that you know that he was our illegitimate
brother. Is not that true ? "

Maria laughed. " You are very cunning," she said ;
but the blue eye was on her, still enquiringly.

" Who told you ? " he asked.

" Lady Emily Seckerton," she said. " What sort of
man was he ? Were you fond of him ? "

" Very much so. I liked him better than any other human being—except you, you know, of course."

" You seem to have taken his loss pretty easily ; I did
not notice that you were much affected."

" I wished to spare your feelings ; I was unwilling to
disturb the happiness of your honeymoon by any exhibition
of grief. Besides, it is one of the traits of my character
that I never do show my grief. The remarkable fortitude
I showed at the death of my father drew tears from the
nurse. She was drunk, and wanted to kiss me ; but I am
sure she was in earnest."

" I suppose you could show equal fortitude at my
death ? " said Maria.

" That would depend entirely on what you did with the
thirty thousand pounds which is settled on yourself. If
you left it back to me, as Christianity dictates, I should

spend five-and-twenty pounds on a cheap tombstone for you, tear my hair, and take to drink. If you let it go back to your family, I should show my fortitude by looking out for another woman with money, as soon as—nay, long before—it was decent."

"Harry! Harry!" said Maria reproachfully, "are you ever in earnest?"

"Sometimes on money matters—on sentimental business, never. So drop it. Now, have you satisfied your curiosity about Poyntz-Hammersley?"

"I have satisfied my own. Now to raise yours. Do you like Laura Seckerton?"

"I love her! She is a paragon of a woman—so beautiful, so discreet, so careful not to wound with her tongue. Oh, I love her!"

"Shall I tell you something about her—your paragon?"

"Do; you will never bore me as long as you speak of her."

"Why, then, I will tell you," said the unhappy woman. "She fell in love with Poyntz-Hammersley; she made every kind of advance to him, which he, for decency's sake, reciprocated. When he was drowned, she took to her long-forgotten devotions, and went into mourning, until her father and mother forced her, with threats, to behave more reasonably. All this time she believed him to be a common groom from the stableyard. I know that she knows no more of him—no, nor does anyone else, except her mother and her father. And this is your Laura: it is the scandal of the place."

Sir Harry drew his chair up against hers, and said, "Say that again."

"Why?"

"Because it is delicious; because it does me good; because it makes me love you. Wheaton shall dine in the housekeeper's room, in the still-room, in the coal-hole, before he insults my peerless wife by his presence! Say it again."

She told the story over, with additions.

" That is very good," he said ; " you love her, don't you ? "

" I hate her ! " said Maria, but said no more.

" And I," said Sir Harry Poyntz, grasping his wife's arm —" I hate her with a hatred which your spasmodic female nature has no power of understanding, leave alone of feeling ! She hates me, and she nearly turned you against me (and your sixty thousand pounds, you know ; let us have no sentimentality). She has used language about me here, there, and everywhere which a dog wouldn't forgive—and a dog will forgive, from his heart of hearts, far more than any Christian. I hate her ! I can ruin her father any hour after six months ; but the pleasure of ruining her will be greater than taking possession of the Court. How are matters going on with Lord Hatterleigh ? "

Maria roused herself, and said : " I expect the engagement to be announced every day. The booby is always there. How long he will take about proposing, Providence only knows. When, where, and how he will do it I dare not think, but do it he will : and she will have him, and stop slander."

" Look here," said Sir Harry, with his wife's wrist still in his hand. " You have said you hated her, and I must do you the credit to say that you never lie, if that *be* any credit. We must let this engagement go on until it is talked of all over the county—until it is in the *Morning Post ;* and then we must revive this scandal, get it broken off, and drag her down in the dust. Tell me, woman (for I am blind about such things), is Hatterleigh, as they say in their cant, man enough to pitch her overboard for this ? "

" He is one of the first men who would do so. But I am not prepared—— "

" Then I will prepare you. It was well done in her to trifle and play with our dear friend, Colonel Hilton, and then throw him over for a roughrider ! "

Maria could not help catching her arm away. " Have I

married the Fiend?" she thought, and Sir Harry Poyntz laughed and left the room.

This interview had opened both their eyes a little. Maria saw, by this last unutterably wicked speech of his, that her husband knew that she had been in love with Colonel Hilton, and that he had tried to see whether that was the case still. He, from the snatching-away of her arm when Hilton and Laura's names were mentioned together, had seen that it was. Alas! he was right. Poor Lady Poyntz had tried to get over it; but the first few days with Sir Harry had opened her eyes, and Châlons and Paris had done the rest. She found herself tied to a hopeless, shameless liar and coward; while that glorious melancholy-eyed hero Hilton had, now that Laura's baleful dark eyes were out of the way, fallen in love with her. It was all Laura's fault; she would have won him in time if it had not been for Laura. So, when her husband had asked her, she had said, " I hate her!"

But had that very unaccountable scoundrel, Sir Harry Poyntz, known anything about the better class of women, which he did not, he would have observed that Maria's " I hate her!" was said in a snappish tone, which, with a very little extra passion, would have gone over the hysterical border, and come to be, " I love her." The fact was that there was nothing more than temper, and a very little matter of that, between her and Laura just now. Lady Poyntz had thought a good deal since she had flown out at Laura on the subject of Colonel Hilton just before she was married: had reflected what a high-minded, noble friend Laura had been to her; how the real fact was that Laura had never encouraged Colonel Hilton, whereas Colonel Hilton had undoubtedly made, in his cool procrastinating dandysoldier way, a considerable deal of love to Laura; and that Laura had only told her the truth about her husband, after all. But still she had a little devil of jealousy and evil temper at work in her heart — a little devil who was sometimes almost powerless, but who got very active and powerful whenever her husband had the management of him.

Sir Harry had just been showing off the paces of that little fiend, and he was full rampant. But even now, in the hour of that fiend's power, poor Lady Poyntz knew in her own mind that she could never bring herself to join her husband in his scheme for ruining Laura. She felt pleasure in the indulgence of her ill-temper towards her, but only in imagination : she knew she would never reduce it to practice, although she went to bed indulging in the anticipation of doing so.

Chapter XXVIII

POOR Laura, terrified, had retired into her shell, and was by no means the genial outspoken woman of old times. Besides, Maria Poyntz had given the first offence, and should therefore make the first advance, which Maria, after the extremely precise not to say demure manner in which Laura had received her, felt very little inclined to do.

"She might surely come and see me?" sulked Lady Poyntz. "I have not committed any crime." But assuredly she did not ; and as sulks grow by indulgence, the chances of a reconciliation seemed to get more hopeless as time went on.

Laura's mother and grandmother were astonished to find all their old influence over her completely restored. They were such very wise women that they never mentioned this astonishment even to one another. They perfectly understood one another, and agreed without speech that the reins now recovered must not be drawn too tight, and, moreover, must be loosened on the first symptom of restiveness. They need not have been uneasy ; they might have driven her hard enough now. Part of her scheme was the giving-up of her own will, and the more they had asked from her the more she would have yielded. One difficulty she had—a comical, foolish little difficulty enough, but one which gave her a deal of trouble: she was determined to yield to the Vicar's wish about fox-hunting, and she dreaded telling her father of this resolution. Moreover, she was afraid of giving rise to remarks. Something occurred, however, before cub-hunting began, which made this matter easy for her.

We were great admirers of the late Admiral Fitzroy, and at one time thought Mr. Burder a most shocking man for doubting his entire infallibility. Certainly, some of the Admiral's hits about the weather were nearly miraculous; but it was a low class of cunning. It was done mechanically, and he was always telling us how he did it—a great mistake in a thaumaturgist. It was almost a low class of cunning compared with the foresight which even an ordinary woman will exhibit, not even empirically, but intuitively, about the social weather. Compared to such a woman as Laura, the late Admiral was quite behindhand, and would have confessed it in a moment.

There was bidden a great picnic party to the place which we, with our fine imagination, have hitherto called "the glen of the hundred voices," but which is marked on the Ordnance Map as "Crab's Gut." They were all to start from the Court at twelve; and when Laura had finished her breakfast, and found herself alone in the room with her grandmother and her mother, she saw that there was something in the wind—that they were going to say something important to her. She couldn't tell you exactly, like Admiral Fitzroy, the process by which she arrived at her conclusion, but the conclusion was no less certain. They were, especially the elder, both well-trained women; and Laura knew that they would take, with their wonderful tact, a long time in telling her. She knew perfectly well what they were going to say, had her answer ready, and wished it done. Nevertheless, she was a ritualist : forms must be gone through. They did not ask her to stay in the room. She looked at them and saved them the trouble, stayed without being asked ; looking at them both steadily.

Lady Southmolton, looking out of window: " What a glorious day for it ! I wish I was going. I wonder if I dared trundle round in my pony-carriage and see you all. I am afraid not."

" You must not think of such a thing, mother," said Lady Emily ; " it would be too much for you." She had by this time come round to Laura, and was stroking her hair.

" That'll do, mamma," said Laura to herself. She said aloud, " I don't think you had better, grandma. It's a long way, and the roads are rough. No, I wouldn't."

" How are you going, dear ? " asked Lady Southmolton, sweetly, as her mother kissed her back-hair, in irrepressible admiration.

" With peas in my shoes. It is Friday, you know," said Laura ; and didn't say anything more, which was worse still. It was abominable and undutiful of her, in the highest degree, to pull out (if one may be allowed a simile, taken from Lady Southmolton's constant occupation) her grandmother's knitting like this ! However, the old lady gathered up as many stitches as she could, and clicked away again. Lady Emily, getting frightened, and being (as was always the case when she was wanted) utterly useless, continued to stroke Laura's hair, till Laura very nearly went to the extreme length of asking her to leave off.

Lady Southmolton got up a ghost of a giggle, and said something about their dear Laura's spirits, which, seeing that dear Laura was sitting before her, looking very stern, and getting paler each moment, seemed to be somewhat misplaced. She was a brave old lady, however, and went on with her business, as per arrangement with Lady Emily —plans rather traversed by Laura's vulgar answer about the peas in her shoes.

"Colonel Hilton is coming with his phaeton, my love ; he would be delighted to drive you." This had been part of the leading-up business, but went amiss : it came in the wrong place, and didn't fit.

Said Laura : "If he don't drive Maria Poyntz he may drive anyone else. But he sha'n't drive me. And if he drives her, I shall not go. Neither would you, mother, would you ? " facing round on her mother at the same time.

Lady Emily kissed her daughter, and most loyally answered, "No, I would not ; " after which she gave the whole business up to Lady Southmolton, and confined herself to kissing Laura at all the important pauses.

" Now go on, grandma," said Laura.

In spite of this traversing of plans by a slightly contemptuous Laura, the old lady nailed the last rags of the original programme to the mast, and fought for them to the end. She had been going to do the thing in the proper way, as that sort of thing was always done. The responsibility of any deviation from the programme should fall on Laura's shoulders. She solemnly played her next card, just as if Laura hadn't just trumped one of the same suit.

" Lord Hatterleigh," she said, in as offhand a manner as she could manage—which was very badly, for Laura had been ' odd ' with her, and she hated ' oddness,' and was nearly eighty — " Lord Hatterleigh has borrowed your mother's pony-carriage, and will be delighted to drive you. Will you go with him ? "

" Yes."

This was worse than before — enough to make Mrs. Hannah More rise from her grave. Here was a young woman with opinions of her own, with some shadowing-forth of a character. That transcendently perfect and angelical muff and ass Cœlebs would never have got on with Laura : a young person who exasperated her own grandmother with such answers as that about the peas, or, failing that, monosyllables like this last " yes," and drove her to make her grand speech before she had half got through the hour's fencing and "beating about the bush" laid down in the programme. It was intolerable! Lady Southmolton came to the "toast of the evening" at once,—

"My love, all that I have previously said, and which you have somewhat impatiently heard, was intended to prepare your mind for this great fact : Lord Hatterleigh has been to see your mother!"

Why does one feel inclined to laugh at a funeral? Laura felt so much inclined to laugh at her grandmother's bathos, that she gave herself great credit for keeping her countenance. Yet she knew—who better?—that it meant a life-important decision. She was all alone, poor girl! Her heart was with Poyntz-Hammersley, who was drowned in the quicksands : that we know well. Her father and she were estranged. It was not a matter for the Vicar's ear, for it was not all her own matter—one half was Lord Hatterleigh's. She had, she thought, nearly done a great wrong to her family, and would atone for it at all risks. No : she had no soul to whom to go to for advice and assistance ; for she had travelled out of the grooves of her mother and grandmother's ways of life and thought, and could not return to them again, try she never so hard. And, above all, she really was fond of that Guy Fawkes Lord Hatterleigh ; she knew his worth, and so she said,—

"Well?"

"Well, dear, we were going to say that in all human probability he will speak to you this morning ; and that if you could give us the very slightest hint as to what answer you would give him, you would remove a great load from our minds."

"I will give him any answer you please ; I will say exactly what you like. What do you wish me to say?"

Lady Emily kissed her and wept ; Lady Southmolton went on. She would not influence her for one moment, she said ; but then went on to point out to her the innumerable advantages of such a match, if Laura could only bring her mind to it, and so on.

" I gather from all this," said Laura, " that I am to say
' yes.' Well, then, ' yes ' it shall be. Now I think I will
go and get ready. Here are the carriages coming round."

Lord Hatterleigh had come over to breakfast that morning, but had spoken word to no one, save salutations—except to Granby Dixon, M.P., the man who knows everybody, and turns up everywhere. Lord Hatterleigh had
eagerly seized on Granby Dixon the moment he came into
the house, had sat next him at breakfast, and talked to him
incessantly and pertinaciously about the Limited Liability
Bill. And that kind and worthy little soul, under the impression that he was doing a goodnatured action by undertaking Lord Hatterleigh, had led him on. Not that he
wanted much leading, however, for he was evidently determined to stick to the Member for Brentford like a leech ;
and after breakfast took him out into the garden, and
stumbled up-and-down beside him, offering a strange contrast to his dapper companion. All this was somewhat
irritating to Lady Emily, who knew what was coming ; but
her wrath rose to a towering pitch when she heard Lord
Hatterleigh say to Granby Dixon, just before they started—

" Come with me, Granby, and we will have it out in the
carriage."

" This is too bad ! " she said to herself. " His own arrangement too ! However, he shall not play with me like
this."

She saw that Granby Dixon had gone upstairs to put on
his boots, and that Lord Hatterleigh was in the porch.
She stood by the stairs. Granby's dandy little boots were
soon heard tripping down the stairs ; him she seized, and
eagerly said—

" Mr. Dixon, my dear friend, don't go with Lord Hatterleigh : *Laura* is to go. I have known you so many
years, I know I may trust you."

He grew grave. " It is easily managed, my dear Lady
Emily ; where is Miss Seckerton ? "

" In the library. Thank you very much ! "

Granby Dixon went after her with his brightest smile and his lightest trip, and found her sitting alone in the library, ready-dressed.

" Lord Hatterleigh is waiting for you, Miss Seckerton," he said cheerily ; and she rose at once without a word, and took his arm. She was rather pale, and he felt her arm tremble just once, but she was perfectly self-possessed when they got among the other people ; and Granby chattered away merrily, and continued to do so until he had packed her into the pony-carriage beside Lord Hatterleigh, who had got in and was sitting on the left side, waiting for Granby himself—having made the last feebly desperate effort to gain a little more time.

Granby saw them drive off, and found his warm little heart nearer to his eyes than he liked. He chattered and made himself agreeable all day to everyone, but at night he said to himself when he was alone in his bedroom—" God help that poor girl ! God Almighty help her ! Oh, it is monstrous—monstrous ! "

Meanwhile Lord Hatterleigh had said to Laura : " Will you drive, Miss Seckerton, as you are on the right side ? " And Laura said " Yes," and away went the pony (an exmoor—that is to say, having a considerable share of Barb blood, and standing fourteen hands) like a steam-engine. They were out of the park and through Winkworthy before either of them seemed to find time for speaking ; but when the pony slackened up the first hill, Lord Hatterleigh laughed, not with his ordinary idiotic cackle, by any means, but pleasantly enough, and said—

" I am glad you drove. I am such an outrageous muff that I can't even drive a pony. This pony would have found me out before this, and run up a tree, or done something or another."

" You should practise," said Laura.

" No good—no good ! I have practised shooting, but I shoot so badly that my own brother swears at me. I was sent into the world with two left sides ; I am an ambisinister. I can't even catch trout—at least I only catch junior and inexperienced trout, and I fall into the water in doing that. Now, who is to answer for this state of things? What is the good of my having fifty thousand a-year if I have two left legs and another man's arms?"

Laura suggested that he might do a great deal with his money. She mentioned hospitals, industrial exhibitions for the working-classes; but found herself dwelling on flower-shows, being in a foolish frame of mind, and naturally harping on the most foolish idea. She forced home the necessity of these flower-shows upon him with considerable volubility; but finding herself somewhat entangled in proving the moral effects of china-asters, she saw that she was talking unutterable nonsense to gain time, and wisely held her tongue until it was all over.

"Well, I do go in for that sort of thing, Laura," he said. "God knows I do heartily whatever my hand finds to do, but I am what they call a muff; and if you married me, you would make me little else. The time is gone by —nay, the time never existed. But, Laura, I am neither coward nor liar, as you will find if you say ' yes ' to the question I am going to ask you. Can you marry me? There is no hurry for your answer. I urge nothing in my own favour, you observe. Give me an answer before we reach the end of the next mile, and that shall be final."

Laura could not help turning and looking at him. She had her answer ready, and was determined to deliver it face to face, with her eyes on his. So she turned; and she saw him as she had never seen him before, and knew him for the first time. Now that he was sitting in perfect repose—now that his fantastic manner was out of the play—she saw what a noble creature he was. She was clever enough to know that his brain was not first-class— that his family was getting worn out; but she had sense enough to see that his face, now that it was at rest, was a very noble one—and to feel that the calm patience with which he waited for her answer, showed that he had a gentleman's soul in spite of his fantastic habits. I suppose it was her woman's instinct which told her that he was in love with her; but woman's instinct is a thing which I don't understand, nor you, and least of all the women themselves.

He soon felt that she was looking at him. He turned on her kindly and, to say the truth, grandly, and said—

"Well, is the answer ready so soon?"

Laura said: "The answer has been ready since this morning. My mother prepared me for all this. The answer is, 'Yes.' If you had asked me at breakfast-time this morning, the answer would have been a complimentary 'yes;' now it is a very decided 'yes' indeed."

"Then you think you can get to love me?"

"Not better than I do at present! I always loved you, Lord Hatterleigh, and I love you better than ever now. I think you are a noble person; but you do not do yourself justice. Let me give you our first confidence. This morning I was ready to submit—now I am ready to acquiesce. I think——"

Ah! that one glance at the wild tide-beaten sands, far below their feet, which showed her that she was speaking falsely, though she meant so earnestly and so honestly every word she said! Step out, old pony, and carry us deep into the green woodlands beside the rushing river; and leave the sands far behind, with the dead man buried in them. The dead man's memory walks there like a ghost, and will walk for ever; but like other ghosts, if not seen, will be forgotten and discredited. On into the woodlands then!

They all met in the glen, at a place where the trees were so high, large, and dense, that you could only see the overhanging cliffs here and there among the topmost boughs. The river, tired of streaming from crag to crag of granite, slept in a deep black pool, over whose surface the foam-flakes slowly travelled in gentle curves. There was silence close at hand all around; but, farther off, the ceaseless rush of water came softly and pleasantly to the ear. About the edge of the water were broad shelves of granite, mostly carpeted with moss; while on the edge which ran farthest into the pool, there stood a great Logan-stone, which seemed as if a child's hand might topple it into the river. The summer sun streamed through a deep boscage of king-fern and hazel. It was a perfect place for a picnic!

Laura and Lord Hatterleigh noticed to one another, as soon as they looked round, that the central figure in the landscape was a very singular one. Sir Harry Poyntz happened to be standing apart from everyone, on the edge of the water, looking about him. He had dressed himself, as he usually did, very oddly, and looked utterly unlike anyone else. With the exception of the blazing breloques on his waistcoat, and the rings on his fingers, everything about him was brilliantly black and white—white trousers, waistcoat, and hat, but a black-velvet coat and lacquered shoes, all in a state of catlike cleanliness and neatness.

" Look how that fellow's clothes are cut, said Lord Hatterleigh. " They won't make such clothes for me; and it's no use my going to *his* tailor. Look at him, Laura! Do you see that he is blowing his nose, and that he has a tinted handkerchief and primrose-coloured gloves, which have the effect of making his waxen complexion look healthy? Did you ever see such a clever fellow? "

Laura had no time to laugh, as she felt very much inclined to do, for Sir Harry Poyntz came towards the pair; and with a smile on his face, but none in the cold shallow blue eye, asked Laura, to her great surprise, if she had seen Colonel Hilton?

" He is not coming; indeed, he was not asked, I believe," said Laura, with the most perfect coolness—a coolness which had the effect of irritating her mother extremely. She wanted to get some hint of the result of the drive in the pony-carriage : " Had that booby spoken ? " Laura gave no sign.

" Oh! bother it all," said Sir Harry; "isn't he coming? Then I shall have to take care of my own wife; this is too bad!"

" I can take care of myself, Harry, I daresay," said Lady Poyntz, bridling.

" Can you?" said he. " From watching you and him together, I should have thought that you could scarcely have cut up your own dinner without him!"

" What a reckless lunatic that man is, George, to speak so to that poor woman!" said Laura, aside, to Lord Hatterleigh.

It was the first time she had ever called him by his Christian name; he turned, and looked at her gratefully; and Laura was astonished, he really looked very handsome. Could this be the booby of this morning?

" Where will this end?" he said to Laura. " What can the man be doing it for? To gird at her in society before they have been six weeks married! I can't endure that fellow, Laura. I know nothing of him, except this, that I *hate* him!"

" You should not hate anybody, George."

" Very like—very like! But I hate that man, however. Are you fond of cats?"

" For the sake of argument, no. But why?"

" Because that man is a cat. Look at him; look at his stealthy grace—look at his perfect cleanliness and neatness, and look at his hopeless, unutterable selfishness. I'll go up, and make him purr for you directly. Did you ever see anything more wonderfully *bizarre* and attractive than the fellow's dress? If he chose to be decently civil to his wife, that sentimental whiskerando Hilton would have no chance with him. Hiltons are as common as blackberries; anyone could manage *him*—there would be no credit to her in dragging *him* at her chariot-wheels. But there is only one Harry Poyntz. If he would only allow her, before society, the reputation of having mastered such a notoriously dangerous tiger as he is, she would be proud

of him, and would get to love him. But he won't; it is
not his game; I can't understand his game the least in the
world. I suspect there is a good deal of caprice and whim
about the man. Those effeminate men acquire feminine
vices, I expect: childish love of power, causeless ill-temper, and cap——"

Laura looked at him with the corners of her mouth
drawn down demurely, and they both burst out laughing.

Sir Harry and Lady Poyntz were having a few words
meanwhile.

"I cannot conceive, Harry," she said, "what you propose to yourself in treating me like this in public. If you
could help it I shall be glad; if you can't I shall retaliate.
I could be very disagreeable, mind!"

"Oh no, you couldn't, my love; you couldn't say anything which these dear friends of ours have not said a
hundred times over. Bless the dear little fool, you haven't
heard half the lies about me yet! But there is no cause
for anger in this case; I only chaffed you about Hilton
because I saw it annoyed Laura Seckerton."

"I wish you would not sharpen your wits on your wife.
Why don't you bring Captain Wheaton, and make him
your foil?"

"The people won't have my helot; my helot gets drunk
and becomes offensive, and what is amusing to me is
disgusting to them. Take care where you are standing,
you will catch fire. By Jove, you are on fire; take
care!"

It was true. The grooms had made a fire on the rock,
as being a necessary part of any picnic; and Lady Poyntz,
in drawing herself up tragically before her husband, had
backed against it, and her flowered muslin dress was send-
up half-a-dozen tiny wreaths of white smoke, just preparing to burst into a blaze.

Laura and Lord Hatterleigh were watching the pair,
and saw the accident. Laura gave a wild scream, and
Lord Hatterleigh a roar. He rose up, tore off his coat,

and, as he hurled his ungainly length towards them, was heard by the terrified spectators to cry out—

" Throw her down, Poyntz ; throw her down into the wet moss. The fool, why does he stand staring there ? Are you fit for nothing in heaven or earth ? Throw her down."

By the time he had relieved his feelings so far, he had got hold of her and fairly tumbled her down, trying with his coat to smother the fire. Fortunately for her, they fell together among deep wet moss at the edge of the water, with the fire underneath. But the fire was strong; and Laura, standing horror-struck, saw his long, lean, delicate white hand in the midst of it four or five times as he tried to smother it with his coat, before his own groom, the first man who recovered his senses, put it out by baling water on it from his hat.

Then Lord Hatterleigh got up, and Lady Poyntz was helped up ; and there was a general shrieking and gabbling, in the midst of which Laura came up to Lord Hatterleigh's side, and found him thanking his groom.

" I am personally obliged to you, Sanders. Your family has served our house for many years now, and has always been distinguished, with one solitary exception " (brother of this Sanders, say the Archives, who got himself bored to the borders of Bedlam, and enlisted in the 16th Light Dragoons—a rebellious Sanders) " for their dexterity and devotion. This shall not be forgotten."

The present Sanders merely touched his hat in acknowledgment, and pointed out to Laura, as being a thing which decidedly concerned her more than anyone else, that his Lordship's left hand was terribly burnt ; after which he went for old Doctor Buscombe, who happened luckily to be of the party, and who was wandering in the wood with Lady Emily, gathering bilberries, and hearing all about Lady Southmolton's symptoms.

Laura took Lord Hatterleigh's arm, and led him away. When she dared to look at his left hand she nearly cried out. It was all burnt up into great bladders—but no more of that. He tried to laugh, but it ended in a feeble cackle.

"Lucky it wasn't the right one—eh, Laura? Shouldn't have been able to write. I should have been obliged to dictate my Limited Liability pamphlet to you; and you're so stupid, you know; you'd have made a hundred blunders, wouldn't you, now?"

"I should, indeed. Sit down here, and let me tie my handkerchief over your hand. I don't like this."

"Don't like what?"

"This, all of this. It is all getting so tragical, and so terrible. Oh, George! George! do, whatever happens, stay by me, and see me through it. Do let me believe that there is one other human soul in whom I can trust. Be friendly to me, George; I have no friend left but you. I always loved you, George—I always trusted you. Be a friend to me, George, for I am all alone, George—all alone, all alone!"

This from his imperial bride, whom he thought so hard to win! It set him thinking. He could think rapidly, and generally to the purpose; besides, to use a term, which I cannot replace by a better term, "his heart was in the right place." His answer was soon ready, rough as it was,—

"Laura, if the Old Gentleman himself comes between you and me, let him take care. I am a peer of England, with fifty thousand a year; that still counts for something, even in these latter days. What is the social status or income of the gentleman just alluded to, I don't know; but let him take care—a British peer is still a very terrible person! Make me your husband as soon as you can, and we will face it out together. Pitch me overboard to-morrow, and we will face it out just the same."

Their *tête-à-tête* was ended. The Doctor was seen approaching rapidly with Sir Harry Poyntz, who was trying to look as if he had been to fetch him. While the Doctor was untying Laura's pockethandkerchief from the burnt hand. Sir Harry spoke to Lord Hatterleigh in a gentle quiet voice, without one touch of scorn, and apparently without the slightest *arrière pensée*—with the strange recklessness of a man who has offended the world past forgiveness, and has become utterly contemptuous of it—

" I have to thank you for saving my wife's life.   That is, I believe, supposed to be a great obligation, although it has cost me thirty thousand pounds.   I am very much obliged to you, and all that sort of thing.   I was utterly taken aback when the accident happened, and she would have been burnt to death before I should have realised it, and then I shouldn't have known what to do.   You have shown an extraordinary amount of courage and sagacity— you must see that yourself.   I have entirely changed my opinion of you.   I always thought you a half-witted booby ; and so did you, you know, Miss Seckerton ? "

It was horribly, viciously true—it was as wicked a thing as ever was said ; but Lord Hatterleigh's quiet beautiful good-humour took the sting out of it in a moment, and made it perfectly innocuous—

" I don't know whether she *thought* so ; I can only an- swer for her having diligently *told* me so for the last ten years.   Eh, Laura ? "

" My Lord," said the Doctor, " we must get home and have this dressed."

" But I don't want to go home."

" You must."

" Pish, Doctor !   I am determined to stay out and enjoy myself."

" Enjoy yourself !   You know you are in terrible tort- ure ? "

" By no means ; I am enjoying myself thoroughly. Take Sanders home, and bring your bandages, your cot- ton-wool, your fiddle-faddles back.   You needn't be gone half an hour.   Home," quoth he—" not if I know it ! "

" Hah ! " said the Doctor to Laura, " the symptoms are worse than I thought.   Fever is setting in ; he is getting *tête montée*.—My dear lord, I am astonished that one who has always taken such care of his most valuable health should trifle with a serious accident of this kind." And here they all three burst out laughing.

"Don't let him chaff me, Laura.—But, seriously, is there any *danger* in my staying out?"

"No *danger*," said the Doctor; "only, if you persist in staying out, I shall think that Sir Harry Poyntz's former estimate of your character was—was—well, I won't say what."

"And Miss Seckerton's too, remember. A half-witted booby, eh? Well, I'll submit; I must act up to my new character. I suppose you couldn't quit this festive scene, Laura, and drive me home? By-the-bye, Doctor, I ought to tell you I am engaged to Miss Seckerton."

"A bad thing for me," said the Doctor.

"Very bad. If you are the man I take you for, you will go and get the pony-carriage for us. I'd do the same for you."

"We shall see," said the Doctor to himself, as chorus, going on his errand, "what stuff there is in this good-humoured gaby. There may be something. He comes of a good stock, and has shown pluck and resource to-day; but I fear he has thought about himself and his inside too long, and that this is only a grand show-off. *Noblesse oblige*, but noblesse and dinner-pills—bah! I can't believe in it yet. He has got that peerless girl to consent to marry him, and he is bent on showing that he is not the miserable effeminate ass which the world has written him down. When the necessity for showing-off before her is gone, he will sink back into his old valetudinarian selfishness again. A man don't study himself for fourteen years, to the exclusion of all other matters, and then turn out a hero at the end. She, pretty storyteller, has been telling him that she loves him—oh, woman! woman! woman!—and he has believed her. When he finds out how she has lied, the last state of that man will be worse than the first."

But when the Vicar heard of it, he said : " I always thought well of that young man from a boy. His mother nearly spoilt him, but he will do now. He only wanted arousing."

Chapter XXIX

AND so Laura was enabled to say, without exciting any surprise, on the day before the cub-hunting began,—

" I shall not hunt this year, my dear father. George has pressed me very eagerly to do so, but I don't think it would be fair on him. He can't hunt himself."

There was, undeniably, good sense in this. Sir Charles sighed and gave up the question, seeing that he should have to hunt his short remaining time by himself. But he found her waiting for him at his early breakfast. She made him his tea as of old, paid the little attentions to his necktie, and made him as smart and as spruce as possible ; and she sent him off with a kiss, and stood laughing at the door in the early autumn morning, as the tall, spare, gentlemanly figure rode down the avenue alone. She noticed how bent he was getting, and said with a sigh,—

" Well, and so there's an end of all *that !* I shall wonder at nothing now. I knew a young lady once, called Laura Seckerton, and a jolly young lady she was ; but I don't know what has become of her. There is the church-bell ! "

The Vicar had been profoundly astonished at this en-gagement with Lord Hatterleigh. If he was in any way offended with Laura for not having asked his advice, he was too sensible, with all his fantastic ritualisms, to show it. He knew that if Laura had ever had the slightest idea of following his advice, she would certainly have asked it. Therefore, when she told him of it, he only gave her his affectionate blessing ; and as soon as he could get rid of her, went and told his wife, saying to her what we have mentioned above as a *per contra* to the Doctor's opinion.

The " Umbrella " was rather more savage about this engagement than she was about Maria Huxtable's. Her life is only noticeable for these few outbreaks, as the history of a volcano is only the history of its eruptions. On this occasion she made an A.D. 63 business of it. After twenty years' quiescence she rose upon her husband, and overwhelmed him ; he being as unsuspecting of such a thing being possible, as ever were the inhabitants of Pompeii, when they saw something like a fir-tree fifteen thousand feet high. Yes, she turned on him for the first and last time. Their servant (probably an idle and un-trustworthy minx, given to leasing) put it about after-wards, that she actually shook her scarlet-gloved fist in his reverend face : it is pretty certain, seeing that he told the whole business to his most excellent gossip Sir Charles Seck-erton, that she " went in on him " very much in this style :—

" This is a most villanous business ! Those exasperat-ing old trots, Lady Southmolton and Lady Emily, are allowing the girl to sell herself. Do they know that she was in love with Poyntz-Hammersley ? "

" With whom ? I didn't catch the name."

" Yes, you did. With Poyntz-Hammersley, the man who was down here in disguise. Do *they* know that—that they are allowing the poor girl to sell herself, for bare respectability's sake, to this tomfool ? I daresay they do. You do ! "

" How do you know that ? "

" I know it now, at all events, because you don't dare to deny it. And knowing it, why didn't you prevent her making this engagement ? "

" What power had I ? "

" None, I hope ; for I should be sorry to think that, if you had any, you would have been such a coward as not to exert it. Why can't you confess at once that you had no power, after all your boasting ? "

" My power is limited at a certain point."

" So it seems ; stops short of the useful point — very short."

" Georgina, you are losing your temper——"

" I am not ! "

" But I could easily forgive you if you were. I don't like it, but will you be good enough to tell me what I could have done ? " ·

Only indignant twitching of the red gloves. The Vicar had administered a puzzler ; and he, seeing his opportunity, dexterously and at once soared up into a vast moral height, and regarded the red gloves, as though through the wrong end of a telescope, in infinite perspective—

" Your instincts, like those of most women, are good ; your capacity of judgment and your knowledge of logic are, as in the case of *all* women, contemptible. I would have prevented this if I could, but I could not. No one knows better than yourself that the wholesome power of the priest is, for the present, circumscribed in a shameful manner."

" You might have done something. You might have gone to dinner there Friday week—fast-day—what is a fast-day to Laura's happiness ? Besides, there were filleted soles and crimped skate—Mrs. Border showed me her bill-of-fare—and you might have spoken your mind. You might have pointed out quietly to Lord Hatterleigh, that he was notoriously the greatest gaby and goose in the Three Kingdoms, and that he never could be happy with Laura ; or you might have wrapped the whole thing up in an allegory."

" As how ? "

" That's entirely your business. You are clever enough at allegories, when you choose. I never know when you are speaking in allegories, or speaking the truth. I thought it was all true about Saint Bristow, till you told me it was an allegory, and the school-children believe it as much as the Babes in the Wood to this day. If you had gone to dinner on Friday week, and wrapped it up in an allegory, the thing would have been stopped. As it is, Laura Seckerton is, entirely owing to you, going to marry Guy Fawkes!"

Chapter XXX

GUY FAWKES, however, as the Vicar's wife called him, made a most attentive lover : he used to ride or drive over from Grimwood every day, and spend many hours with Laura, interfering sadly with the regularity of her life, and her methodical arrangements ; and of course she submitted uncomplainingly.

Nay, more. These interruptions of Lord Hatterleigh were far from unpleasant. Those good folks who said to one another, " How can that noble girl endure that booby for ten minutes ? " knew very little either of Laura or of Lord Hatterleigh. In the first place, all her hundred-and-one rules and regulations, though bravely persisted in, were, so far from being any relief, becoming intolerably irksome. They had always been tiresome to her in the old times ; but she had grown into the creed that the only difference between an Englishwoman and a foreign woman, the only difference between an immaculate saint and an ordinary sinner, consisted in the adherence to these aforesaid rules. That the immaculate saints, when they did fall, made a far worse mess of it than the ordinary sinners, who had not pitched their pipes too high, she had long suspected ; but she had been brought up to consider that the only life possible for a decent woman was that of the well-regulated British female of the superior classes, and on to this belief she had engrafted the Tractarianism she had learned from the Vicar. Whether the creed she had knocked up, between Hannah-More regularities and ultra-high-church regularities would not hold together, or whether her mind had all along been too extremely ill-regulated for either, is a question we must leave to abler hands to decide. We have only to do with results; and the results were, first and last, unsatisfactory.

Last, more particularly: when she had that terrible fright about Poyntz-Hammersley, she began to believe her grandmother once more, and fled back to her old formulas. She found them deader than ever—so very dead, that when she recognised that the submitting to Lord Hatterleigh's attention was part of her duty, she found at the same time that his babble was the only thing in life that she cared for. When he was absent she went on with her other duties—her regular reading, her poor, her schools, or what-not. But as day after day went on she began to look more eagerly for his coming, and, to his great delight, to chide him for being late. She had always liked the man, and she liked him better day by day. Though he at first gobbled like a turkey-cock, and blundered about like a hobbled donkey, yet what he said was far better worth hearing than anything else she heard; and as for clumsiness, he improved rapidly.

" I wish," he said once, " that I could put you on your horse."

" Why ? " she asked.

" Because then we could ride together; and it seems so shameful to me that you should have given up your riding on my account."

" Would you like to ride with me, then ? "

" I would give anything to do so; but I should pitch you over. And I can't ride."

" You ride well enough, and the stud-groom can put me on. Do you desire that I should ride with you ? "

He laughed, and so did she. " I make a formal request that you ride with me."

" I obey, of course," she said. " Will you ride with me to-morrow ? "

" Shall we go with your father to the meet ? " he said eagerly. " I know you would like it."

" What can we want at the meet, my dear George ? Every man can't ride to hounds, and you can't. I don't love you or respect you one whit the less for it, but I don't want you to be sneered at by all the horsebreakers and horse-dealers on that account. Come with me over the sands."

So they went—farther and farther each day ; poor and schools being more and more neglected for a week. At the end of that time, Laura made her appearance one night in her father's dressing-room, as of old, and, putting her arm round his neck, said—

" George and I have got such a quarrel with you, you wicked and unfeeling old man ! "

" My darling, why ? "

" You never come and ride with us ; you treat us like the dust under your feet. If you want us ever to speak to you again, you will come and ride with us to-morrow."

He could only kiss her and cry. Poor old gentleman ! with all the ruin hanging over their heads, and he afraid to realise it to himself, still more afraid to tell Lord Hatterleigh the truth. But he came with them day after day, and, for the first time for so many years, was sorry when a hunting-day came, and they were separated. He forgot that he was ruined during these rides ; he only remembered it in the dark watches of the night, while the unconscious Lady Emily murdered sleep by his side. They rode everywhere these three, Sir Charles pioneering—by the river, through the woodlands, up the glen, on the mountain ridge, along the sands. They talked of everything—of hounds, politics, other folks' housekeeping, Constance Downes' match, bullocks, ploughs, cottages and their improvement, horses, and servants. But there was one horse they never spoke of—" The Elk ; " there was one servant they never mentioned—Poyntz-Hammersley ; and there was one ride they never rode—the bay under Leighton Castle, where " The Elk " lay dead on the morning after the dark night in which Poyntz-Hammersley had been lost in the quicksands.

Chapter XXXI

" It is all getting so terrible and so tragical," said
Laura once before. So it was, though she knew nothing
of her father's impending ruin. She could see that her
mother and her grandmother knew nothing, or would
know nothing, of the great tragedy which was being
played around them : of her state of mind, for instance, ·
with regard to Poyntz - Hammersley and Lord Hatterleigh ; or, again, of the relations between Sir Harry
Poyntz, his wife, and Colonel Hilton ; which last were getting horridly confused in Laura's mind. Whatever happened, she was sure that they would have a respectability
handy, and would get over it : " My dear, he was a handsome fellow, and Laura behaved with great discretion—far
better than poor dear Lady Becky ; " or, " My dear, he
used her shamefully, and she went off with Colonel Hilton. She must never be mentioned again." Laura was
right. If they had known of Sir Charles' difficulties, they
would only have said, " Poor dear Charles has been living
too fast ! " That would have been their formula for ruin ;
and they would have gone to Baden with the utmost com-
placency, and without any loss of dignity. The thing had
happened before to dozens of people in their rank of life,
and with their way of living ; therefore, there was nothing
shocking about it — nothing particular to grieve about.
Laura knew this, and knew that it would be a more shocking thing, in her grandmother's eyes, if Sir Charles had
sold his grapes or his game, than if he had lived beyond
his income in doing usual extravagances, and had landed
them all *au premier* at Brussels.

She had done with these two ladies, and she felt less inclined to renew her confidence with them every day ; for
she had found a friend—Lord Hatterleigh. Every day
she felt more respect for him, and every day she felt more

and more that, with that noble, high-minded, highly-educated oddity at her side, that she could face the world in arms. There was not perfect confidence between them, and that made her at times uneasy. Much as she loved him, he was no lover of hers. One night, while Sir Harry Poyntz was walking up-and-down his room, and thinking when he should begin to poison Lord Hatterleigh's mind against her, she was tossing on her bed, brimful of the resolution of breaking off her engagement with Lord Hatterleigh, and taking him for her friend. She never did so. She let things drive ; she did not move in the matter any more than did Sir Harry Poyntz. They both bided their time.

But the pleasure she felt in the confidence and conversation of this man was very great ; she revelled in it. She told him everything (save that one, and got to forget that, and to act about it as she did when it first happened —to shove it back into her deepest consciousness, with such success that she thought it was going to stay there). She told him of her systematic bringing-up, and her early rebellions—and he laughed ; of her religionism—and he spoke gravely and well, praising her and blaming her confidentially and sensibly : showing her the absurdity of running into these extremes, and, in the end, persuading her to return in a moderate manner to her old routine ; and, as part of it, took to going to church on saints' days with her himself. Her grandmother could not have been more discreet than this youth ; sometimes, however, she was forced to laugh when he got too priggish. There was perfect equality between them ; it was all give-and-take. He was a strong anti-Tractarian — would have been, if he could, leader of the Oxford Liberals ; and they had many a fine fight over that matter. She, on the other hand, was merciless about untidiness, and bullied him systematically about his personal appearance, until he got to put on his clothes in a decent manner, and to come into the room without falling into the fireplace. In short, they did one another a great deal of good—as any two honest people may, if they will only speak the truth to one another. She by degrees laughed him out of his sententious Daniel-come-to-judgment way of talking; and he, though sometimes in a fantastical way, put more good sense and knowledge of the way in which the world wags into her head than ever had been there before.

In the full luxury of the new-found confidence between them, the following dialogue took place one day when they were riding together :—

"George," she said, " there is something very near my heart, and you must share it."

He said—&c. &c. &c.—just what you or I would say.

"Don't cackle ; and you shouldn't giggle after such a speech as that ; and you have got your feet too far in your stirrups, and are turning your toes out. Men who don't hunt shouldn't ride like grooms. Keep your toes in as if you were in the Row."

"Is that what was so near your heart ?"

"Now, pray, don't be funny ; remember the bull in the china-shop."

"I will—and turn my toes in too. There ! Now then, Laura ; if you are going to be serious, be so."

"I am not at all sure that you are in a fit state of mind to be consulted with ; you are a trifle rebellious, and I have a good mind——But, George dear, let us be in earnest ; I want to speak to you about Maria Poyntz."

Lord Hatterleigh looked over his shoulder to the groom, and said, " Go home to the Court, and borrow me a clean pockethandkerchief from Sir Charles' valet." And he went.

"What about her ?"

"Is there nothing to be done ? Is there no way to warn them—to warn her ?"

"Do you wish to try ?"

"I only want your sanction."

"Then you have it. God speed you !"

Chapter XXXII

" Is Captain Wheaton come in ? " said Sir Harry Poyntz to his valet one day, about half an hour before dinner.

" He has been in some time, Sir Harry; he is smoking in the library."

" He has no business to smoke there, unless I am present. Did you tell him that he was to come to me the moment he came in ? "

" I did, Sir Harry."

" Then why the devil didn't he come ? Lawrence, that man is getting too much of a gentleman for us; he must have a lesson."

" The best lesson you could give him, Sir Harry, would be to pack him about his business."

" But who is to do the dirty work—the spying, informing, mischief-making, gaining information, and so on ? *You* won't. I have asked you more than once, and you flatly refused. Who is to do it ? "

" Nobody, Sir Harry; leave it undone."

" Ah ! but you're a fool, you know. There is not a man or woman within ten miles who is not a rogue—except you, you know, of course, and my Lady Poyntz—of course I except my Lady Poyntz—and roguery must be met by finesse. Send him up."

He soon came, whistling : an evil-looking creature, with his eyes too near, too deeply set, and too shifty, and a nasty grin on the mouth of him, which fortunately could only be guessed at, not seen, under his beard.

" I'll tell you what, Wheaton," said Sir Harry ; " I'll give you five pounds if you'll shave."

" What for ? "

" I love my money better than anything in this world—except, of course, virtue, and my Lady Poyntz ; but I would give five pounds to see your villanous face without all that hair on it: only as a matter of curiosity I would. I hate this beard-and-moustache movement. One used to be able to tell a rascal by his mouth ; now one has to look at his eyes. However, it don't much matter in your case ; in more difficult ones it might be different."

" Have you called me up here to insult me ? " said Captain Wheaton.

" Yes : partly that, and partly to hear your report of your rascally eavesdropping expedition."

" The devil is on you strong to-night; Lawrence had better sit up with you again. Bedlam ain't such a nice place as Poyntz Castle."

" Bedlam, you fool ! In the first place, I am not in the least degree mad ; and in the second place, I have had another attack of angina pectoris this morning, so you'll soon be in Newgate. You won't be out of jail six weeks after my death, and I can't last many months. Now then, report progress, and let us have no more nonsense."

" I went," said Captain Wheaton, " at your desire, into the pleasance and watched Miss Seckerton and Lady Poyntz, and I was lucky enough to hear some of their conversation."

" Sagacious touter ! And neither of them horsewhipped you, as the boy Custance did at Newmarket ? And how did the fillies gallop ? "

Wheaton never looked at him, but went on : ' I heard their conversation. Miss Seckerton was telling her what a fool she had been to pitch Colonel Hilton overboard, loving him as she did, in a fit of ill-temper, for such a worthless, effeminate, shallow knave as you."

Such a silly lie ! But he, who disbelieved every other word the man said, believed this. He had exasperated himself against Laura : this man Wheaton had helped in it to his utmost, hating her with his deepest hatred for the utter scorn which always shone on him out of her eyes ; and Sir Harry Poyntz believed him.

" I really must play the deuce with this young lady—I

really must. I am very sorry, for I rather like her when she is wicked. Go on."

"And then I came round the corner on them."

"What an infernal hang-dog scoundrel you must have looked! What did they say?"

"Do you want me to drive a knife in you, you brute?" cried Wheaton, rising in a catlike rage. "I'll do it some day if you go on torturing me and insulting me like this. Do you think I can't feel?"

"If I thought you couldn't feel, I shouldn't do it."

"You make my work too hard for me. I didn't mean to lose my temper. You are ungenerous—you are ungentlemanly to use me so. And it is such bosh! You can be kind enough at times. Why do you madden me against you like this? You know you ain't half such a devil as you want to make out."

"Silence! You interrupt my line of thought. Well, I won't do it any more; if you weren't such a hound I shouldn't do it at all. About this young lady: I'd let her be Lady Hatterleigh, and madden her life away when she found out the truth, only I shouldn't be alive and shouldn't see it. Besides, she's a shrew, and I hate her; but she is too good for that. I think I shall merely administer a severe castigation, which I shall have the pleasure of seeing, and teach her to keep her tongue between her teeth. I shall not give you any money to-day; I will not be threatened with knives."

"That's it! Devil's pay! You never gave me anything for making the huntsman drunk, and getting him to tell me that he saw them kissing one another in the garden; and now you are going to ruin her on my information."

"There is scarcely a word of truth in what you say. In the first place, it wasn't in the garden—it was in the shrubbery; in the second, they didn't kiss one another, but fell together by the ears, and blew one another up consumedly; and in the third place, I am not going to ruin her at all, but only to give her a lesson about the management of her

tongue. Saving her from Lord Hatterleigh cannot be ruining her. She can marry Bob ; he would take her with any
reputation for the sake of the estate. Lastly, if either you
or the huntsman say one word—you know what I mean—
I will pitch you overboard (and you know what that
means) ; and I will ruin his master, and take uncommon
good care that that rascal Robert shall turn him off the ·
estate."

" About Lady Poyntz and Colonel Hilton ? "

" Silence, sir. My domestic affairs are none of your
business."

" Are you going to sell up Sir Charles Seckerton ? "

" That is a matter of detail. Go and ask Lawrence for
my cheque-book." (He brought it.) " You don't deserve
anything—you and your knives. How much do you want ?
Want, I say ; what matter is it how much water one pours
into a sieve ? "

Wheaton mentioned five-and-twenty pounds.

" Then you will want the dogcart to drive to Exeter, and
I charge you five pounds for that ; that makes twenty. A
man of any gumption would bring back a couple of hundred. But you can't play billiards, and you never will.
Why do you go on trying? None of you catfaced men
ever can play. I would give you points, and have all this
money back to-night, if you dared to play me. Here's fifty
pounds for you ; in the name of decency take a fortnight
in losing it ; I don't want you before that."

Chapter XXXIII

" YOU have got your hat on the back of your head again,
George," said Laura, one afternoon. " I wish you wouldn't ;
I am always telling you of it."

" Why shouldn't I ? It's very nice."

" If looking like a lunatic is nice, that's nice. No one

does it out of Bedlam; it makes you look as mad as a hatter."

" —— does it? " He mentioned a statesman, at the sound of whose name the earth quakes to its centre.

" Then *he's* mad," said Laura, " and ought to be locked up."

" You can think better when your hat's like that," said Lord Hatterleigh, " and I was thinking."

" What about ? "

" I was thinking when we ought to be married."

" That's my business. I have thought about that, and come to a decision. My decision is, next year."

" I will see if I can make you alter it."

" There is not the least use. George, I want time. George, I must and will have time. Do you accept my decision ? "

" I suppose I must."

" So I suppose. Now go and dress for dinner."

" It is very early."

" Use the interval in abstraction from worldly affairs and contemplation. No great work of art is accomplished without that. Put the whole force of your intellect into the subject for the next half-hour, and then, when your valet comes to you, you will have grasped the subject yourself, and will not be dependent on a mere expert. Get to feel yourself safe without your expert. Why, if anything was to happen to him, you wouldn't be able to dress yourself and would have to put the thing in commission. Look at the Admiralty, will you ? "

And with these whirling words she left him, and went in, but not to dress just yet. She went upstairs past her own room, higher yet, to the room which old Elspie inhabited with Lady Emily's maid, and she found her alone.

" Elspie, dear, how are you ? "

" I'm braw, my bonny bird. And I'm as strong as maist of these southern lasses yet, praise be to God ! And how is my Lord ? "

" He is very well—and he is very kind and very good, Elspie, which is better still."

" Bless him ! A noble heart ! I wish I had had the nursing of him. Your feckless queans of southern nurses —see what they've done with him ! His heid gangs ane gate, and his legs the ither."

" He is mending, Elspie ; he is mending."

" I'd mend him ! Why does his Lordship keep the Tullibardie Moor, that his brother Lord Charles should kill the grouse, and send them south to him ? Why does he no go north, and brush the bare lean legs of him through the heather ? When he came south again he'd be for kicking your Colonel Hilton downstairs. Laura dear ? "

" Well ? "

" When you are married, take his Lordship to Scotland ; and oh ! my darling, take me with you. It's a bonnie country, this England, and I love it ; but let me see Scotland again before I dee. I am an auld fule, and I'll confess that Fern Tor is grander than Schehallion, and that Wysclith is bonnier than Tummle ; but take me back to Rannoch, darling, once more, before I dee. I'm a hale old woman, I'll no dee on the road. If I dee there—I *will* dee there, Laura, and lie with him on Tummle side, with the roar of the Waxing Burn in my ear, until the dawn which knows no night begins to wax in the Cairn of Schehallion——"

" That's all about long ago, and about long to come," said Laura, looking out of the window across the sands. " Elspie, tell me this : how long does it take to live down love ? "

The old woman had risen, and had been getting a little excited, as the images of the crystal mountain, the longdrawn lake, the snarling river, the whirling snowdrift, the crashing thunderstorm—all the wild incidents of that wondrous fairyland, Perthshire, came flashing on her aged brain. But she sat down now suddenly, and watched the back of Laura's head with her keen grey eye.

" How long does it take to live down love ? " she repeated slowly. " Weel, that just depends on the person ye speir of. There was Luckie Macdonald of Dall; Sandy Macpherson of Aberfeldy died in the snaedrift aboon Rosemount, coming over to see her, and she married Rab Grant, one of Lord Breadalbane's keepers, before her second sacrament. (The deil mend the pair of 'em !) Then there's my ain case, again. I have been forty years forgetting him, and have not done it yet ; but then I have no tried, ye ken. Of whom were ye speiring ? "

" Of no one in particular ; of such a person as myself, say."

" O, yersell. Oh, forty-five hundred and saxty-seven years ; and ye'll no do it at that, lassie. Gang down and dress for dinner. Mistress Bridget will be here the now for her tea. I'm loth that she should hear you talking your nonsense. Gang down—gang down to my Lord."

Chapter XXXIV

TIME went on, until the months had nearly made up another year ; but nothing happened of any sort worth relating, and only two things progressed which are worth mentioning by us.

One thing which progressed was Sir Charles Seckerton's ruin. There was no doubt now that he was in the hands of Sir Harry Poyntz, for the interest on the mortgages was openly paid to his man of business; yet neither man took any step. Sir Charles lived on the same as ever, and Sir Harry Poyntz never made the slightest allusion to his affairs. That some contraction in the household expenses must be made, and that the hounds must go, was pointed out continually by Sir Charles' man of business, but entirely without effect.

" I am cheating no one ; they will all be paid with interest. I want to keep my daughter and my hounds one year more; when she goes they may go. *Laissez-aller.* I have lived with all these faces round me, and I don't want to see the old style changed, and the old circle broken up. Either in my time, or soon after it, the Yorkshire money will set everything straight."

" Not at this rate, Sir Charles."

" Pish, man ! Lord Hatterleigh is a model young man, who knows every sixpence he spends. He will put the whole matter right, after my death."

" The smash may come any day, Sir Charles."

" Well, I shall not make the smash myself; I am not going to take to shambling about the pump-rooms at Aix-la-Chapelle till I am forced."

No sense could be got into his head. The old prestige had become too dear to him. A grand handsome crash would have pleased him better than saving himself by any retrenchment. He even stopped the ordinary cut of timber that year, to the actual detriment of his woods. And it seems curious enough that he confessed afterwards, to a certain acquaintance of mine and of the reader's, that the man towards whom he had the greatest jealousy—the man from whom he most jealously and proudly concealed his difficulties, was his old tried friend Sir Peckwich Downes — a man who would have lent him a hundred thousand pounds on moderate interest, and put him square.

His man of business, in despair, made a schedule of his liabilities, and tried to get him to look at it, but he refused point-blank—

" I know in a general way that the estate will pull through, if we get time. I'll make the change when Laura is married. There will be an excuse then. I shall miss my daughter, and so on. At all events, I will go on for another season ; and there are fifty contingencies in my favour — Lord Hatterleigh — the Yorkshire property — I know not what. Let be."

" But if Sir Harry Poyntz comes down ? "

" Let him. Let me hear no more about it ; only keep the whole thing quiet."

That was all his distracted man of business could get out of him. In some unlucky moment that most innocent attorney had bought and hung up in his parlour Hogarth's print, in " Marriage à la Mode," of the morning after the rout, in which the old steward is going out of the room with only one bill on the file, and all the rest in his hand. It became so offensive to him now that he had it removed. He could do nothing more, except wonder at the extraordinary reticence of Sir Harry Poyntz, and the equally extraordinary insolence of Sir Charles Seckerton towards Sir Harry, the man who could ruin him at any moment.

For Sir Charles was riding the high-horse with his neighbour of the Castle. The relations between Lady Poyntz and Colonel Hilton were not pleasing to Sir Charles Seckerton. They were going about too much together ; Colonel Hilton had got his leave of absence unreasonably prolonged. The whole state of affairs between those two was of a sort which had never been tolerated in this extremely moral county of Devon : and Sir Charles found it incumbent on him to put on fawn-coloured pantaloons, a buff waistcoat, a blue coat and brass buttons ; and mounting his most solemn cob—the property of a late bishop, picked up for a song (sixty guineas) at that prelate's death—and followed by the most solemn and handsomest of all his enormous choice of grooms, mounted on a vast hack (another bargain), he rode round to the Castle to give Sir Harry a piece of his mind.

The solver of difficulties says, in his reckless way, that both this horse and this groom went into the undertaking trade—the one as a hearse-horse, and the other as a mute. He talks too fast sometimes ; but there is no doubt that Sir Charles on the Bishop's cob, followed by the hearse-horse and mute, looked most awfully and severely respectable, and would have frightened anyone except that strange, fantastically incomprehensible creature Sir Harry Poyntz, who, as he viewed the enemy's approach from the window, broke into an uncontrollable fit of laughter, which he was unable to stop.

"*You're* going to catch it," he said to his wife. "I wouldn't be in your shoes for a hundred pounds. Just look at the solemn pomposity of the old fool, will you, Maria? What have you been up to, eh? Hallo, it's me he wants! I hope I shall keep my countenance."

After a solemn shake of the hands, Sir Charles went gravely into his business, more in sorrow than in anger. Sir Harry listened patiently, and made reply,—

"I assure you I think you labour under a great mistake. I cannot say how much I think you are mistaken. I have honestly the fullest confidence in Maria—dear me, the utmost confidence, not only in her, but still more in Hilton."

"Well, I have done my duty. I have known you from a boy, and have taken the liberty of telling you what the county said."

"The county are a parcel of cackling idiots—all except, you know—in short, with the exceptions which common politeness requires. If they knew anything about present society, they would know that every woman of any pretensions to fashion has a follower."

"It is a shameless custom!"

"I don't see it. You at all events should not complain of it in this case. You knew all about me from a boy, and it was you who sold the girl to me, and it is you who are spending the money now."

The poor old gentleman rose up deadly white, and laying his hand to his heart, gave a pitiable groan. Such a bitter, bitter stab!—so reckless, so needless, so horribly cruel, and yet so bitterly true! He turned towards the window, and leant his head on his arm.

Sir Harry Poyntz rose at the same time. He cursed himself and his own tongue with a refined sort of blasphemy which none of us need guess at. He cried out to Sir Charles to witness that he was a fool, a lunatic, who didn't know what he was saying ; and, lastly, besought his pardon on his knees.

Sir Charles turned on him at last and said : " Leave me alone a few minutes, and I am at your orders. Let the pain of the wound go off a little before you give me another."

And Sir Harry went back to his chair, and took up a book of pictures—no other a book than our " Tom and Jerry ; " and when Sir Charles turned on him after a considerable interval, he was to all appearances deeply engrossed in it.

He knew that Sir Charles had turned towards him, and instantly began the conversation—

" The cleverest thing in this most marvellous book is the figure of the beggar scratching himself. Now, did your Hogarth beat this man ? "

" I want you to be serious, Harry."

" I'll be perfectly serious, my dear Sir Charles ; I have much more to be serious about than you have."

" How can that be ? "

" I have been to London to the doctors—real doctors, none of your tin-pot, twopenny-halfpenny, secondhand leech apothecaries, but Savile Row, you know. And they say I am dying ; I have angina pectoris. I could have told them *that*. But it appears that my brain has been softening for years, and that if the one thing don't carry me off I shall die a drivelling idiot. It appears that I can seldom have been sane since I was sixteen, and that my lucid intervals will get rarer. Do you forgive those wicked words I said to you just now ? "

" Most heartily, Harry ; but I can never forget them— they were so terribly true ! "

" Fiddle-de-dee !—you'll forget them fast enough. I'll send you out of this room six inches higher than you were when you came into it. Sit down."

Sir Charles did so, wondering what was to come next.

" You feel humiliated. Of course you do. So you
ought, if you have any of the feelings of a gentleman left.
You see I can be keen enough in my lucid intervals. You
thought, forsooth, that you were going to incur pecuniary
liabilities, and then march out of the whole business at
twelve-and-sixpence in the pound, with your nose in the
air. Now, no man with the feelings of a gentleman ever
did that yet, and you have the feelings of a gentleman. I
am sorry I spoke so cruelly to you just now, because I love
you very much; but it is an uncommonly good lesson for
you. You lay it to heart, and don't get yourself up in the
heavy-father style again, and come here to lecture me."

" I take my rebuke, Harry. But be merciful; I am an
old man. You shall have your bond to-morrow; I will
announce my ruin to-morrow morning. But don't say
any more cruel things."

" Announce your ruin! For God's sake, Sir Charles,
don't be a lunatic! I have got this pain in my chest coming on again, and I cannot talk much more; this attack
may kill me. Listen to what I say, and go home and
think about it, without any further discussion. Your
daughter Laura irritated me, in one way and another, beyond what my temper could bear. I had a plan for ruining you and disgracing her. But I have given it up. I
am a bad fellow and a great rascal, as you, who have
known me from a boy, well know. But I am ridiculously
superstitious, and I want to die without leaving anyone
anything to forgive. Come, there is nothing foolish in
that. I could ruin you to-morrow, but I won't. While I
live you are safe. (Why you don't retrench I don't know—
that is your business.) But during my lifetime you will
have mercy, afterwards none. What do you know of my
brother Robert? Come, speak out."

" I have heard that he was very dissipated and wild,
but that we attributed to——"

" To false reports spread by me? Come, speak out,

man; you don't know how much depends on it. ˙Is it not so?"

"Yes."

"Ask anyone who knows him—but you don't know anyone, though—if I am not right, half spendthrift, half miser. Even I had to send him off. You will get no mercy from him; you'll be sold up, body and bones, as soon as I am dead."

"You are not dead yet, Harry."

"Ah! but I may die to-night. Have you not brains to see your only course?"

"I can't say I do."

"Break off this match with Lord Hatterleigh," said Sir Harry, looking very keenly at Sir Charles. "I was going to do it once from far other motives, but will do it still if you hesitate. Break off this match, and marry her to my brother. He will come home from India in a most marriageable frame of mind. Those two queer rumpty-tumpty old trots of yours, Lady Southmolton and Lady Emily, would have him to book in a week."

Sir Charles passed over this disrespectful mention of his womankind, but rose in wrath on the other side of the question—

"Sell my daughter, sir? Never!"

"Hang it, old fellow! You know," said Sir Harry, nursing his knee, "you sold Maria to me, as you have confessed. And you have sold your own daughter to a Guy Fawkes who wears his boots hind-side before. Surely you can do it again? But whether or no, you think of it, and bring your mind to it. It seems shocking now; but it is wonderful what you can bring your mind to, if you only put yourself *en visage* with it soon enough. Now go home, and don't say a word to me, or I shall die before it will be convenient to you. Only remember this: break off this unnatural match between your daughter and Lord Hatterleigh, or else I shall have to do it myself."

Sir Charles rode back again. The groom and the horse

which followed him were as portentously solemn as ever ;
but Sir Charles sat huddled together in an undignified
manner, and rode badly. And the cob stumbled once or
twice—a thing we must attribute to the uncertain hand of
poor Sir Charles ; for when ridden by his late master, the
Bishop, that cob had never been known to stumble. But,
then, his Lordship was a man so certain of his conclusions, that his certainty communicated itself to his horse ;
whereas poor Sir Charles was in a perfect sea of bewilderment. No wonder the pony stumbled !

Chapter XXXV

THIS last conversation must have taken place nearly a
year after the eventful midsummer on which we have had
to dwell so long—not long before the time when fresh and
startling changes took place ; which changes conclude
that period in the lives of our friends which seemed to me
worth speaking of, and which also bring my story to an
end. It is now my duty to speak somewhat at large of
Colonel Hilton.

"What business he had here at all," said Lady Emily
one day, "was a thing which no one could find out."
But, whether he had any business here or no—here he
was ; and we must decidedly agree with the county that
he had much better have been anywhere else.

He had returned invalided from the Crimea, but had
soon got well; and had found himself in the course of
duty at Plymouth, doing some work or another, nothing
very much the matter with him. He was in a deservedly
high position, and was able to take things very comfortably.
He was asked, of course, to Leighton Court ; and at once it
occurred to him that it would be a very nice thing to fall in
love with Laura, which he immediately did—in a sort of
way. What was unfortunate was, that Laura did not fall in

love with him; and, what was worse still, Maria Huxtable did, and, not being so well-formed a young lady as our poor Laura, let him see it. Of course he was flattered and pleased by this; though to himself he said that it was a most unfortunate and unhappy business, that a very beautiful girl with sixty thousand pounds should have shown herself ready to be asked by him, as it was impossible that he could return her affection, and all that sort of thing. He pitied the poor girl extremely, and was very kind to her indeed.

Fall in love with her he could not. She was vulgar beside Laura, he said; and she had a dog-like way of following him about and persecuting him, which exasperated him to the pitch of madness. If the poor silly girl had only waited for him to make love to her, instead of making play at him, she might have been Mrs. Hilton. But she wouldn't. She had no mother, and had had no training. She thought, in her simplicity, that her little artifices to get near him, to touch him, to get him to speak kindly to her, were utterly unsuspected; while Hilton was driving back in his dogcart to Plymouth, and saying, "Hang it all, that girl is worse than any girl who ever made a dead set at a man in India! It is perfectly sickening. The women in England are losing all sense of modesty. But I like her better than the other one, after all."

For his imperial majesty, after having bound himself to Laura's chariot-wheels for a few weeks, and having received nothing but impertinence from that young lady, had begun to dislike her amazingly, and to show it. He had got a certain sort of contempt for her. She sets up for strength of character, but she lets herself be led by the nose by a priest. She is positive, and will never confess herself wrong; but she is as often wrong as right; and she has such a deuce of a tongue! Colonel Hilton, after all his knockings about, did not feel at all inclined to "hang up his hat," as the soldiers say, with Laura. Besides, he did not want to marry at all, if it came to that.

A few weeks made a great change in his sentiments about marriage. Hitherto he had been getting all the kicks and none of the halfpence of this world. And now, just when he could look about him, he neither felt inclined to tie himself for life to such a very positive and contradicting person as Laura, or to a jealous spaniel of a woman like Maria. He went back to his work, leaving Maria, who had created a fiction that Laura had stood between him and her, in a state of jealousy and anger against Laura.

It gave him a pang, however, when he heard that Maria was married to Sir Harry Poyntz. Everyone knew everything about Sir Harry Poyntz except those most concerned. Hilton, who knew that she was in love with him, was shocked and distressed at such a shameful sacrifice; and while at Châlons, hearing that the Poyntzes were at Paris, left his duty to see——what? Who can say? Let us put it thus—to see how they were getting on together.

Sir Harry had received him with a most cordial welcome. He found in him a most agreeable companion, not only for himself, but for Lady Poyntz. He could not, would not, pay much attention to her—Hilton was able and apparently willing to do so. He knew she had been fond of him, but with that strange unreasoning recklessness which was part of his disease, he, merely because he took a great liking to the man, pressed his friendship on him, and as a matter of course thrust his society on his wife.

The mischief must have begun very soon, probably in the rush and roar and glitter of Châlons, for he got off going to America on the score of his health; and those who knew and loved him best were grieved to see the Hero of Assewal obviously malingering, and getting himself talked of with another man's wife.

The county, as we know, strongly rebelled, but no one dared to speak. Some said that Sir Harry connived at it —others said he was a besotted idiot. The last opinion was more nearly true than the former. Sir Harry's head was going. He began to find that he had not brain to execute the schemes which his cunning had originated. He had early confided what was the matter to Hilton, and Hilton had often acted for him. But something happened once which gave him firmer confidence in Hilton, and which gave Colonel Hilton supreme power over Sir Harry.

Poor Sir Harry began to get into a new phase of his disease. His fits of irritability became more acute, and began to develope into violence. His wife one night irritated him extremely; she had no tact whatever, and he threw something at her. The ridiculous part of the matter was that it was only an antimacassar; but the pathetic part of it was that the poor fellow had cunning enough to see that he had by that act overstepped a certain boundary, and that he could never step back again. He was on his knees before her directly, and she, not having wit to see, laughed at the whole matter, and threatened to box his ears. He said nothing more to her; but he rode over to Plymouth, and told the whole business to Colonel Hilton.

" If it had been the poker, you know, Hilton, it would have been just the same. And it would bein the highest degree ungentlemanly if I laid my hand on that woman. She hasn't behaved badly, and she brought me, first and last, sixty thousand pounds. It's an awful nuisance, isn't it ? "

" Why did you marry, Poyntz ? "

" Heaven only knows ! Why the deuce did they let me ? If they had all done their duty they could have stopped it. My character was bad enough to have justified the county in burning down the Castle."

" Poyntz, I can't make head or tail of you ; you are the most confusing fellow I ever met."

" I know I am a disturbing cause among you sane people. You generalise from an accumulation of facts which you consider as sufficient, and then *I* come cranking in, and send your calculations to the four winds of heaven—make you all in your bewilderment a hundred times madder than myself. For instance, *you* are all mops and brooms now. You don't know what to do—*I* do. I want watching, and someone ought to watch me ; someone I respect and like ought to have his eye on me. If it was only once a week it would be something."

"Go home and fight against it, man ; you have plenty of resolution and plenty of brains, though they are most decidedly addled, God help you! I never saw anything like you in all my born days," cried the Colonel, in a bewilderment which would have been comical under any other circumstances. "Go home and keep your temper, man."

"But will you speak to Maria, and persuade her not to exasperate me to the pitch of murder?"

"Well—— Yes, I will. What did she do to you?"

"She kept on agreeing to every word I said. I tried to make her contradict me for an hour and a half, but she wouldn't. She sat there smiling, and agreeing with every word I said till I thirsted for her blood, and hurled the antimacassar at her. I talked of everything in heaven or earth. I turned high-churchman and low-churchman, Whig, Tory, doctrinaire Radical, pothouse Radical—pitched into Popery, pitched into Whalley ; but there she sat and smiled, and agreed to every word I said, till at last I did what can never be undone—I used violence towards her."

"You haven't hurt her much, have you?" said Hilton, laughing.

"Don't be a fool! If you can't see the importance of what I have told you, leave us alone!"

So Colonel Hilton thought it his duty to see more of that establishment, as being the only person who had any power over Sir Harry. He made very light of this antimacassar business ; Sir Harry was so fantastic about it. A circumstance which happened a few days afterwards showed him that the poor fellow (we may call him so now) was right, and that a strong head was needed in that house.

Sir Harry Poyntz had lately drunk nothing but water ; he was a very abstemious man. Therefore one evening, when Colonel Hilton was over at the Castle, he felt no anxiety when he left Captain Wheaton and Sir Harry alone over the wine (Captain Wheaton drinking like a fish, and Sir Harry eating grapes like a famished hound), and went up to the drawing-room to Lady Poyntz.

He had hardly been there ten minutes, when Wheaton came in, as pale as a ghost, and called on Colonel Hilton to defend him.

Hilton thought he was drunk. " I thought I had—that you were forbidden this room, sir ? "

" For God's sake come and help us ! Sir Harry is going to murder me ; he has gone for his revolver ! "

Hilton went at once ; from a noise he heard he directed his feet towards Sir Harry's bedroom. There he found three or four servants round the door, begging Sir Harry to be calm ; he, in a furious rage, had just finished loading his revolver.

" Now, clear out of the way ; I'll shoot the first man who stands between that dog and me ! "

All got out of the way except a young footman, who cleverly kept his eye on the pistol, intending to run in on his master. He was just going to make a dart, when he was thrust gently on one side ; and Colonel Hilton, walking calmly in, took the pistol away from Sir Harry as if he was a child.

" You can all go. Thomas, you have behaved uncommonly well ; Sir Harry will reward you. Now, Poyntz, how did this come about ? "

" He was drunk, and he amused himself by irritating and insulting me the moment you were gone."

" Didn't you begin nagging at him ? "

" Nothing of the kind, I assure you."

" Well, we must take care it don't happen again. You have pretty well frightened him this time."

" He would do it again when he was drunk ; we had better kick him out."

" I think that ought to have been done a long while ago ; but—I beg your pardon, Poyntz—are you quite sure you mean what you say ? "

" Quite sure ? Yes."

" You are quite sure the fellow don't know too much—is not dangerous ? "

" Oh, dear no ; he knows nothing more than you do. I certainly did keep him on, partly because I did not want it known that I was odd in my head ; but the main reason was that I liked to tease and insult him, and see how much the dog would stand. As far as I am concerned, kick him out to-night ! You are not afraid yourself, are you ? " said Sir Harry.

" What should *I* be afraid of ? What is the dog to me ? "

" He will blacken your character and, I fear, Maria's too. But anything is better than murder ! "

" I will give the rascal a hint of my vengeance if he dares. I will go now and send him off."

And so Captain Wheaton got what he elegantly called his " walking ticket," and disappeared. Instantly on his disappearance, rumour got tenfold more busy with Lady Poyntz's name, with Hilton's name, and with Sir Harry's name. Lady Poyntz was an abandoned woman, and gambled ; Hilton was lost to all honour, and drank ; Sir Harry was abandoned, gambled, drank, and was a dangerous lunatic all at the same time. Of course these reports were set about by our friend Wheaton, but most people believed them ; and not long after Wheaton's departure, Sir Charles Seckerton had the interview we know of with Sir Harry Poyntz, and came home with his feathers ruffled.

Meanwhile Sir Harry clung more and more closely to Hilton, as the only man in this world whom he could trust.

And Hilton hung on about the house, and saw more and more of Maria, till now he and Lady Poyntz were standing on the very verge of ruin unutterable.

Chapter XXXVI

" Did you see Lady Poyntz this morning, Laura ? " asked Lord Hatterleigh, as he and Laura met on the stairs, going down to dinner, and dawdled together for a chat.

" Yes ; I saw her and walked with her, but there was no result. She held me completely at bay, and talked and rattled on just as she has done since I went back to her to try to gain her confidence. She is perfectly friendly, but will talk nothing but commonplace. I must give the business up, George."

" Don't do that ; persevere, my love. Think for a moment what is involved in giving her up."

" You are right. I will persevere on the mere chance of some accident giving me my old hold on her. George, there was a time when that woman hung on every word I said—when I could have made her jump off the keep or turn Roman Catholic."

" How did you lose it ? "

" You are rather provoking ; but I will stick to our bargain, and tell the truth. Through my own conceit and folly, not to mention my tongue ; I bullied her too much."

" And she thought you stood between her and Colonel Hilton at the time you encouraged him to pay you so much attention ? "

" If snapping his nose off every time he opened his mouth meant encouragement, you are quite right."

" I know," said Lord Hatterleigh, giving one of his own " Alcedo gigantea " guffaws. " I used to watch you. What on earth made you hate the man so ? "

" The same thing which makes me dislike you so much
—he is a gaby ! "

" I don't think he is a gaby at all—at all events, not
such a gaby as I was."

" I never examined into the degrees of gabyism."

" Bless thy sweet tongue, Kate ! And you wonder you
lost your power over Maria Poyntz ? "

" Bless thy sweet temper, George ! Did anyone ever
make you cross ? I have tried hard enough."

" No, I never was cross. My mother remarks it in public often—a great deal too often. She damages my reputation, and makes people take liberties with me, by always
representing me a lamb. It would do me infinite good in
the world if people could be got to believe that I was a
terrible tiger at bottom ; but they won't. By-the-bye, do
you remember that you told me once that the reason you
hated Colonel Hilton was that he agreed with every word
you said ? Now that is singular, isn't it ? "

" Come to your dinner, will you, and don't stay exasperating me on the stairs. The cases are utterly different.
You contradict me, and argue with me in perfect good-
humour ; he flattered one until he made one contradict
him, and only opposed one when he was thoroughly angry. Now that is quite enough to carry you on for the
rest of the evening ; I cannot be always flattering you."

" Very well ; I can take care of myself."

" They are coming to-night," said Laura.

" Who ? "

" The Poyntzes and Colonel Hilton. That is the last
civil thing I shall say to-night. As an illustration, you
knew who I meant well enough, only for the chance of
another spar you pretended you didn't."

They both burst out laughing. There was something
very pretty in the friendship between these two. They
sparred at times, but Laura always lost. She sometimes
lost her temper, for instance, which that sweet-natured
gorilla of a nobleman never did. They did one another a

deal of good. She civilised him to an extent which his own mother had never conceived possible ; and he, by his persistent good-humour, broke her of her petulance, and cured her of her unfortunate habit of speaking her mind. When on this occasion they had both done laughing, she answered him—

" The Poyntzes and the other gaby—you know whom I mean by the first one—are coming. Now."

" Pax, be serious ! I am in earnest, Laura. I want to speak to you ; I want to consult you. There, now let us be wise."

They were at once as wise as Solomon.

" I wish he was gone from here," said Lord Hatterleigh.

" We all wish that."

" If he has a spark of honour or manliness left in him— and the man is a noble soldier, Laura—he will go after hearing to-day's news."

" What news ? "

" News ! " cried Lord Hatterleigh, and looking sternly at her. " Heavens ! have you heard nothing ?—that India is lost ; that the Sepoys have risen, and are driving the British before them like sheep ; that the European men and women are being shot down like dogs, and treated worse ; that the whole remnant of British rule in India consists in a few hopeless garrisons, shut in, with their women and children, in the principal towns, holding out, through thirst and hunger, lest a fate worse than death befall them ? India is lost—gone—hopelessly gone ! "

" That is very dreadful, Hatterleigh ! Are we really to lose India ? But we shall get on pretty well without it, sha'n't we ? "

" Heaven Help her ! " said Lord Hatterleigh, addressing a case full of stuffed birds, which stood in the hall close before him. " My mother was right ; I can't lose my temper. Laura dear, you can understand this. We have suffered a fearful disaster in India — more fearful, more

terrible, than you can understand! I will teach you to understand it, dear, and you shall be as angry and as fierce
as I am. But this terrible disaster strikes home here in
two ways."

" As how? I cannot understand."

" Colonel Hilton's brother is there in the thick of it.
Surely the danger of his only brother, his favourite, will
be sufficient to rouse him from this unmanly sloth? Surely
he will exchange into some regiment ordered for service,
and quit this place for ever? "

" It would be an excellent solution; let us hope so."

" Then there is Poyntz's brother Robert. He is in the
thick of it too. Now would be the time for someone to
say a kind word for him to his brother, and to reconcile
them."

" Is their quarrel very bitter? "

" Very so. He was very wild. There, your mother has
rung for dinner; we shall catch it."

" Not we," said Laura, laughing; " my mother never
scolds you."

Chapter XXXVII

DURING dinner, and after dinner, they talked of only one
thing—the Indian Mutiny; and more particularly that part
of it which was illustrated by a wonderful letter just received by Sir Peckwich Downes from his son George, who
was in the heart of the whole matter.

The party was complete, with the exception of Colonel
Hilton, who could not come. Sir Peckwich looked seven
sizes larger than usual, and tried to be as pompous as ever,
but failed. A radiant genial smile overspread his features
continually; and more than once, like our dear Sir Hugh,
he manifested a mighty disposition to cry. All the best
part of the man (and he was a noble man enough) was coming out of him as he talked of his son's heroism, and his

son's friend's heroism. And Lord Hatterleigh and Laura noticed, as a curious thing, that he addressed himself almost entirely to Sir Harry Poyntz, to whom he had hardly deigned to speak before. He appealed to him, and he flattered him : when he told the most exciting part of the noble story, as he did by request half-a-dozen times over, he addressed himself almost entirely to Sir Harry Poyntz. Once, when his utterance was stopped, and his great chest began heaving, he sat calmly looking at Sir Harry, until he had succeeded in smothering the sobs which were trying to rise. And Sir Harry, with his shallow pale-blue eye, sat watching and listening to him with his head on one side, like a parrot. No one but Hilton could have read that intense look : it meant, " My brain is getting dull ; but I think I know what you are after, old gentleman ! " Lord Hatterleigh couldn't make it out at all.

The gist of the story was this : The garrison of Gorumpore, reduced to about sixty European soldiers, one hundred Sikhs, and the civilian volunteers, had, finding their position untenable, made a glorious retreat, with the women and children, back in safety to a nucleus of the army, which was now sufficiently large to retreat the next day into communication with the base of operations at Calcutta —and this through masses of swarming Sepoys. You can read a hundred such stories. Their rear had been sorely pressed by rebel cavalry. The handful of mounted Europeans and Sikhs had charged back, against overwhelmingly superior numbers, time after time through the burning day. At last, at evening, when the main body were just getting into safety, within hearing of British bugles, George Downes, in command of the party, had ordered one last charge. But the rebels, getting more reckless as they saw their prey escaping, were too strong for them—the British got the worst of it. Several of the Sikhs went to Paradise with closed teeth, laying about them like glorious fellows as they are ; but the rest cut their way through the rebels, and, led by a certain Cornet, were in a fair way to get home ; when this Cornet, now their leader, looking round, missed Downes, and, crying out to the rest of his handful of Sikhs and Europeans, turned bridle and rode back again as hard as he could go.

The main body of the rebels had found themselves too near the British bugles, and had retreated. But in the centre of the plain there were left somewhere near fifty of them, riding round and round one another in a circle—the inner ones of them cutting and slashing at something with their sabres. The Cornet, sailing straight away into this embroglio, never looking as to who were following, and making himself felt right and left, discovered that the something they were cutting at was George Downes, standing, dismounted, over the body of a wounded British trooper, fighting the whole fifty of them single-handed.*

The Cornet dashed at the whole of them alone ; and whether it was that he laid about him so stoutly, or whether the mere appearance of " an angry sahib "—which, as Mr. Trevelyan tells us, is sufficient to produce any amount of panic among Indians—caused it, we cannot say : at all events there was a general " skedaddle," which is one fact ; and another is, that we agree with Mr. Trevelyan that an angry Englishman is a very terrible business indeed.

However, the Cornet and the Cornet's tail got Captain Downes out of his terrible situation in triumph, and that was the story.

" And what I say is," thundered Sir Peckwich Downes, " that nobly as that most noble boy of mine has behaved, the Cornet has behaved more nobly still. Just think of it,

---

* I have not drawn on my imagination here. I met a quiet man at a country dinner-party, not many years ago, on whose dresscoat I detected the Victoria Cross. In the half-hour before dinner I got introduced to him, for the purpose of having a look at his shabby bit of gun-metal, a decoration which I had never seen closely before. A few years afterwards I saw his sword-arm, and then I began to understand what war meant. He had eight-and-twenty sabre-cuts in various parts of his body.

by Jove!—coming back after poor George—all alone, single-handed, by Jove! And you talk to me of your ancient
Romans," he continued, turning with sudden asperity on
Sir Charles, as if that innocent and perfectly silent gentleman had just finished a string of highly offensive classical
allusions—"your Quintus Curtius, your Leonidas, your
rubbish! What were they to this glorious self-devoted
Cornet—eh, sir? Go along with you, sir; don't talk that
nonsense to me!"

"A glorious fellow truly," said Sir Charles; "a noble
fellow—a hero among heroes!"

"We have not had his name yet," said Laura. "Let
us have this noble man's name."

"Ask Sir Harry Poyntz," said Sir Peckwich, with a toss
of the head and a puff.

Laura did so, with her eyes flashing, and her whole face
animated by the glorious story. Sir Harry looked at her
steadily, and thought, "I shall have to play the mischief
with you to-morrow, my dear young lady — I shall indeed;" and then said slowly, aloud—"I do not know his
name. I know nothing of the story but what I have heard
here. But I begin to make a guess, from Sir Peckwich
Downes' exceedingly personal gaze, that this hero is no
other than that lunatic young rascal, my brother Bob: it's
exactly like a piece of his tomfoolery."

"Right, by Jingo!" said Sir Peckwich, bringing his fist
on the table with a crash: a piece of vulgarity which,
coupled with the lowness of the remark which accompanied it, would at an ordinary time have raised extreme anger
in the aristocratic soul of Lady Downes; but she now
only sat, flushed and proud, looking so really noble that
Laura remarked it, and pointed it out to Lord Hatterleigh.

"Wonderful!" he whispered; "and such a *very* com-
monplace-looking person on ordinary occasions!"

"We have all got a little extra fire in our eyes to-night
—not one of us but looks nobler," said Laura; "but the
proud mother beats us all. I wonder whether that strange

creature Sir Harry will notice his brother now: he is going to speak."

"It was not a difficult guess of mine, Sir Peckwich. I know now that he must have changed into that Clanjam fry because your son was there. They were boy-lovers at Eton, you remember."

"I congratulate myself on the result," said Sir Peckwich.

"I say," said Sir Harry, with some show of interest, "what does one do in these cases?"

"What do you mean?" said Sir Peckwich, puzzled.

"In these cases, when a man's brother or son distinguishes himself like this: do you send them a present, or merely write them a complimentary letter? What are you going to do in George's case, for instance?"

"I shall write to him, sir, a letter he'll remember to the day of his death. And I shall pay a thousand pounds into Cox and Greenwood's, for him to spend in the way he likes best. That is what I am going to do, sir."

"Oh, indeed! You are going to do that. Should you say that in my case half would be enough?"

"Give me your hand, Poyntz," said Sir Peckwich; and the other did so, laughing.

"Much obliged to you for giving me a precedent. Bob has never done so in his own person. He has never behaved in any way approaching to common decency till now. Here's my difficulty about the letter: all the letters I have ever written to him have been of a violently exasperating and abusive nature, and now to begin gushing ——. However, it must be done."

By-and-by a servant came in and announced "Sir Harry Poyntz's boat."

"It is very early," said he.

"I think you are wanted at home, Sir Harry: something about Colonel Hilton."

"Is anything the matter with him?"

"Is he dead?" said Lady Poyntz, in a voice which made them all start.

" No, my lady, I believe not—nothing at all the matter with him."

But she passed out, very pale ; and Laura went with her to wrap her up, for the night was chill. Her husband stayed behind, and paused while wishing Lord Hatterleigh good-night. He was a little more fantastic than usual—

" Good-night ! I hope you will sleep well to-night."

" Thank you—I generally do, Poyntz—thank you," said Lord Hatterleigh.

" And I hope you will sleep well to-morrow night also. Inside all right now ? "

" Quite right, thank you," said the other, laughing.

" Hah ! don't let it go wrong again, if anything happens to you. Put a bold face on it, you know. Good-night !"

" Put a bold face on what ? " asked Lord Hatterleigh.

" On anything that may happen," said Sir Harry. " Don't think so much of your inside. Bless you, there is no greater mistake in life than beginning to study your inside ! If I had done so I should have been in Bedlam ten years ago. Short of turning Papist, I know of no superstition so mischievous as that of believing one's inside to be in an exceptional and abnormal state. That is the great temptation of your life ; don't you yield to it after you get my letter to-morrow."

At the door Sir Harry came across his wife, Laura, and Sir Charles Seckerton. He bid Laura " good-night," and paused with her as he had with Lord Hatterleigh.

" That was a fine story about George Downes," he said.

" A noble story ! And your brother too !"

" And my brother Bob, eh ? A fine fellow—a fine fellow ! I will send him five hundred pounds, and I'll bet another hundred that he makes that five hundred go further than scatter-brained George Downes does his thousand. A fine fellow, Bob, after all, Sir Charles ; only one fault, he is such a miserly screw !"

" I can hardly believe that about such a hero," said Laura.

"You'll have to believe it, Miss Seckerton. And now, as we shall never meet again in this world, let me say good-by once more. Reserve your judgment of me; all I ask of you is to reserve your judgment of me."

And before puzzled Laura had replied, he was down the pleasance-walk after his wife; and soon they heard the throb of the rowlocks, as the boat carried them across the tideway towards the dark Castle which threatened in the westward before the sinking moon, "Seen him for the last time! Reserve her judgment on him! The man was mad!"

Chapter XXXVIII

IT was a cold night, and a cold and wailing wind came down the river from the moor; but it was hardly cold enough to account for Lady Poyntz trembling and shivering as she did.

"How you shake, old woman!" said Sir Harry; "you have caught a cold. Take my coat."

"I am warm enough, Harry; at least I shall get warm walking up to the Castle. I hate dining at the Court! I shall catch my death crossing this river some night. However, here we are."

She sprang on shore; and the moment they were alone together, she said,—

"Hilton has got some ill-news, or he is going to India. Go and speak to him."

"India! For God's sake don't let him go away from me! I shall be ruined. I can't do without him now. I tell you fairly, I have no one who will act for me but him."

"Go to him, Harry; see if anything is wrong."

"I wish you would go," said Sir Harry. "I hate a scene. Besides, you have ten times the influence with him that I have. Do go, to oblige me."

"Let it be so then," she said, with a sigh.

" Thank you ! I will go to my room."

Colonel Hilton, the servant said, was in the library. She passed quickly to the door, and paused when she had her hand on the handle.

She felt sick and faint ; she was terrified beyond measure. The poor woman knew that, although as yet innocent, she was on the edge of a precipice, and that any movement might be her ruin. What was Hilton doing ; why had he sent for them home ? She knew, poor creature, that she was in his power ; that he had got perfect control over her ; and that if he was scoundrel enough to say the word this night, she would follow him to the ends of the earth ! She wished she was dead ; she wished that she had never been born. At last she said to herself, " Oh, if he will only have mercy ! "

She let the handle go. A thought came into her head so maddening, so terrifying, that she nearly screamed aloud. Her father ! For one moment in the darkness she saw the dear old face, as it would be when he got the news ; incredulity, horror, and a wild grief which was beyond wailing, were torturing each sacred line. The ghastly vision was gone again in an instant ; and she stood gasping for breath before the door, knowing that she must enter to her fate.

She was terrified suddenly by a sound in the room, at the door of which she stood trembling : a word—a word in Hilton's voice—a loud, furious, terrible oath ! She went in now, and as she looked at him, she thought her doom was sealed.

He was perfectly white, and his hair was disordered, and hung over his forehead. On his face there was a scowl so fearful, so utterly unlike anything she had seen there before, that her terror was almost lost in amazement. He was standing with his back to the fire and his face towards her as she came in, and so she took it all in at a glance.

" Is that you, Lady Poyntz ? " he croaked out,

" Yes, it is I ; you sent for us."

" To hear the news, the gallant news, my Lady Poyntz. Have you heard the news of my brother Jack, of my bonny little Jack, the lad I swore to protect, to my mother on her deathbed ? Only he and I left in the world together!"

" Has anything happened to him ? "

" Murdered ! " he shouted, in a voice which rang through the silent house, and startled the distant servants. " Murdered, foully and cruelly, by his own men, while I, like a thrice-cursed fool, was mincing here ! That is brave news for you, my Lady Poyntz ! "

She could only weep—she had nothing to say.

" But, Maria, I will have vengeance for this — sweet, noble vengeance ! I am off to-night ; I only stayed to say good-bye, and before you see me again, I shall have waded knee-deep in blood. Our fellows are at the glorious work now, and I am away to join them. And now good-bye once more, Maria ; say good-bye to your husband for me. I have been here too long already." And so, without another word, he was gone.

A sad frame of mind for such a genial noble creature to find himself in. It is easy enough to be philosophical over this state of feeling, and to be shocked at it at this distance of time. We, however, have nothing to do either with excusing it or condemning it ; all we need say about it is that it existed to an immense extent, and that its existence in the breast of Colonel Hilton probably saved him and Lady Poyntz from hopeless ruin.

She was saved, and she knew it. Half an hour after Hilton was gone, her husband, prowling round the house with catlike tread, came to the library-door and looked in. Lady Poyntz was kneeling at the table, with the light in her face, and her hands held before her as though she prayed ; while her lips, though moving rapidly, did not disturb the beautiful smile which was settled on her mouth. She had not been weeping, for her magnificent lustrous eyes were as clear and more brilliant than ever ; but what was more noticeable than anything, was a look of unutterable joy which overspread her face, and had its origin in too many infinitely intricate sources for it to be possible to analyse it, or to say it was expressed so, or so. There was something so solemnly beautiful about her, that Sir Harry drew back, and looked on puzzled—

" How wonderfully beautiful she looks ! Why is she glad Hilton is gone ? I hope I have not been too careless. She is looking like her dead mother now. I never saw her mother, but I know she is. Well, it is no good trying to get her to help me in this business while she is in this saintlike frame of mind; I might as well ask that madonna there. I see I must do it all myself."

And so with catlike stealth he crept away through the silent house, and left her kneeling with her hands before her, indulging the long - lost but new - found luxury of prayer.

Chapter XXXIX

LORD HATTERLEIGH came over earlier than usual the next morning. Laura heard his horse come to the hall door, and heard him come rattling along to the door of the breakfast-room, where she sat alone. She thought he was in a great hurry, but until he had shut the door behind him took very little notice. When he had done so she looked up, and was filled with astonishment and fear.

Poor gentleman, he was a sad spectacle ! He looked pale and wild, and, what was more extraordinary, all the latent " Guy " element in the man had come out stronger than ever, as the doctor said it would on the first strain of circumstances. He had got his hat on the back of his head, his necktie was on one side, and one of his shoe-strings was untied. Laura saw that something had happened, but she preserved her equanimity, for she had really no anticipation of anything overwhelming. She spoke first—

" What is the matter, George ? "

" Oh, Laura ! Laura ! I have got such a dreadful letter."

" Is that any reason why you should keep your hat on, not to say wear it on the back of your head, like a lunatic ? Sit down, and tell me all about it."

" I hardly know where to begin," said poor Lord Hatterleigh, sitting down.

" Begin anywhere ; and as for leaving off, leave off as soon as I order you."

It was the last piece of her kindly shrewishness which she ever gave to him or anyone else. Lord Hatterleigh saw the old effort to be smart and epigrammatical, and saw the failure also. She was frightened. He paused before he went on, and there was a dead silence. She would not speak, and he was forced to begin. He sat, and looked steadily and kindly at her, and began speaking. She thought he had never looked so manly, so noble, or so good as he looked now, when every word he spoke was like a dull blow on her heart, which by God's mercy deadened its sensation, and prevented her going mad.

" Laura," he said, " do you remember once that you turned to me suddenly, when I, to tell the truth, was not prepared for your doing so ; when I, in fact, was only hoping that you could get to love me after getting used to my uncouthness, and finding out by degrees my better qualities ; you remember that at such a time once you turned to me spontaneously, and told me that you had always liked me and trusted me ? "

" I went further than that. I said I had always loved you ; and so I always did, and so I always shall in a sort of way. I always laughed at you, and, unless my heart is broken and the wells of laughter get dry, I always shall whenever you are ridiculous. I would laugh at you now if you were not so serious. Go on."

" Do you remember that you said to me on that occasion, that you had no one left whom you could trust to but me ; and, moreover, that I gave you my knightly word of honour, as a Peer of Great Britain, that whatever happened would make no difference to me—that I would stand by your side and see you through it ? "

" I remember all that.   Go on."

" Now I wish, before you see this letter, to renew that vow, and to tell you that this letter makes no difference to me ; that I swear by my title, by my position, by my fifty thousand a-year, that no cloud shall come between me and you !   Will you read it ? "

" I had better.   I would have made you a shrewish joke about the absurdity of your swearing by your income, but I fear I shall make few more jokes in this world.   Give it to me ; and give me one kiss, George, before I read it."

He tried to kneel to her, but she would not have it. " We must be very cool over this matter," she said.   " If we were only Jemmy and Jessamy it would be different. You are Lord Hatterleigh, and I am Laura Seckerton. Now for the letter ; I suppose the signature is Harry Poyntz."

Lord Hatterleigh gave it to her without a word.   It was infinitely worse than she had anticipated ; there was ruin in the first two lines of it.   She had often laughed to herself at the idea of her, with her secret, being received into the bosom of a family so rampantly offensively particular as that of the Hatterleighs, and she had lately determined that it would not do.   She knew that she loved the dead Poyntz-Hammersley still : and her plan had been to keep Lord Hatterleigh dangling after her, nominally engaged to her ; to form him as well as she was able, to cure him of his Guy Fawkes habits, and so by degrees show him that their engagement was only a thing of words ; to quietly dismiss him as soon as an eligible young lady appeared in the field, and to keep up a platonic friendship with him for the rest of her life, while she herself went into the high-church nursing-sisterhood business. That was her programme—not a bad one if that unaccountable bedlamite Sir Harry Poyntz had not drawn a wet sponge through the whole matter. As she read his letter to Lord Hatterleigh, she saw that her engagement to him must come to an end at once; and, what was more, that there was left, over and above, a frightful personal scandal against herself. She had not read three sentences of it before she looked up at Lord Hatterleigh, and said—

"I wonder why he did this. I cannot conceive what his motive can be. But a lunatic has no motives. Perhaps it is better that he has done it." And then she went on, finished it, folded it up, and gave it back to Lord Hatterleigh, with a sigh, saying: "Well, that's all over!"

The letter was as follows:—

"MY DEAR HATTERLEIGH,—I have been waiting for someone else to perform this exceedingly unpleasant task, but as no one seems inclined to do it, I must open your eyes myself.

"Miss Seckerton's close intimacy with young Hammersley—a noble young fellow, certainly, but only huntsman, or something of that kind, to her father—renders it impossible and ridiculous for her to become your Countess.

"One particular and private meeting which took place in my shrubberies was witnessed. The indiscretion in this particular instance will, I suppose, accomplish my object.   Yours very sincerely,
          "HARRY POYNTZ."

"And what do you think of that for a false villain?" said Lord Hatterleigh. "You must commission me to go to him and give him the lie to his face!"

"I can't do that; it is all true enough," she said, wearily.

"All true enough!" he cried, aghast.

"All true enough to ruin me, I mean," she said; "though of course, my Lord," she added, suddenly and fiercely, "you understand that I acted with the most perfect discretion throughout the business."

"Of course you did. Did you dream that I distrusted you?" Lord Hatterleigh answered, proudly. "I only ask you to explain so far as to enable me to go and tell that villain he lies in his throat — not a word more than that!"

She liked him better now she had lost him than she had ever liked him before. She had intended to break off her engagement; Sir Harry Poyntz had done it for her, and ruined her besides. The world seemed all such a ghastly, weary waste! Only one hand seemed held out to her, and she was going to cast that hand away—

"I can give you no explanations. As he has put the matter it is utterly false, but I am wearied of the subject, and it is hateful to me. Our engagement is at an end!"

"It is nothing of the kind; I will not have it so for an instant."

"Do not you see that it is wholly impossible for you to continue it if I refuse you those explanations? And I do refuse them. Here is your ring."

"Laura, one moment before it is too late——"

"Not another word until you have taken your ring."

He was forced to take it, and said, "What have I left to live for now?"

"Much," she answered. "Now we can talk as friends. You have me to live for; I am in want of a friend."

The poor gentleman did not accept his position at all kindly, but sat ruefully silent.

"I can speak no more on the subject this morning," she said; "I am ill. Go away now. What can I have done to make Sir Harry Poyntz use me so cruelly?"

She said this as she passed out, and said it in such a pitiable tone, that it went to Lord Hatterleigh's heart. He thought a few minutes, and then hurled himself down the stairs out of the room, across the hall, and out of the house.

" Send my horse and groom after me," was all he said to
the wondering butler, and strode away gesticulating across
the park.

Chapter XL

LADY EMILY and her mother sat alone in the library,
no more suspecting that there was anything wrong in their
domestic affairs, than believing that the granite tors of the
moor were breaking from their bases, and coming crashing about their heads.   They had never had a hint of Sir
Charles' difficulties ; and he used to see them day after day
utterly unconscious, cheerful, and peaceful, in a circle of
circumstances, which to them appeared a well-kept English
gentleman's establishment, but which to him seemed only
a ghastly heap of fraudulent bankruptcy and ruin.

They were talking, as they always were now, of Laura's
approaching marriage, and were indeed getting busy about
it.   It was very charming to Lady Emily to have the
management of such a great affair, and not less pleasant
for her mother to be consulted (as she was a hundred times
a-day) on every detail, and not only consulted but im-
plicitly followed.   The presents were dropping in.   The
Downes only the day before had sent in a magnificently
ostentatious offering from Howell and James, and there it
stood ; even Lady Downes and Constance Downes' com-
paratively humble contributions towering above all the
others on the table, while Sir Peckwich himself was represented by an almost offensively beautiful centre-piece for
flowers, which, like Sir Peckwich himself, was head and
shoulders higher than the other two.

" I hear Laura's footstep : she is coming to look at the
Downes' presents."

If she was she had made strange preparations for doing
so.   It would seem much more likely that she had been
getting herself ready to act the part of " Medea."   She was

deadly, ghastly pale, and somehow—perhaps by some frenzied motion of her body, perhaps by the mere clasping of her hands to her heated head—one large band of her hair had come down and hung across her face. She was very calm, and her mouth was set firmly; but the instant the two ladies looked at her, they saw plainly enough that she would never be Countess of Hatterleigh.

" I am come to tell you both that I have broken off my engagement with Lord Hatterleigh, in a manner which renders all reconsideration impossible. Will you tell people about it for me, and all that sort of thing? I am very tired, and am unable to speak any more on the subject."

" If Lord Hatterleigh has dared——" began Lady Emily.

" Lord Hatterleigh has not dared anything, my dearest mother! The whole thing is of my doing—my fault from beginning to end. Lord Hatterleigh has behaved like a very noble and true-hearted gentleman, and has left me very unwillingly."

Lady Emily immediately went down on her knees. " Laura," she said, " let your own mother on her bended knees implore you to say the one word to that unhappy young man, which will bring him back to your side, and save us from the intolerable ridicule which always attaches to the breaking-off a match when it has gone as far as this one has ! "

" Mother, get up."

" I know this is your doing. I know that Hatterleigh was too infatuated—loved you too dearly. Oh, say the word—oh, say the word, and save us ! "

" Mother, I think I can bear what I have to bear. You may make it harder for me by these scenes, but I will try. I wish you to understand, once for all, that it is all over between us, and that no power on earth can ever make me alter my decision."

She left the room ; and Lady Emily, getting up from her knees—by no means so easy a process as going down on them—turned to her mother, and said, " Here is a pretty business ! "

" I never thought it would do," said Lady Southmolton.

" I am aware of that, my dear mother; I have heard that before," replied Lady Emily, with perfect truth, but with more tartness than was necessary. " The question is, what is to be done? "

" Nothing that I am aware of, except writing to Jane Clark."

" Jane Clark is dead," said Lady Emily, still snappishly. " Do you mean to advise me to sit down under this ? "

" Whether I advise you to do so or not, my dear Emily, you will have to do so. You had better stop any further expense."

" The milliner will put it all about London."

" Not she : a hundred others will have done it for her," said Lady Southmolton, who had never been spoken to sharply by her daughter before, and had no idea of standing it.

" It is so sudden," said Lady Emily; " and we have had it talked about so much. It was in the *Post.*"

" It is the most sudden and scandalous business I have ever had to do with," replied her mother. "I thought I could have crept to my grave without being mixed up in a business of this kind. But I will not complain; I will bear my cross, Emily."

" You seem bent on driving me out of my mind, mother. Will you tell me what to do? "

" With the greatest pleasure. Was her veil ordered? "

" You know it was."

" Then you must compromise. The milliner is a most excellent woman, and will let you off your bargain much cheaper than Madame Muntalini would ; but I should tell her all the circumstances of the case, out of mere courtesy. Then you must write to Gunter and tell him all about it; say you don't want the cake. Then you will have to tell Harry Emmanuel about it, and so on."

"Mother! mother! why are you so cruel?"

"Because I am angry with you, Emily!" said the little old lady, stamping her foot upon the floor. "Would you have dared to rebel against *me* in this manner? Why don't you do your duty as a mother, and send for Lord Hatterleigh yourself? Why do you allow Laura to dictate to you in this shameful way? Order Laura to her room, and sit down and write to Lord Hatterleigh yourself." (The little old lady had shaken and wagged her head, and stamped her foot so much by now, that she might almost have frightened a rabbit.) "Do you think that at Laura's age I should have so far forgotten every moral and religious duty as to allow you for one instant to behave as Laura is behaving now? Never!"

"I know you would not, mother. But I am afraid of Laura; I dare not speak to her!"

Old Lady Southmolton was so filled with unutterable contempt by this expression of weakness, that she had nothing to say. She looked up to heaven as though praying for patience.

"Do speak to her yourself, mother, and make her obey you," said poor Lady Emily.

At this very alarming proposition, Lady Southmolton came back to earth again with the most startling rapidity; she actually tumbled down, headlong. Her first act on arriving on this earth, after a serene contemplation of the deterioration of the human species since the days of Hannah More—after falling suddenly, from a height of moral speculation, down on to the floor of extremely disagreeable personal practice—was, so to speak, to sit up and look round her, to see if her daughter was in earnest, or was daring to make game of her. Poor Lady Emily was perfectly in earnest—there was no doubt in that. Lady Southmolton said, quietly scornful,—

"She is not *my* daughter; she is yours. I am not her mother, any more than my sainted Southmolton was her father. I wash my hands of her! Do not drive me to say that I wash my hands of you—of my own daughter!"

The idea of Lady Southmolton washing her hands of her was so dreadful to Lady Emily, that she went through the action of washing her own, and moaned and wailed herself into silence, as ladies do in such cases. When everything had been quite quiet for a quarter of an hour, from Lady Emily's last sob, Lady Southmolton, solemnly but on the whole in a conciliatory manner, said,—

"Emily!"

Lady Emily threw herself on her mother's bosom, and went through the sobbing business again—but three octaves lower, and many minutes shorter; after which they talked together in a reasonable manner. But all that they arrived at was that girls were not as they used to be, and that dear Laura was very strange; that, on the whole, they—they—were both horribly afraid of her, could not in the least degree calculate what she would do next, and so had better leave her to herself : which they did.

Chapter XLI

Sir Harry Poyntz was sitting at his library-table turning over his papers. This became day after day a more difficult and tiresome business for him. He knew that his brain was softening, and he had submitted to his fate in that matter with that quaint godless fatalism which possibly was part of his disease. He had told Hilton that the only thing which annoyed him was, that those fits of irritability were beyond his control. He said, in his queer way, that it was so unutterably exasperating to find that he couldn't keep his temper. But these fits had grown milder as the disease went on, and had altogether ceased; but as they ceased a new cause of irritation seemed arising. He had always been the most methodical as well as the most catlike cleanly of men, and now he began to find that his papers got wrong, and that he was getting untidy in his dress. This vexed him considerably.

He was in a mess with his papers this morning. He had found himself getting angry, and, being fearful of one of his old fits of fury coming on, had dismissed the steward with a sweet smile, on pretence of a headache. He had made an effort to bring his mind to a focus, and to get his papers in order; but he found that the effort was beyond him—and there was no one to help him.

"The game is very nearly up," he thought; "I wish Bob was here."

Suddenly there came, as there will in such cases, a sudden activity of brain, a more rapid passage of blood, or if not that something else. He suddenly saw, in one instant, that he was all alone, without a single friend in this world, and utterly without hope or belief in the next. The first effect of this flash of intelligence was infinitely mournful —the second most ghastly and most horrible. There came on him, for one moment, that sense of illimitable distance from others, which no man can feel for many seconds and keep his reason. The nightmare passed away, and left him sitting there careless, stupid, and desperate.

When the brain quickened again, he began thinking about his brother Robert, and wishing that he would come back, and that he might hear that Robert had forgiven him from his own lips. He did not acknowledge to himself that he had been to blame in their life-long quarrel; he only wished that Robert would tell him they were good friends. "I wish we could start afresh. How was I to know that Bob was a hero? I suppose," went on the poor fellow, "that I must be wrong. Everyone loved him, and everyone hated me. Why did he always hate and despise me so? Why did he irritate me, and make me hate him? Well, Master Bob, I have brains enough to be even with you yet!"

Someone laid a light hand on his shoulder. He said,

"Bob, I'll be even with you. You'll be devilish sorry for me when I am gone." And then he looked up and found his wife standing over him.

"Maria, I am glad to see you ; I have had the nightmare. Do *you* wish me dead ? "

"Harry ! Harry ! give up talking so wildly."

" I am not talking wildly at all. Maria, do you think, for the short time we have left to live together, that you could be friends with me ? It is so horrible to die without one single friend ! "

" I will be a faithful and good wife to you, Harry. We have both made a mistake. You have so often and, let me say, so coarsely put that before me, times innumerable, that I have no delicacy in speaking about it. I have been saved from unutterable woe by God's providence, and my heart is tender towards you, my poor Harry—very tender ! Why are you so hopelessly wicked as to make it impossible for me to love you ? "

" What have I been doing so unutterably wicked lately ? "

" Harry, why have you ruined Laura Seckerton ? Why did you write that horrible letter ? I have just been with her ; she seems the same to the world, but you have driven her half-mad. We have come together again after all our misunderstandings, and I tell you, Harry, that she is broken-hearted."

" Serve her right ! " said Harry Poyntz, laughing ; " she wanted a lesson. Let her keep her tongue between her teeth another time."

Maria was so exasperated by this brutality that she rose up, and paced up-and-down the room in furious heat, denouncing him. There was nothing she did not say of him. When she had somewhat cooled, she, in a very imperial manner, without in the least degree thinking what she was about, declared she would live with him no longer, and formally demanded a separation. Meanwhile Sir Harry laughed louder and louder as she went on, which, however she might conceal it, drove her nearly wild.

"Separation!" he said at last, amidst his laughter. "Why, Sir Charles Seckerton came over here once to represent to me your goings on with Hilton. I knew and trusted *you*, Maria, and I sent him back shorn. Come, Maria, be sensible; come and hear all about it. Let us have no nonsense."

Poor Lady Poyntz had nothing more to say. She was obliged to listen, however indignantly; innocent as she was, she was obliged to be calm. She came and sat down beside him.

"Maria," he said, "I did write that letter."

"No one doubts it; you signed your name to it. I came in here to-night in a softened mood, to behave as a wife to you; and you, by your hopeless wickedness, have exasperated me to that extent that I have utterly lost my temper with you. Why have you ruined Laura?"

"You mean, why have I broken off her engagement to that Guy Fawkes booby, Hatterleigh?"

"You may put it as you will. Why have you involved her name with Hammersley, sir?"

"Because," said Sir Harry, calmly, "I want her to marry my brother Bob. I have bought up every mortgage on that estate, and I could sell Sir Charles up to-morrow. By my arrangements, Laura, with her damaged reputation——"

"Her damaged reputation, sir!" blazed out Lady Poyntz. "How dare you, sir?"

"I am aware of her perfect discretion, but I was not speaking of that; I was speaking of her reputation. With her reputation she will be glad to marry Bob, and the two estates will be joined, you see; and her father's creditor will be his own son-in-law, and they will all live happy for the rest of their lives."

"It is a cunning scheme," she said, "and I so far like your part in it as to see that you mean well by your brother. But you little know Laura ; she would sooner be burnt alive than marry a man under such circumstances."

" But I have put her reputation at zero ; I have told others about it. I tell you she will be glad to marry anyone."

" I have no patience with you ! You have ruined her for nothing. All she will do will be to go into a convent."

" I thought she was a sound churchwoman."

" A desperate woman soon gets over a few little difficulties of creed. Besides, another thing will show you the absolute folly of your plan. Your brother Robert—he—this heroic man, with all the pride and bloom of his heroism fresh upon him, is to marry this woman, whose reputation you have so carefully undermined. You have gone muddling and scheming on, until you have done irreparable mischief, and ruined a noble woman."

She turned and left him in indignation, and looked back after she passed the door. Sir Harry was looking at her with a half-silly, half-sly expression, and was laughing at her. There was more about him than she could understand. She was sorry to have lost her temper with him, and she went back and kissed him. After that she passed out, and left him sitting in his chair.

Chapter XLII

THE next morning Laura had risen early, had taken her sketch-book, put some food in her hunting-canteen, and walked away alone through the park to the Vicarage.

The Vicar was away that morning—she knew that well enough ; but she only wanted the Vicar's wife, whom she found alone.

" I only want the key of the church."

Mrs. Vicar hardly spoke, but seemed to think the more.

She had actually given the key to Laura, and Laura was turning away, when the two scarlet gloves were whipped suddenly round her neck; and she found herself violently kissed, and the next instant "The Umbrella" was standing before her, flourishing a scarlet fist within an inch of her nose.

"Oh, if I only had the trouncing of some of them! Oh, if I could get Tom Downes to play Benedict to a certain gentleman's Claudio!"

"Hush! hush!" said Laura; "there is no one to blame. Just think of what you are saying; how very dreadful!"

"I am not an image," said the Vicar's wife. "I am not a stone gargoyle, to have a mouth and never speak. I am furious, I tell you."

"Quiet—quiet, old friend," said Laura; "you should help me to be quiet, and not make me angry."

"I should, but I can't," said she of the red gloves. "Oh, Laura, if I only had Lord Hatterleigh here!"

"What would you do with him?"

"I would give him such a piece of my mind. Oh, Laura, they have used you so shamefully!"

"Indeed, my dear, I cannot see that at all. In the first place, Lord Hatterleigh: Do you know that I might be Lady Hatterleigh now, in spite of all that has passed, and rule him with a rod of iron? Do you know that Lord Hatterleigh is the most perfect gentleman and the most high-minded man I have ever met? My dear soul, I have committed an indiscretion, and am suffering for it—that is all!"

"There is a villain somewhere, Laura."

"I don't see why Sir Harry Poyntz should have been so cruel. But it is all for the best. Now, give me the key."

"Why are you going into the church?"

"To practise the organ. All my old habits are cut away. I will not ride again. I cannot look at the poor people; they *will* sympathise with me, and I cannot cure them of it ; and I won't be sympathised with. They have no manners, those poor folks. And the regulation of hours of business won't do now. Your husband and my grandmother would recommend it, I know, but it won't do ; I have got the ' snatches ' on me too strong for that. And I have tried to paint, but—but what is the use of losing your temper over a thing of that kind ?—and so it is all gone but my most wickedly-neglected music, and I am going to try that ; therefore give me the key, and I will call at the school for a boy to blow, and I will see what that will do."

And so she went ; and she of the red gloves said to herself—" They have played old gooseberry with a very fine girl among them. Why," she said indignantly to the ambient air, as if the very winds of heaven were to blame, " there wasn't a finer girl than that in the Three Kingdoms ! What have you been doing with her, you two old trots " (which was personal), " and you extravagant old zany in topboots ? " (which was more personal still). " I wish I had the trouncing of you ! Got nothing left but the organ, and can't play that ! If I was her I'd go to Rome, out of sheer spite ; that would be the way to exasperate them."

If the Vicar could only have heard her ! But he was away at Exeter at the Visitation. They called her, in joke, " The Umbrella," partly from her figure, and partly from her inanimate submission to her husband. She let him do as he would with her ; the red gloves were a case in point. But sometimes, to everyone's astonishment and confusion, " The Umbrella," so to speak, put herself up, and refused to be got through narrow high-church passages and doorways after her husband, or to be put down again—a most obstinate old umbrella with a very rusty spring.

Laura, laughing to herself, went into the church ; and soon afterwards the boy came, and she began playing. The church was very dear to her, and she wished to get back once more into the old church-routine. Nothing had

ever satisfied her so well as that, after all. As for communicating—as for returning to the old pretty woman's
ministrations (in the way of ornament, and so on, about
the altar), that was impossible to her. There was a vin-
dictive chord in her heart, which was vibrated twenty
times a day; and at every vibration she said, " Oh, if I
had a brother!" The old church-peace was not attainable,
now that she had fully put before herself her utter exasperation against Sir Harry Poyntz. He came to church,
and she could not kneel and pray with him. She hated
him, and she did not in the least conceal it from herself.
He had gratuitously ruined her, and she hated him !

She had tried all her old round of duties and pleasures,
and they were all dead and dull. She had a fancy to shut
herself up in the old church and play the organ—to take
once again to her long-neglected music. The poor girl was
hunted and illused, and she had nothing else to look to.
" I will practise, and then I can play on Sundays, and so
have some part in the worship ; and I can sit here behind
the curtain, and *see* them communicating. It is better
than nothing."

So she in her Galilee. She was not very clever, or very
devout, or very sentimental ; but she was very truthful,
very brave, and surely as hard beset as a woman need be.
The chords all went wrong : her hands had got strong
enough with her riding to grip any keys ever made, but
she had lost the fingering of the keys, and the trick of the
stops, and what-not; and she could get no harmony out
of the old instrument, which she had heard sounding so
sweetly under other hands. Her foolish fancy of speaking
her sorrows by the organ to those of the congregation
who still dared approach the altar was gone; even this
quaint fancy, her last hope, was unattainable. There was
no resource left. She sent away the boy who blew the
bellows, and began to cry. It is hard to laugh at an
utterly lone woman crying over the keys of an organ. I
cannot, and I am quite sure that you cannot either.

To find her father beside her was no surprise. She only said, in a low, indignant, almost objurgative tone, " I have forgotten my music, now I wanted to play for them in church. But I can't play—I have lost everything. I have behaved so well, too. What have I done that I should be treated so ? I have told Hatterleigh everything, and he would have me now if I had not been so honest as to refuse him. What have I done to Harry Poyntz that he should ruin my character ? "

" Laura," said her father, " Harry Poyntz is dead ! "

" What ! " she cried, starting up and looking at him. " Come out of this place ; let me hear no more here. Come into the churchyard—no, not in the churchyard, out on to the mill-green. Dead is he ? Who has killed him ? Oh, father ! father ! there has been nothing between him and Hatterleigh ? "

Her father looked surprised, but went on—

" He was found dead. Lady Poyntz had left him sitting in his chair, and soon after the servant brought him a letter which a man on horseback had brought over from Plymouth. Harry went and lay on the sofa to read it, and very soon after the man heard him laughing uproariously. He laughed so loud and so long that the servant feared he would hurt himself. At last he was silent, and silent so long that the servant went back——"

" Well ? " said Laura.

" He was quite dead, my love. He had gone off with a spasm of the heart, perhaps brought on by his laughter— a strange end to a strange life ! "

" Oh, may God have mercy on him ! " said Laura. " Oh, Harry ! Harry ! I forgive you so heartily."

" They sent for me early this morning, and among other things showed me the letter which had caused the poor· fellow such amusement. It was from Hatterleigh. He called Harry liar and coward, and informed him that he waited for him at Dessin's, at Calais, with a friend."

" And he only laughed at it ! You see that he died in

charity with him, at all events. Poor fellow, what could I have done to make him use me so?"

"Laura," answered her father, "it is time you knew the reasons for his line of action. He had set his heart on your marriage with his brother Robert, and the union of the two estates."

"How did he dare——! I forgot. But he must have been mad, for I never saw the man, and the man never saw me."

"I am aware of that; but Harry has broached the idea to him, and he has taken most kindly to it. In fact, there is nothing whatever to prevent you becoming Lady Poyntz, if you feel any inclination for such an honour."

"Oh, father! father! how utterly you would despise me if I did so!"

"I really *cannot* see why," he angrily broke out; "I really, God grant me patience, cannot. It is high time you were settled in life—you must be aware of it. We have none of us said a word to you about your behaviour to Hatterleigh. You might have had him and his fifty thousand a-year back by saying one word, and you wouldn't say it. I don't believe you would say it to save your old father from ruin. Now I tell you once for all, that if Sir Robert makes you the subject of this magnificent offer, and you refuse him on sentimental grounds, it will materially alter the relations between yourself and the rest of your family."

Laura had become very pale, but her heart was going fast and furious.

"Now look here," she said, turning to her father and forcing him to look at her; "you talk about altered relations. They are altered—they have long been altered. And as for this Sir Robert Poyntz, I would not marry a royal person on such terms. Who is he that he DARE make me a part of one of his schemes for increasing his estate, the least important element in which seems to be considered my consent to marry him? It is monstrous— the whole of it—monstrous!"

Poor Sir Charles was now driven to despair, and spoke as a desperate man, lost to sense of shame, but with a dim hope of his object beyond a sea of degradation, and determined to plunge in and wade through. As he went on, Laura was shocked and frightened to see how his nature had given way under the wear-and-tear of concealed difficulties, and that the best half of it seemed to have disappeared. She remembered a noble, grand, upright gentleman—the worthy magistrate, the generous patron, the courteous host, the wise friend—whom she had loved and called " Father ; " she saw before her a miserable, bent, selfish old man, unable to look his daughter in the face, who went through his wretched part with the air and the whine of a begging-letter writer.

" Laura, I must tell you at once that, if we cannot make this arrangement with him, your poor unhappy old father is ruined ! "

" Ruined ! "

" Ruined utterly ! Our existence in this place has been a fiction for a year or two past. Sir Harry Poyntz spared me in hopes of executing his darling scheme. If we disappoint this man, there is no hope whatever ! "

" Let me sit down," she said—" I cannot stand any longer ; " and she sat down on the root of a tree, and heard him go on.

" He is my only creditor ; the arrangement would be actually perfect in every way. I would give up the hounds, if he insisted on it. Nothing stands in the way but yourself. And what is all that your poor father asks of you ? To make one of the finest matches in England, and save a father from ruin ! "

" Cannot we do anything ? Is there no hope elsewhere ? "

" None ! "

" Has grandma no money she can lend you ? "

" She has twenty thousand pounds, and I want eighty thousand," said Sir Charles, curtly.

" But other people get ruined. I should not mind it except for you. And I would take such care of you, and work for you—— Believe me, father, we might be quite as happy without all these miserable superfluities! Dear father, do think——"

" You speak like a child, my poor Laura! There is one other point which you force me to mention, though I would rather have avoided it. With this ruin will come disgrace!"

" Disgrace! what disgrace?" asked Laura.

" You may spare your father, Laura. It is hard to have to make the confession—spare me the details. It should be enough for you to know that it is disgrace so deep that none of our name could survive it. Now you know all!"

She sat perfectly silent for a long while; he could not tell whether she had yielded or not. When she spoke at last her voice was changed, and she spoke in a hard resolute tone. She rose, too, without any help, and seemed perfectly firm—

" We will talk no more of this; the subject is distasteful. I suppose Sir Robert Poyntz will have the tact and propriety to behave as if he knew nothing about these arrangements; and I hope that a proper time will be allowed to elapse. Now I will go and look at the church. I think I should prefer to walk home alone, please."

So she went back towards the church; and, when she came to the gate, turned and saw him walking away, with bowed head, under the shadow of the elms.

" I *must* save him," she said to herself; "and, what is more, I must not think, or I shall go mad. I only want a little more hardening, and it will come easy enough. I must be as Maria was when she married poor Harry—if I can. She might help me, but she is so strangely changed and softened—— I must go through it by myself. I must become desperate, lest my father's blood should lie at my door."

She was alone, desperate and forlorn; the dead, so much happier than she, lay all around her, and she envied them.

She sat on one of the green mounds, and thought of her position.

" I would have been so good if Hammersley had never come " (for she was getting desperate, taking leave of her better self forever, and concealed nothing), " but he came and spoilt it all, and ruined everything. And I know now that I love him still as well as ever, and should have done poor Lord Hatterleigh a wrong. I saw that after I broke with him. And I put all thoughts of him aside so loyally while I was engaged to George, and only thought of him again when I was free; I thought they might have left me alone, and not driven me to this pass. I am sure I don't want to accuse anybody; but why has my father gone on with this selfish ostentation until he is obliged to sacrifice the creature he loves best in the world—to put on his own dear daughter's face a brazen defiant look, which she must wear till her death? And my mother and my grand-mother, how much do they know of this horrible business of my father's ruin? They will stroke my hair and praise me for being dutiful, while I am getting hardened and desperate. I shall have to dress and to flaunt it out. I can stare down Constance Downes, but I can never face Maria Poyntz in her new mood. I shall die if that woman turns her great eyes on me. She has been through it all, and has come out again with a face like a saint; and I, who was so bitter and harsh with her, must go through it all, with those eyes of hers eating into my soul. I wish I was dead—I do wish I was dead ! ''

She rose up and went into the church, and looked round. Their seat (Sir Charles was lay impropriator) was in the chancel; but she would not enter what was to her, in her belief, the more sacred part of the church—she thought herself unworthy. She went round the building, and wished the dear old place good-bye. She had always loved the church from childhood, as a solemn peaceful place, which seemed to hold the very presence of God. She had sat there year after year, under long weary services and dull weary sermoms, with the sunlight sloping on the tombs, and glimpses of the wild moor—the fairyland of her childhood—seen through the windows; building fancies about the dead Poyntzes, Seckertons, and Downes's, whose effigies crowded the chancel; and since the Vicar had come, she had got to love it better still. In spite of all his fantastic ritualisms, the man knew what a church was originally designed to mean, and had taught it to her. Then she had taken a new delight in it—had decorated it with a wilderness of glowing flowers at Easter, and carefully-woven patterns of box and holly at Christmas, believing that she was doing good service the while. Now the hard world had come crashing in, and had thrown down her dear loved images. All that was past and gone, and could never come back again; but the remembrance of those times was most melancholy and most pleasant. She took one last farewell of the old place, put on her new look as well as she could, locked the door, and passed out of the porch :

To meet the Vicar leaning against a grave-stone: who said, looking keenly at her,—

" You are at your old pious duties, I see ? "

To whom Laura, trying to look hardened and worldly, answered, " Not at all; I was taking my farewell of the church. I thought you were away."

" So I was, but I am at home now. My wife told me you were here. Have you been saying farewell to the church ? Are you not coming to church any more, then ? "

" I suppose I may," said Laura.

" You suppose you may ? " said the Vicar. " To-morrow is the feast of St. Ebba of Moorwinstow. Are you coming to-morrow ? "

" No, I am not," said Laura.

" Are you coming to confession this week—eh ? "

" Certainly not."

" Then are you coming to church on Sunday ? " asked the Vicar. " I would if I was you : everyone does."

" I may or I may not—I am not well—most probably not."

" I think I shall see you at church on Sunday," said the Vicar. " I say, Laura, don't be down-hearted over this business."

" What business ? "

" This business ; you know what I mean."

He looked so good, and so kind, and so little *prêtre*, that she felt very much inclined to melt, and tell him everything. But it would never do to begin like that. She put on the new and hitherto unsuccessful hard look again, and said,—

" I cannot be expected to understand you, Vicar."

He laughed—a right jolly laugh too, and said,—

" Have you heard the news ? "

" What news can matter to me ? "

" None, of course ; but I will tell it. Sir Robert Poyntz has arrived at the Castle."

She saw he knew all. In trying to tell him how cruel she thought him—in trying to tell him that it was mean in him to laugh at her, she broke down, and bursting into tears left him standing where he was.

" Poor child," he said, as he looked after her, " she has been hardly tried ! But it will do her good—and God has been very merciful to her. Many a woman has had her heart broken for less before now. Well, let her go ; I really can't pity her so very much."

The Vicar took a turn round the churchyard, and stopped against Hammersley's tablet, and said, " Hum— ha ! " Going closer to it he noticed that someone had chipped off a little angle of the stone. " Now I would bet a hundred pounds that she did that," he said. " And what the curious part of it is, it hasn't been done a week. I wonder if she *did* do it ! Well, we shall see. It is all in God's hands now. Heaven help us fairly through it ! "

Chapter XLIII

LAURA soon wiped her tears. All the world was banded together against her, but not one of them should see that she had been crying. She had to make her face hard ; she had to be cool and defiant towards the world in future. Maria Poyntz had done it, and she, who had six times her brains, could surely do it also !

Why, no—at least not without practice, for the tears which had been dried began to flow again. Lady Poyntz, with less heart and fewer brains, could manage the matter better than Laura. Powder as she would, her eyes were red at lunch ; but she was singularly cool and self-possessed, though her mother and her grandmother nearly drove her out of her mind.

They were wonderfully high-bred women, *Tact* with them had become almost a science. They had no *written* rules of tact, but they had so many unwritten laws of that great science that it was almost reduced to exactitude. They, especially the elder, could pronounce in an instant whether a person had tact or had not ; the consequence was that they had no tact at all. They had infinite *finesse* doubtless, all according to rule. It is humiliating enough to hear a costermonger telling his wife what he thinks of her in the vernacular, but it is still more humiliating to a quickwitted person to watch a woman, who has forgotten her art, trying her miserable little *ruses* upon him. Laura was such a quickwitted person, and saw in two minutes what these two good ladies knew, and what they did not know. Her feelings towards them, as in some other cases were—first curiosity, then contempt, and then indignation.

Their buoyant and pious gaiety in the first instance, though not overdone (they knew better than that), was perfectly obvious. There was no reason for this exhibition of Christian cheerfulness. Poor Harry Poyntz had died dreadfully the night before; and on any other similar occasion her grandmother would have kept her room except for meals, and would have improved the occasion as soon as her soup and glass of sherry had put life enough in her to talk. Therefore, why did she twitter like an old dickybird the moment Laura appeared? Moreover her mother, the inferior actor of the two, was arch. Now, if there was one thing Laura hated more than another, it was archness. She saw in the first three minutes that they knew all about Sir Robert Poyntz's intentions, and were, as far as that went, in her father's confidence.

That they knew nothing of the impending cloud of ruin hanging over their heads, she saw well enough also. "Poor father!" she thought, "he has behaved badly enough, but he *has* confided in me, and I will serve him. *They* would merely sell me to the highest bidder to-morrow." She saw, moreover, that they were both afraid of her, and she behaved, in manner only, with a cool recklessness which they must perfectly have understood.

One wonders if they had sense to see her own terror—a terror which grew on her as minutes went on: the terror of first seing this *bête noiré*—this detestable Sir Robert Poyntz, to whom she was sold like a sheep, to save her father from ruin. I doubt if they had; Laura's honest, cool recklessness puzzled them, I fancy. But the terror was there. At one time she hated him; at another time she made wild schemes of throwing herself on his generosity—appealing to his manhood to——she knew not what. She saw her own folly, while she nursed the hope of its success. She was like a hare in a snare—deliverance would only come with death.

And this man was within three hundred yards of her. She had once coolly asked where her father was, and they had told her that he was over at the Castle with Sir Robert. Would her father bring him home to dinner? she asked herself. Of course he would; she would see her fate at seven o'clock.

The man had acted heroically in India. Yes; but there were heroes and heroes, as she knew well. One man, whose glorious deed of arms in the Crimea had sent her wild with enthusiasm, had been quartered at Plymouth. Her father had asked him over. She had dressed herself with extra care to meet him, and had conned a pretty speech for him. She found her hero — a scowling, ill-tempered, vulgar fool, with no visible quality save ferocity.

So as the afternoon went on, and time got shorter, she found herself hating and dreading this man beyond conception. She discussed with herself whether she could best face it out by coming down to dinner first or last. Last she thought, on the whole; and so she let the second gong sound, and after five minutes' law came sailing resolutely into the room, "all eyes, mouth, and black velvet," as the Vicar—who was there—described her to his wife.

Sir Robert was not there. She chafed at this new prolongation of her misery, but she was calm, cool, and polite. There was another fifteen hours of anxiety before her. The Vicar, who knew everything, says that she behaved with the courage of a lion. Her father hardly spoke to her, and the weary evening wore through, the Vicar staying long and late, doing his duty like a man.

The next morning she knew her fate. She slept long and heavily, as the men who are to be hung at eight generally sleep—a forgetful, dreamless, Sancho-Panza sleep. At ten o'clock she was in the breakfast-room alone, trying to read "Adam Bede," when she heard the hall-door opened, and the footsteps of two people crossing the flags straight towards the room where she sat.

The butler threw open the door and said, " Sir Robert Poyntz, Miss " — and then shut it again, which was the best thing he could do; and although he had been bribed for doing so very heavily, he did it well. She was alone in the room with him.

She ought to have risen to receive him, but the thing was

sudden; and she felt faint and ill, as women do sometimes. She half turned her head towards him, bowed, and
said, "My father is in the library."

"I did not come to see your father," he said; "I came
to see you. I have bribed all your father's servants to
watch you, that I might catch you alone; and I have succeeded."

It was partly the sound of the voice, and partly an in-
definite feeling of anger, that made her rise and look at
him. She saw before her the most magnificent man she
had ever seen—a man of extraordinary beauty, with a high,
square, resolute forehead—a man so young that the golden
beard which was beginning to mantle his cheeks and his
chin had no shadows in it as yet; you could still see beneath the golden haze that his beautiful mouth was parted
in eagerness, curiosity, and admiration.

Why did she put her hands before her eyes to shut out
the sight of him? Why did that quaint little sound—half-
moan, half-cry—rise from her overloaded heart? And
why did her lips begin to murmur a prayer of thanksgiv-
ing? Questions easily answered. This detestable Sir Robert Poyntz—this inexorable creditor—the man who held
them all in the hollow of his hand, and who stood before
her in all the promise of a noble manhood—this man was
the only man she had ever loved, and for whose love she
had suffered so much. It was Hammersley himself, risen
from the dead, with the wild lurid light of his Indian glory
still blazing in his eyes.

Chapter XLIV

HE spoke first. "I have done as you bid me," he said;
"and I have come back to ask you if I have done it amiss."

She had no answer ready. The poor girl was so utterly
undone by her last day's misery, and so deeply happy and

thankful at the discovery that the terrible Sir Robert was no
worse a person than the one she loved best in the world,
that she had no answer for him, and could make no fight.
She was, or ought to have been, very angry ; she had a
hundred things to say to him. But she was taken by surprise—was like one awakening from a horrible dream, to
find himself in the world once more ; and she had nothing
at all ready. She should have made her fight at once, no
doubt, but for these reasons she could not. It simplified
matters immensely.

It gave him hope. He saw that his wild dream was like
to come true—nay, would certainly come true if he could
only help speaking too fast (which he could not : a man
just come out of such a wild dark hurly-burly as the Indian
Mutiny could not be expected to be so very cool). From
the moment he saw her sit silent, after her recognition of
him, he began to be certain of her. He knew she loved
him once, but he did not know what had happened since.
He would have been less eager—would have let matters
take their course for a much longer time—if it had not
been for Laura's emotion at seeing him again. That made
him push on fiercely, and forget all his worldly-wise resolutions. He saw that affairs were as he left them ; but he
was far too wise to claim any acknowledgment of love from
her. He did not know all. He little thought for whom
she was prepared, and for what she was prepared.

" I have come back again, Miss Seckerton, to know
whether I have done enough to gain your respect." Some
sudden impulse or instinct showed him that he must
change his tone before her tears were dried, and he knelt
at her feet and said, " Laura ! Laura ! you loved me once ;
do you love me still ? "

She found her voice : " Yes ! yes ! But why have you all
used me so cruelly ? "

*   *   *   *   *

When they had done being sentimental—which was very
soon, seeing that a great deal of sentiment had been

knocked out of both of them in a somewhat rough school —they returned to common-sense, of which both had a considerable stock. He began by asking her what she meant by her having been used cruelly.

"Never mind that now," she said. "Once and for all, tell me how all this has happened? You have surprised me into an admission by the suddenness of your appearance; it is only due to me to explain your incomprehensible conduct. Let what I have undergone through that conduct pass for a time; I only ask you to explain."

He did so, of course—partly in narrative, and partly by question and answer. I must be allowed to shape his story for him, only giving Laura's remarks when they are at all illustrative:

"You have heard of my father, and I wish to say little about him. He has, I fear, not left a good name in this part of the world."

"We need not begin so early," said Laura. "I have heard a great deal about your father."

"You must not believe all you have heard. He had very good qualities; I cannot bear to hear my father ill-spoken of. There were many worse men than my father. In time I will make you know my father as he really was; you have only heard the worst side of him yet. He was a very clever man, and very pious latterly. As for his riding —I think there would be only one opinion about that."

Laura loved him the better for his silly breakdown in trying to whitewash the memory of that most miserable old sinner his father, but she would not help him out. She had admitted more than she meant to already; she sat silent.

"But that is beside the mark, possibly," said Sir Robert. "Friends of the family, whose judgment I would be the last to impugn, but whose advice was certainly never asked, were of opinion that his establishment was not on the whole calculated to raise the moral tone of such an exceedingly ill-conditioned and turbulent boy as myself. Now, I look on this as being an exceedingly fine point in my father's character ; and I am sure you will agree with me about this. Although my father had never asked these people's advice, yet he yielded to it. Their advice was forced on him in the most offensive way. Tom Squire (you know him) was in the room when it was forced on him, in the most eminently offensive way, by Sir Peckwich Downes and someone else—never mind who. They said, ' You are a most disreputable and wicked old man ; and you are lost to all sense of decency if you bring those boys here.' That's what they said to him ; and see how nobly my father behaved ! He took their advice, at least as far as concerned myself. He used to have poor Harry down, as you know yourself, having met him here."

" Never mind your father," she said.

" But I *do* mind my father. My father is an ill-understood man. What are the accusations against him ? That he used to drink, and have in the servants to drink with him. And Harry, poor fellow, used to deny it in the strongest terms. No servant ever sat down before my father except old Tom Squire, whose mother was our nurse. Who is your Downes, that he is to dictate to a man in his own house ? "

Laura didn't know.

" He *had* Harry down. Who is your Downes, that he is to part a father from his eldest son ? Me he never had down. One of the best points in my father's character, one that showed his knowledge of human nature best, was that he couldn't bear the sight of me."

Laura burst out laughing, but she had to stop it again, lest she should get hysterical ; recent events had been too much for her.

" I mean what I say," continued he. " I was one of the most turbulent, ill-conditioned young rascals that ever lived. The whole aim and object of my life, till six months ago, seems to me to have been quarrelling with my own brother. Laura, I never hated him ; but his better and higher and gentler nature irritated me."

Laura gave a start. Had she given her heart to an absolute fool?

"I never saw this," he continued, without having noticed her start, "until six months ago. I did something in India, no matter what; they have given me the Victoria Cross for it, so it counts for something; and that dear fellow who lies dead across the river wrote me the kindest and tenderest letter that ever one brother received from another—a letter written to me, who had never done anything but vilify and backbite him!"

"About this letter?" said Laura. "Attend, please. Did he never vilify and backbite you?"

"Harry had an infirmity," said Sir Robert. "From childhood Harry was very acute about money-matters, but I never held Harry accountable. He had an infirmity—his brain softened, you know—he used to forget what he said last. It might happen to you or I to-morrow, you know."

"About this letter once more," said Laura; "did he say anything about me in it?"

"Not a word."

"Did he ever mention me to you in any of his letters?"

"Never! I never had but one. He never said one word to me about you. Now I will go on with my story.

"My father, you must know, for some reason of his own—I *think* because he never liked me—left me entirely dependent on Harry, who I always thought liked me still less than my father did. Now, the most unfortunate thing was that Harry and I never got on together. My excuse for this is that Harry would be master, and I would never submit. I was sent to Eton to be out of his way, and kept from home. As we grew up we got on worse and worse, and at eighteen I found myself left in the world—free certainly, but entirely dependent on Harry.

"My father left me no guardians; I was entirely in Harry's hands. And now I must allude to another infirmity of the poor fellow's—I must, in justification : he had such a terrible tongue ! "

" Ah ! well I know it," said Laura.

" He used to say such horrible things, and then laugh at them, that he drove you almost mad. I have heard him use his tongue so to that poor creature Wheaton—who, by-the-bye, must be provided for — that I wonder he never murdered him. He soon gave up this habit to me, at all events, as a general rule. But it would come back to him ; he couldn't help it. When we were boys I used to thrash him for it. But when we got too old for that, his fear of me left him, and he was pretty near as bad as ever. After our father's death he told me, with a stinging insult, that he would allow me three-hundred a-year—that I might go anywhere, and do anything. I thought this a somewhat grand revenue, and went to London an independent gentleman.

" What did I do there ?—Why, I went there with three-hundred a-year, and spent nine-hundred. How did I spend it ?—In muddle. You know how our family vacillated between extravagance and stinginess, often in the same individual. Well, I was in the economical mood when I went to London, and I apportioned out my income carefully—so much for my rooms and living, so much for my horse and groom, and so on ; and I left a margin of 50l. a-year for contingencies. At the end of the year I was six hundred pounds in debt. I struggled and floundered on until I made it up to a clear thousand, and then I wrote and told my brother. He was furious : he paid it, but stopped my allowance, formally renounced me, and left me to shift for myself with a hundred pounds.

" I had been living a very pleasant life in London. Many of my Eton friends had not gone to the University —more than one of them was in the Guards. Their families received me very kindly—most of them from mere goodwill, but some because they foresaw what has actually happened—that Harry would die without a family, and that I should be rich. So, boy as I was, I was not merely had out for my dancing, which is admirable, but as a lad whom it was worth while to have one's eye on. I have been very civilly bespoke, do you know, by very great people indeed — political people, I mean. Harry seemed to me always to be a *known man*, I cannot tell why or how; it is a puzzle to me. Whether it was his tongue, which he could use in one case like a delicate poniard, and in another (when among his dependents and relatives) a brutal cudgel; whether it was his credit as a pushing unscrupulous man, who must rise in spite of a reputation even then damaged; or what it was, I cannot tell. There was something odd about Harry which made him a well-known man. I have, in the corners of drawing-rooms, and on staircases, among the men, heard him called every name under the sun. What puzzled me was that he should be so known, so talked about, and—what seemed to me stranger still—so feared."

" Did you never speak up for your brother?" asked Laura.

" No; it was impossible. Harry had earned his reputation, and he had it. I have not learned to lie yet."

" This fits well with your extravagant praise of him ten minutes ago. I thought that he was the saint then, and you the sinner."

Sir Robert laughed aloud, and did not stop quickly; and as poor Laura found that she could laugh now without crying, she joined in. They should not have laughed, you think, so soon after poor Sir Harry was dead. Well, they did: most of us have laughed between a death and a funeral.

Sir Robert went on: " I never made him out a saint, save by contrasting him with my own wicked self."

" You are coming to your confessions, then. Pray, did you ever meet poor Harry in society?"

" Never but once. I was only in society part of one season, and all that time he was getting the family affairs

together. Near the end of my only season I was at a ball
at Tulligoram House, and was attending to poor old Mrs.
Smallwood. I had got her an ice, and was talking to her.
The crowd was very close, and I noticed that she was
back to back, at very close quarters, with Gordon Dunbar,
a six-foot guardsman. His back was towards hers, and
he pushed her so close to me that she had to eat her ice
under my nose; for the Righter of all Wrongs and the
Poet of the Domestic Affections were backing me up from
the other side. All would have gone well had not the big
guardsman who was backing up Mrs. Smallwood been introduced to someone. He made such a low bow, that he
shot Mrs. Smallwood on to me headforemost, and me on
to the Righter of Wrongs, who from his physical and
moral elevation apologised. When I had finished blush-
ing, and had got her right, I looked Gordon-Dunbar way
again. It was my brother he had been introduced to ;
and my brother was standing in the centre of a circle looking at Gordon Dunbar : perfectly dressed, perfectly at
ease, looking at the guardsman, with an expression on his
pale puffed face, and his shallow blue eye, which said
plainly, ' Now what is *your* métier ? How much are you
worth ? ' "

" Did they speak to him ? "

" Oh yes, they spoke to him ; but they seemed to look
on him as some dreadful curiosity. Do you know, he did
look very curious. His dress, to begin with : it was only
black and white, of course. I can dress myself as well as
any man alive ; but he could beat me. I dealt with the
same tailor (who, by-the-bye, must be paid), but I never
could *wear* my clothes as he did. You know the story
about ' Good heavens, sir, walking trousers ! Why, you
have been sitting down in them.' It illustrates what I
mean—Harry wore his clothes marvellously well. And
add to this, he had a calm *look* with him, not a *stare*,
which did wonders. When anyone spoke he, by some
twist in his neck, some turn in his eye, gave all present

the idea that this fellow might be worth listening to or might not, and then, with a quiet but very slight turn-up of the chin, decided in the negative. I tell you, Laura, solemnly, that no angel in heaven has the temper which would have borne with him. The unutterable exasperation which he was capable of——"

"Hush! hush!" said Laura, "we must forget that. Did he speak this time you met him?"

"Yes—to Gordon Dunbar, in his usual style. I never would have dared to say what he said: ' You have made a great mess of it in the Crimea. You have let the French beat us at all points. We seem to have as much pluck as they, but we want the brains—at least, I mean our army seems to want brains. Our system is wrong altogether. No man enters the Army, either as officer or private, who has the chance of a career elsewhere.'"

"Did he dare say that?"

"He dare say anything."

"Did Gordon Dunbar strike him down?"

"No; he is a gentleman. And he carried in his own person such a refutation of Harry's nonsense, that everyone laughed. Dunbar only bowed, and withdrew from the discussion."

"Did poor Harry say anything to you?"

"To me? No. But he behaved so queerly. He looked me perfectly straight in the face, and then began talking to Mrs. Smallwood, with his face almost touching mine, *about me*. He gave her my character, speaking of me as ' my brother here,' but not addressing himself personally to me, or even after the first look glancing my way. He told her (this was to my face, mind!) that I was idle, extravagant, and, he feared, deceitful; but that I was generous and brave, and that (so he said—don't laugh) my extraordinary personal beauty would make me friends everywhere, and that he hoped those friends would not find themselves deceived. And then he walked on."

"Poor Harry was mad, you know," said Laura. "No sane man ever acted or spoke like that."

"Do you mean what he said about my personal appearance?"

"Yes."

"Well, shall I go on with my story?"

"I think so. I want to hear, sir, what you did when you were left in London with your debts paid and one hundred pounds to spend."

"I say, by-the-bye," said Sir Robert, looking at his watch, "do you know, Laura, that I have been with you *tête-à-tête* an hour and a half? I must go to your father."

"And leave the story of Cambuscan half untold: is this what you call an explanation of your extraordinary conduct?"

"No; you shall have it. You can surely trust me. But let me go to your father. Laura, you shall have every word; but there is a dark passage or two to come. Let there be no cloud over to-day's sun."

Chapter XLV

THEY say that a large proportion (I am sure it is one-third, and think it is more) of all the folks who go mad, are driven so by long-continued anxiety about their pecuniary affairs. Whether Sir Charles Seckerton would ever have gone mad I cannot say: we know that his relief had come, but he as little dreamt of it as he deserved it.

There seldom has lived a man with a sweeter disposition than had he. His careless, generous, *laissez-aller* temper had been one cause, though only one, of his ruin. But it was a very sweet temper. No one had ever seen the dark side of it but Laura; and she only once, for a minute, on the occasion when he proposed to her a marriage with Sir Robert Poyntz, and she resented it. Sir Charles' character among men was that of a perfectly determined person, thoroughly trustworthy, sensible, and decided—as well able to manage his own affairs as any man in the County. The truth never leaked out—circumstances saved that. Tell any man in that part of the County at this day, that Sir Charles had been recklessly extravagant, and had only saved his position in the world by a scandalous sale of his own daughter; and tell them, again, that the beautiful glorious Lady Poyntz was at one time hunted and driven into such a state of desperation as to acquiesce in the arrangement—tell them this, and they will laugh at you. But so it was.

Sir Charles' temper had lasted till this very day, and this very day it had given way. He had borne the misery and anxiety of debt, with a tolerably certain prospect of ruin, well enough. I have no doubt that he would have gone to Baden most decently, had it not been for that irrepressible Sir Harry Poyntz, who showed him how he could retrieve everything, or at least keep the whole thing in the family, by the marriage of Laura and Robert. His fate was in his daughter's hands. The first symptom of temper he had ever shown was when she rejected his hint about that matter with scorn. She had seemed to agree on that occasion, but had said not one word this last two days on the subject. He could not tell for certain what she would do; if she rejected him there was ruin; if she accepted him all would be well, in a sort of way; but he could not trust her. He had seen her obstinate as a child, and since; he had seen her show fight to more than one person; suppose she were to do so now? Ruin!

He had not recognised Sir Robert, to that young gentleman's vast amusement. He had "seen the likeness," but nothing more. Tom Squire, the huntsman, had come up to him this very morning, and Sir Charles had mentioned the likeness to him: adding, to poor old Tom's puzzlement, that poor Hammersley was the better-looking fellow of the two. Tom had been set on by Sir Robert, and told poor Sir Charles, with many exaggerations, the passages he had seen between Laura and Hammersley. Tom couldn't make out, for the life of him, what Sir Charles knew and what he didn't. He played his part faithfully, and left him.

Sir Charles knew that Robert was coming this morning, and he was deeply anxious to know how Laura would receive him. He determined to make one more last appeal to her. He could not make up his mind what she meant to do. For two days she had kept silence, but she had worn a hunted desperate look, which gave him infinite disquiet in every way. He could see plainly that she had made some resolution, but what was it? Did she mean to acquiesce in the arrangement, or had she determined to lay the whole matter before Sir Robert Poyntz? I don't know what put that last idea into his head, but it was there, and would not go away. It got stronger as the two days went on—got so strong now that it seemed a certainty; and in going to seek for Laura he felt that he was going to hear his doom from her lips.

" Where is Miss Seckerton? " he asked of a servant in the hall.

" In the breakfast-room, Sir Charles. Sir Robert Poyntz is with her."

" How came he there? Who showed him in? "

" Parker (the butler) showed him in, a quarter of an hour ago," said the guilty-looking man, turning scarlet.

" Who opened the door to him? "

" I did, Sir Charles."

" You and Parker pack out of this house in an hour! How much did Sir Robert give you, you rascal? "

" Only two sovereigns, sir ; upon my soul, only two sovereigns ! "

" Go and tell Parker to be out of the house in an hour— never to set face on me again ; I shall do him a mischief if he does."

And so he was too late ! And Laura was alone with the

man—at this moment, in her desperation, betraying her father's cause to Sir Robert. What was actually passing in that room we have seen already. Meanwhile Sir Charles' temper and judgment had both given way, under the long-continued strain of anxiety; and he strode towards the drawing-room, believing himself ruined, to announce his ruin to his wife and her mother.

They were sitting in their usual places—Lady Emily writing letters, and Lady Southmolton, having just finished her devotional reading for the morning, knitting. The dear old lady had three times the quickness of wit of her daughter. She no sooner set eyes on her son-in-law's face than she rolled up her knitting, stuck the pins in it, put it aside on the Bible, and folding her hands, said, "My poor Charles—my poor dear Charles! Come, tell us all about it quietly; what is it?"

At these words Lady Emily looked up, and when she saw her husband's ghastly terrible face she began to cry. All the training in the world would never make that fat silly body into a heroine, like her mother. She was almost entirely in a state of useless collapse in the conversation which followed.

"I want to ask you two some questions, and to tell you some news. First, I want to ask you this: Had either of you any idea that Laura became attached to that unfortunate young gentleman Poyntz-Hammersley, whom I, like a ruined old lunatic as I am, admitted into familiarity?"

The old lady did not answer Sir Charles at once. She addressed herself to her daughter, who, as her experienced eye showed her, was making every possible preparation for making a fool of herself, and was very nearly ready to begin the performance. She said: "Emily, my love, there is nothing like the most perfect calmness in family affairs of this kind. If you do not find yourself equal to being calm, I shall use such influence as I possess as a mother to persuade you to leave the room."

Lady Emily went no further with her preparations. She

merely, forgetting that weight had come with years, cast herself into an easy-chair, which creaked, but bore up nobly, and bided her time. A little bird tells me that at this time, feeling safe under the guidance of that noble old generalissimo her mother, her face assumed an expression of the most intense curiosity; but this is merely hearsay tittle-tattle.

The old lady turned then to her son-in-law, and said : " My dearest Charles, you take us utterly by surprise. That sort of thing has happened, I know, and will probably happen again; but with regard to our Laura, I won't believe a word of it."

" Why was the match broken off between Laura and Hatterleigh ? Had this anything to do with it ? "

" *Laura* broke off the match. Neither of them have ever deigned any explanations; but this had nothing to do with it. It is utterly untrue from beginning to end. May I ask what grounds you have for such a monstrous question ? "

" You are very good to me. Why don't you upbraid me with my insensate folly for allowing them to ride about together ? It is all too true ! "

" Charles, come here and kiss me." (He did so.) " My poor dear boy, who has been putting this nonsense into your head ? Come, tell me."

" Squire."

" A tipsy old goose ! Let us dismiss the subject; it is so utterly below our contempt. What on earth has made you bring up such a subject, at the very time when we are all so anxious that matters should go well with our gallant young friend over the water ? "

" I fear it is terribly true. Now let me ask you, what sort of mood is Laura in this morning ? "

" Now we are coming to common-sense," said the kind old lady. " Why, I am sorry to say our Laura is not in one of her best moods—a trifle rebellious against our designs for her happiness. I don't suppose for an instant that *you* have let those little designs of ours reach her; but they *have* reached her, and she is in a mood. She must not meet that man at present. You must take us to London, and all will go well. Time! time!"

Sir Charles leant his back against the chimney-piece. "I have told her," he said quietly, "with my own fool's lips, all those little designs for her happiness; and he has bribed my servants, and at this present moment is closeted with her in the breakfast-room."

Lady Southmolton lost her self-possession, for the first and only time in that part of her history which we have to relate. She unfolded her two white hands, and spread them abroad before her. "Then I can only say," she said, in a tone which was almost shrill, "that the whole thing is off, and that we may give it up utterly and for ever! Laura is in a mood this morning which I decline to describe. She has turned on her mother and on me, and has denounced us for selling her to the highest bidder; has told us to our faces that if there was such a thing as an Anglican convent, she would enter it to-morrow. She said that all which prevented her entering a Papist one was, first that she loathed Popery, and secondly that there was some other reason—in short, got incoherent in her anger. My sweet Charles, it was a good scheme enough; but since that foolish young man has chosen to treat her as he would have treated a girl sent out to India to marry the first man she could catch, the whole thing is over. It was a pretty scheme, but it is a scheme of the past. Think no more about it. We shall do well enough with her yet."

"Have you any idea what Laura's second reason for not entering a convent was?" asked Sir Charles.

"Not the slightest."

"I can tell you. Robert Poyntz is my creditor for eighty thousand pounds. He can 'annex' this estate whenever he chooses. Our only chance of pulling through was his marriage with Laura."

At this point Lady Emily did make a fool of herself. I

don't think that anything would be gained by describing a silly woman in hysterics. It was her first trial, and she broke down under it. I only wish the reader to understand that she did it thoroughly, and took her time about it.

But she was quiet enough at last to let the conversation proceed. Lady Southmolton—who had risen from her chair, and had helped Sir Charles to pacify her—was the first to resume the conversation. She took her old attitude and said, with her kind old smile—

" Well, my dearest Charles, my dear friend and son for so many years, and so you are ruined ? "

" Utterly ! "

" Well, son, we shall have to go to Germany, and live on my money. The principal thing we have to think of is where. *I* should like Brunswick ; but the Duke is not married, and he is horribly rich ; and it is *not* cheap, whatever they may say. Dresden, dear, is very pleasant and gay, but it is horribly cold in winter ; and I am a fanciful old woman, and object to the statues of August der Stark—they are an outrage to public morality ! Hesse is dull, Ems and Wiesbaden dissipated."

" But is there no hope from Laura ? " asked Sir Charles.

" Not the least," she answered. ' She is in one of her obstinate moods. I don't blame your family. The Seckerton blood, my dear Charles, never shows any obstinacy. This is the Sansmerci blood, which I have unfortunately transmitted to your family, and for which I owe you all apologies. She is behaving to-day so exactly like Southmolton's father, that I am ashamed to look you in the face. She has not certainly put the red-hot poker in the coalscuttle, as Lord Southmolton did to annoy me, the first time we went and stayed with him ; but she shows the blood. It is all my fault, Charles. Come, can't I make you laugh—— ? Well, then, listen to an old woman, and let us return to the subject in hand. My dearest boy— Brussels—— "

The dear old lady's quaint consolations came to an end

here, and were never resumed again. The butler—the proscribed and banished Parker—threw open the room-door, and announced

"Sir Robert Poyntz!"

Chapter XLVI

SIR CHARLES was still standing with his back against the chimney-piece : Lady Emily had sunk back in a chair, and the old lady was as she always was. Sir Charles advanced with *empressement* : Lady Emily rose and bowed, but was in terror of her red eyes. The only one of the three who kept their presence of mind was the old lady. She resumed her knitting very carefully, and said : " Now, here is Sir Robert Poyntz, for instance. If he has his family's manners, he will back an old woman up against both of you. Don't you think Brussels the most charming place on the Continent, sir? You have never been there—well, you may admire it for all that. I have never been to the Mauritius ; but I admire ' Paul and Virginia.' "

" What do you want me to say, Lady Southmolton ? " said Sir Robert, laughing ; " I will say anything you wish."

" You are very *maladroit*, young gentleman. India is a good school of arms ; don't force me to say that it is a bad school of manners. You should have *known* what I wanted you to say ; or, failing that, should never have committed such a *gaucherie* as to ask me."

" I am very sorry," said the young fellow, laughing ; " but something has happened this morning which has made me forget the few manners I ever had."

" We can see that, sir," said Lady Southmolton. " None of your Indian manners here, sir! Do you know, sir, that I am one of the most terrible old women in England ; and that if you forfeit my good word, society is closed to you, sir? You are behaving with the most unbecoming levity in my most awful presence, sir; what do you mean by it?"

" I am not a bit afraid of you, Lady Southmolton," said Sir Robert; " I am afraid of no one this morning."

The kind old lady looked round, to see if any more of what some folks call " chaff " was necessary. No; the brave old lady had held the field long enough. Sir Charles and Lady Emily were both perfectly calm; but as she looked round, her eye lighted on the face of Sir Robert Poyntz. She said at once, " Come here to me, immediately; I want to look at your face."

He came, and knelt before her. She looked into his face three or four times, but she was baffled. She recognised his wondrous personal beauty in a moment; and she saw something else at once which puzzled her extremely—it was the look of his eyes. *She* knew well enough what was the cause of that tender brilliance in those eyes. The man was a successful lover—she could see that fast enough. And the man had just been closeted with her own Laura, with a previously-declared intention of making love to that imperially obstinate young lady; he had come from that audience-chamber with that flash in his eyes, instead of looking like a whipped hound. Had Laura been false to all her teaching? Had she allowed this man to be successful with her after his declared intention, on the very first interview, instead of decently fencing him off, for weeks, for months, to save appearances? Her own Laura could never have done that—it was a monstrous impossibility! Yet there was that light in the man's eyes, which she could not mistake; and then came, sudden and swift, the thought, " What if Laura *had* acted up to my teaching—what else could she have done ?" If she had ruined all her future prospects of happiness by allowing herself to be won too easily by this man, whom had she, poor Laura, to thank for giving herself to this enraptured fool, Sir Robert Poyntz? No one but Lady Southmolton herself. She was puzzled and frightened.

She said, " Get up, sir, and tell your story—you puzzle me. I am an old woman. Get up, and explain that light in your eyes."

He rose up, and turned to Sir Charles Seckerton. " My dear Sir Charles," he said, " I am your debtor for five hundred pounds."

" It pleases you to say so."

" I owe you five hundred pounds for a horse of yours, which I borrowed, and which was drowned. I mean ' The Elk.' Do you really mean to say that you have not recognised me yet, and I laughing in your face all yesterday ? "

" Are you Hammersley ? "

" Of course I am. Has my beard altered me so much then ? "

Lady Southmolton cared to hear no more. She went on with her work. The story had lost its interest for her, for she had read the *dénouement* in Sir Robert's eyes. Her only thought was, " Can I get these three to hold their tongues? Everything has gone well, and will go well if they will only talk about the weather and the crops, and let the Laura business stand over for a month. This man must have made it safe with her, when he was down here masquerading. What did Lady Herage mean by deceiving us so shamefully? And to think of the madness of Charles! He must — unless he is blind, unless he had got utterly idiotic over his pecuniary affairs—have seen the whole of this going on under his own nose, at the very time that he believed this young gentleman to be penniless and illegitimate. And Laura! This accounts for much, however. One never knows these girls. I would have gone bail for her discretion—in fact, I did so not ten minutes ago. I hope to goodness there will be no declaration for a month: we can defy the world then! I wonder how far she went with him ? And the man was drowned, and buried—at least had a stone put up to him, which is the same thing. I am not in the habit of being utterly puzzled: but I am now. I wonder if the four have brains enough among them to avoid any sentimentalism for a month?"

They had. Sir Charles had shown his wish to have no further explanations at present, by testifying the most elaborate commonplace surprise and pleasure in a humorous manner. Lady Emily, after having done the same thing in a less degree, left the room and returned with Laura, who was formally introduced to the man who had kissed her a quarter of an hour before, as an utter stranger. Laura! Laura! you artful young lady, you carried the farce too far, when you looked at him with languid curiosity. You overdid your part, my Lady Poyntz; and very nearly caused your outraged grandmother to forget her manners for the first time in her life, and burst out laughing.

"Will you walk, my dear Sir Robert?" asked Sir Charles; and it appeared that he would. They went out on to the terrace together, and then Sir Charles said, turning suddenly on him—

"I must have explanations, Robert, on all except one point. That I can't allow to be touched. I—I can't explain. Now I have *you* to deal with—Hammersley to deal with. I—I *won't* explain. I am not afraid of you. I am Sir Charles Seckerton of Leighton Court once more, and you are little Bob Poyntz, the ill-tempered boy. I won't explain what point I refer to. I have been looking at your face, and I am puzzled. I know how you bribed my servants, and where you have been: on that point I will not have one word of explanation."

"Not for worlds!" said Sir Robert. "You must be very angry with me. I have served you very badly. We must leave that point quite alone at present; then we can defy the world! *Are* you very angry with me, sir? Can you ever forgive me?"

"One will try to forgive a man to whom one owes as much as eighty thousand pounds."

" So much as that ! Then I must take the hounds from you as soon as —— What am I talking about ? I was trespassing on forbidden ground. Dear Sir Charles, what explanations do you want ? "

Sir Charles wanted to know his history, and how he had come here.

Poyntz told him the same story he had told Laura, up to the point where he was left nearly penniless in London.

" And what did you do then, sir ? " said Sir Charles, severely. " I must have everything explained ; my position demands it."

Poyntz looked once at the old man, and did not know whether to be pained or pleased. He knew the awful strait that Sir Charles was in ; and he did not know whether to be pained or pleased at this fresh self-assertion on the part of the poor old gentleman, the very first moment he felt himself safe. Knowing everything, he was a little pained, on the whole. Knowing everything, he could not help wishing that this extravagant and somewhat selfish old gentleman had tried, after the terrible lesson he had had, to develop himself into something better and newer, instead of trying to reassert himself back into his old position. As the day went on, Sir Robert Poyntz wished this more and more, as Sir Charles grew more and more stilted and pompous ; but, shrewd as he was, he did not know everything. Sir Charles' self-assertion for the next week was only what vulgar people call " company manners." It was the height of discretion. Things had to be hushed up, and among them all they hushed up the matter most perfectly—the proof of which is that no one but you and I know the real truth of *it*. The Downes faction don't know the truth yet. " He vowed he would win her. He came down disguised, disclosed himself to her father and mother, and won her affections. He fled to India to avoid his creditors." That is Constance Duchess of Pozzi d'Oro's story to this day.

Poyntz said, while walking on the terrace, " You ask me for explanations about my life after I was left destitute ? You have no right to do so *now*. Do you understand that ? "

" Most perfectly, Robert—most perfectly."

" But in a week or so you *will* have the right. Do you understand that also ? "

" No," said Sir Charles. " Don't you see, my dear boy, that, under present circumstances, I mustn't understand that ? Your good sense will show you that I am Sir Charles Seckerton and you are Sir Robert Poyntz for the next three weeks, or, if the women don't object, say a fortnight. Before a fortnight has passed I couldn't outrage the County by understanding anything of the kind."

" Well, then," said Sir Robert, with a laugh in his eyes, which would have been visible in his mouth also had it not been clouded with his golden beard, " will you receive my explanations as a dear old friend of our family ? "

" No, Robert. I demanded them as my right in my position as chief man of this part of the County. Consider me as dead, and that you are making them to Downes, who will succeed me. But go on."

" Do you remember me as a boy ? " he asked.

" I can remember you."

" Was I not a fearful young ruffian ? "

" You and your brother used to quarrel and fight a great deal."

" I was a fearful young ruffian. Perhaps it is complaisance, perhaps it is want of recollection, which makes you shake your head, but it is true. Shall I prove it to you ? When I had been about two months at Eton, the master of my house and Hawtrey were talking about me. My master said, ' That boy is more like a devil than a human being ; I cannot think what to do with him.' ' Shall I expel him ? ' said the Doctor. ' No,' said the other, ' for he is not vicious, and would burn his right hand off sooner than lie ; but he's so fiendishly fierce and wild.'

'Won't the others lick him into shape?' said the Doctor. 'No,' said the other; 'there is no one in the house dare face him; he is the most fearful irreclaimable little savage I ever saw.' So they spoke of me that day. That night was probably the most eventful of my whole life.

"The last thing I did before I went to bed was to have a perfectly causeless fight with a boy a stone heavier than myself, about a matter provoked entirely by my own evil temper. He thrashed me at last, and I went to bed swearing, and when I was alone sobbed myself to sleep with impotent rage. I had slept but very little time when I was awoke by a light in my eyes; and I started wildly up, with clenched fists, thinking they were come to bully me.

"There was a touch, sir, on my clenched hand which made me open it. Ah, sir, I can feel it now—the touch of five long delicate bony fingers, very warm and dry, but very gentle. I sat up in bed, and looked into the face of the owner of those fingers, and grew still, and stayed the curse which was on my lips. I never uttered that curse, sir, and (I speak no romance) I never spoke to that person before then or since.

"It was Lorimer, one of the biggest boys in the school: a tall, gaunt, weak boy, who could never play, but who must have played at some time or another, for he was appealed and referred to in almost everything by the others. I had noticed him about often. I had seen him gently making the peace between little boys, and preventing their fighting. I had seen him walking with masters. He had been ill once, and I had heard all the boys asking one another how the 'Colonel' was that morning; whereas other boys had died, and there had been no great talk about it. I was so utterly unpopular that I had no confidant to ask about him; yet I had got up a sort of languid interest in him. He was not in my house, and yet here he was, sitting on my bed, holding the candle to my face, and stroking my hair.

" I spoke not one word—he began. He told me, word for word, the conversation he had overheard about me, between the Doctor and the Master, but I remained perfectly dumb ; then he said—

" ' My poor fellow, try to do better. I know you can if you choose. Such a one as you were never made for destruction. Has no one ever told you of the Christ who died for you ? '

" Before heaven, Sir Charles Seckerton, nobody ever had, save one—old Mrs. Squire, my nurse, the woman at whose deathbed I first met Laura ! With the exception of her quaint Calvinistic teaching, I was as utterly neglected, as regards religious thought, as any wretched boy who sweeps the streets. I knew my Catechism, Old Testament chronology, and so forth, just as I knew my Ovid ; but with regard to my religious teaching, hers was all I had ever had, for my tutors had given me none whatever. What wonder that I shook my head at him ? "

" ' Will you come to me, my boy, and let me talk to you ? '

" I remained silent as Memnon at midnight. He little dreamed how soon the sun would rise on me, and raise harmonies from my dead granite. He gave me one more melancholy look from his large brown sunken eyes—I shall never forget those eyes any more, Sir Charles——"

A long silence. Two turns up-and-down the terrace, without a word spoken on either side.

" His footfall had scarcely died away upon the stairs when I arose. I was at that time, poor little wretch of thirteen as I was, in a general rebellion against the world. I think that my idea was, that anything in the shape of constituted authority was a thing to be opposed, kicked, bitten, and generally defied, by every person of the least spirit. I don't know why I took that resolution into my head, but I know that I held to it with the most astounding resolution—with as great resolution as I did to the new line of conduct on which I had determined when I got out of bed, lit a candle, and picked up my Riddle and Arnold and my Livy out of the corner where I had hurled them in a paroxysm of rage, before I put out the light. Part of my plan had been to refuse learning anything, to make myself celebrated as the very worst boy in the school, and revenge myself on the world by getting expelled. I never slept that night till my work was finished.

" I rose in the morning a perfectly different person. I rose in my class. I was very gentle and civil to everyone ; I gave way in every direction. I made no concealment, nor any assertion of the change in me ; and before a fortnight was gone, I began to be recognised as a good fellow. The bitterest thing of all was that they said, in my hearing, that it was the thrashing Yelverton had given me before I went to bed that had changed me so. Could you have stood that and made no sign ? "

" No ! I couldn't have stood that."

" *I* did ; and won popularity in spite of it. You wonder at this sudden change—indeed, I do myself. You say ' he was more like a fiend than a boy, by all accounts ; and yet, because another boy sat on his bed for ten minutes, he turned out one of the best-remembered fellows at Eton.' You *know* I was popular."

" Indeed, Willy Downes represented you as being most popular."

" I don't know that one ought to wonder. I am very resolute—I was very resolute to prove myself a *mauvais sujet*, and was equally so to make myself the most popular fellow in Eton—equally so after somebody said something which sent me to India. I wish someone would guide my resolutions—I will be answerable for carrying them out. Besides, poor Lorimer's visit had a sentimental effect on me. Do you know that I am a bit of a poet, and have written verses ? "

Sir Charles, not seeing what else to say, said that many other perfectly respectable people had done the same thing.

" I know," said Sir Robert. " But I want to tell you

about Lorimer again. I never spoke to that fellow, and never would speak to him. Not one living soul in the world, except you and I, knows that he came to my bedside that night. I made one of my mulelike resolutions; and I said, ' He shall see the fruits first, and then we shall talk more as equals.' The last time I saw him was nearly the end of the half-year. I had been doing what I had often done lately—making peace between two boys, one of whom had called the other a liar. I did not succeed, because one must fight over that, you know; but I was trying to get a retraction, and I said, ' What is the good of giving the lie ?—He believed what he said—Do be reasonable, old fellow,' and all that sort of thing; when I turned round and saw Lorimer. *He* stopped the fight, and then he turned smiling to shake hands with me. But the half-year was not over, and I was perfectly resolute in my mulishness; I turned away. I never saw him again."

" Left, I suppose ? " said Sir Charles, who was thinking of a good many things.

" I went away for the holidays to our cousins, the Dorsetshire Poyntzes (where I always went for vacations), who were exceedingly sorry to have such a young ruffian foisted upon them. But I won the battle there, sir. The girls cried when I came away. I was resolute that they should love me, and I made them. Then my half-year's silence with Lorimer was finished; and I girded up my loins, and ran from Slough, in nine minutes forty seconds, to meet him, leaving my things to come on in a fly."

" And I guess that he had left ? "

" Dead, sir—dead of consumption! When it was announced in school they wondered why I burst into such a tempest of tears. Others cried too, a few of them, but none like me. And that interview betwixt him and me is known only to you and I—to God and himself. The fellows of my time, at Eton, believe to this day it was the thrashing I got from poor dear Yelverton the night before."

Several turns were taken up-and-down the terrace before either spoke. Sir Charles had by this time found out that things were going well with him. He was the first to speak—

"Now, I am going to have no more sentimentality. I have adjured you, on your allegiance to the County, to tell me, the head of that County, what you did with yourself that year in which you were missing. You have practically refused, and put me off with romantic stories which have made me cry, whereas I want to laugh. Come Bob, old boy, tell me all about it. I used to tip you; let me have my fun for my money. What did you do?"

"I had rather not say; I am ashamed of myself. But what *could* I do?"

"Out with it."

"Well, I rode steeplechases. Let's have no more of this."

"I suppose I mustn't ask your imperial highness how it was you favoured *me* with a visit; and what the deuce Sir George Herage meant by sending you here under false colours?"

"I hardly know what you mean. The facts are these. I was riding a horse for sale there, and Sir George Herage recognised me, and I rode some horses for him; and he promised to hold his tongue about me, and who I was; and then there was a confounded row about one of the girls—I never said six words to the girl; and then Harry came to stay there, and there was a general row. Harry denounced me in the stableyard; and then Sir George told me privately that you wanted a fellow, and I thought I would come and see the old place, for I was hunted to death; and I came, and no one knew me but Tom Squire and his mother. I was very happy here. I got very fond of you. I bullied you royally, though, didn't I?"

"You did indeed. But they said you had hunted at Pau?"

"That will pass for truth; I was there six weeks."

"Steeplechasing?"

"Oh, hang the steeplechasing! Don't bring *that* up again."

"But we were always hearing from your brother that you were in India?"

"A pure fiction of Harry's, which he put about when I disappeared from society. It was convenient enough for me. *I* never contradicted it. I never went to India, as you will hear, until a year ago."

"There is one other thing I must ask you. Lady Herage sent us word that you were the illegitimate brother (don't laugh) of yourself and Harry; that is why I received you as I did?"

"That must be poor Harry's doing; that bears his mark altogether."

"Is there such a person?"

"There is. Harry wrote to me about him the other day, asking me to take care of him; but I have never seen him in my life. Now, I want to ask you one thing. When you take into consideration how utterly lonely and neglected I have been all my life, do you pronounce that I have done well or ill?"

"I think you have done wonderfully well!"

Chapter XLVII

"IN time," said Sir Charles, "we shall find out how you came to be drowned. How pleasant and old-timelike your voice sounds to me, Robert! I was very fond of you."

Sir Robert laid his hand on the old gentleman's shoulder and went on—

"I was very happy here. I could not have stayed after Harry came, of course, but my visit was cut short accidentally."

"Indeed!"

"Yes. It happened all in one minute, that an irrepressible sense of my degradation and uselessness came over me—was forced on me. I took one of my sudden resolutions, and in ten minutes was turning old Squire out of bed to put it in force."

Sir Charles asked no questions about the cause of this singular resolution, but thought the more.

" I wanted him to get me ' The Elk ; ' I ordered him to do so. I need not tell you he would sooner obey a Poyntz than a Seckerton. In ten minutes more I was in the saddle, ready for a wild ride of five miles across the sands to Berry Head, before the flowing tide."

" In the name of heaven, what made you so mad ? "

" I partly wanted to fly from the place, and partly I wanted, with my usual impetuosity, to get into action at once ; and the doing something desperate and wild suited my humour too. Tom Squire did not know where I was going until he saw me turn for the sands ; and then he startled the night with a cry which I should have thought would have reached you, and ran after me. When I was a few hundred yards out on the sands, I turned. The Point was black behind me, and nothing was distinguishable under the dark hanging woods ; but there came a wild shout of despair from them, which was repeated twice and died off into a wild wail ; and I was alone far out on the sands, with the crawling sea on my right. I steered by the light on Brinkley Cleve. When I looked back I could see only one light—that from a window in your house. It was the only light for very far, and I waved my hand in farewell to it."

" It was the light in my daughter's room ; we calculated on the circumstance at the time."

" When I was, as I guessed, about half-way across, I began to see the utter folly of which I had been guilty : before I guessed that the water was less than two hundred yards off, it suddenly slid past the horse's feet ; and though I managed to splash out of it again, it was only for a moment, for it was all round. My pace became a walk, and

I was, I guess, two miles from shore. I had a presentiment, which almost amounted to a certainty, that I should come to no harm; but things began to look very awkward indeed, and I began to shout. The water was above the horse's girths before a boat was near enough to answer me. I got on board. The poor horse neighed to me, as though to ask me by what means we had come into this strange position, but contentedly followed the boat out into water deep enough for him to swim. I held his bridle, and encouraged him with my voice; but the swell was a little too heavy, and before we were half-way to the shore his head went down; and I, finding that I was only dragging a deadweight, let go of the bridle, and that was the last of 'The Elk.'

" Now a new idea seized me, which was in many ways pleasing to me. I determined to disappear, leaving no traces of myself. By giving the men—who were Teignmouth men, not likely to land here—a couple of pounds, and pretending that I should get into trouble about the horse, I persuaded them to say nothing about it. They, after a night's fishing, landed me at Teignmouth. I immediately went off to London, to Harry. I threw myself upon his generosity, and asked him to get me a commission in a regiment going to India. The negotiation would have gone right from the first, if I had not somewhat foolishly threatened, in case of his refusal, to disgrace the family by enlisting in a dragoon regiment. To my dismay he jumped at the idea, and was very much taken with it indeed. He said it was a capital way to make an ass of myself without any expense, and strongly urged me to do so. He saw he was teasing me, and went on ; but my imperturbable patience was too much for him, and he yielded. I think you know everything now."

" Are you going to stay in the Army ? " asked Sir Charles, in an offhand manner, as if it was no concern of his.

" That is exactly as Laura chooses," said the heedless Robert.

" I beg your pardon," said Sir Charles, quickly.

" I was saying," answered Robert, reddening, " that it is just exactly as Lawrence chooses—Sir John Lawrence, you know. He has been kind to me, and I shall be entirely guided by him in this matter."

Sir Charles said " Yes, I understand;" and the next time that Robert made a joke he laughed at it very loud and long, to make up for his self-denial on this occasion.

There remains but little more to tell. Another chapter, and our tale is finished.

Chapter XLVIII

A YEAR or more passed by, and the Great Indian Mutiny had burnt itself into darkness and silence. It was all over, except telling the tale of the dead. Still, in London and elsewhere, after each mail houses would be seen with the shutters up for a week; and bevies of girls, who but a week ago were dancing in their finest clothes, would begin to creep out at dusk in deepest mourning, and say, to those who knew them well enough to speak to them in their grief, " that mamma was not so wild to-night, but oh, that it was so very very dreadful——! "

In these times—the times when the excitement had died out, and the dull grief was making itself felt, and we were beginning to count the cost—it so happened that Lord Hatterleigh was spending the last few days of his honeymoon at Dover.

He had married a lady who was pleased to call herself Scotch, for what reason I am unable to explain. Her father, the Marquis of Ericht, had certainly large possessions in Scotland; but if he claimed to be of any particular race, it should have been to be Scandinavian-French. However, he chose to call himself Scotch, to wear a kilt, and to have that other barbarous English invention, the bagpipes, to play to him at meals. His daughter also was a perfect devotee on the matter of Scotch nationality, and it was no one's business but their own ; and therefore we will yield so far, under protest, as to say that Lord Hatterleigh had married a Scotch lady—and an excellent good business he had made of it.

With her we have nothing to do. She was a lady at all points, and we can or need say no more. With regard to him we may say a few words :—

He had grown into a big and somewhat handsome man ; now that he had let his long black beard grow, he would pass muster anywhere—nay, do more than pass muster. His broad shoulders were still so loosely hung, that one could not help wishing that some drill-sergeant had taken him in hand, and forced him to hold his really fine head higher. There was only one symptom of his old muffishness left about him. He had clung to that old valetudinarian self-considering creed, which he had got, after all, from his mother, as long as he could ; but he had been driven from point to point of it—first by Laura Seckerton (now Lady Poyntz), and secondly by Lady Jane Portobello, his present bride—until he had hardly any of it left. The old creed was very dear to him, but he had been laughed out of it. He made a stand at a certain point : he took to wearing spectacles. That there was nothing the matter with his eyesight he had to confess to Bradbury, at whose shop he bought his spectacles. And so Bradbury gave him a pair with flat glass lenses. These spectacles were only the last appeal for extra-consideration by a man who had been taught by his mother to appeal to the pity of society, and who was growing out of that humbug rapidly. What need to say more of Lord Hatterleigh ? Some say they know him, and that he is showing an honesty and, what is more, a power which is making itself felt. You could count on your fingers the men who are able, so well as he, to remember old inconsistencies, and to hang them up to ridicule.

Leighton Court

It so happened that Lord Hatterleigh and his wife were walking on the pier at Dover, up-and-down, taking their airing in the full blast of a south-easterly wind, when they noticed a movement among the sailors on the quay, and at the same time saw that a large ship was coming into the harbour. He asked the reason of the harbourmaster, who was known to him.

" It is the *Supply*, my lord, with invalided troops from India. We sent a boat out to her, and the officer commanding the soldiers has persuaded the captain to put in here. He prefers taking his men on by rail to Chatham, to forcing the ship round to Chatham by sea. There are many dead, and many dying."

" My love," said Lord Hatterleigh to his bride, " we had better go home to lunch."

" George," she said, " I must see these men land. I don't want to go back to lunch ; I must see this."

" It will not be at all a fit sight for you," said Lord Hatterleigh. " Your mother would be furious if she heard of it."

" But we needn't tell her," said Lady Hatterleigh.

" But my mother would never forgive me," said Lord Hatterleigh.

" Then tell her to mind her own business. Do let me stay, George ! "

After this appeal there was no more to be said, and there never is. When will women gain the secret of power ?

The ship was alongside the pier by this time, and the London, Chatham, and Dover Company had a special train ready for them ; and the victims of the war began to creep ashore—some nearly well, but looking like old men ; some maimed, walking on crutches ; some beyond everything, carried with hanging limbs in the arms of the sailors. But there was one among them on whom everyone looked with greater interest than the others, and that was the officer in command of this regiment of ghosts, himself the most ghostly object there.

He was a very tall and handsome man, in full uniform, covered with Crimean and the older Indian decorations. One armless sleeve was looped up over his breast; but it was not that which drew all eyes to him, for there were plenty like him in that respect—it was his face. There were pale faces there, but none so deadly white as his; and there were sad faces too, but none so sad and worn as his. Lady Hatterleigh called her husband's attention to him, saying—

"If I look at that man much longer I shall begin to cry."

Lord Hatterleigh turned and looked the way she indicated, and as he did so exclaimed—

"Bless me, how dreadful! It is Hilton; and his arm gone."

His good-natured soul overflowed at the sight of his old acquaintance in such a plight; and he made towards Hilton, and took his solitary hand in both of his. A very faint smile came over Hilton's face when he recognised Lord Hatterleigh behind his beard and spectacles, but it died away again.

"Come, you can laugh still, you see; was it my spectacles you were laughing at, or my beard? I won't ask how you are, for you are very ill indeed, and must be taken care of. You must come to Grimwood instantly, and my wife shall nurse you. I am married now, you know. Hilton! Hilton! what have you been doing with yourself? You have been at death's door. You must come home with us to Grimwood directly, and be nursed. The women will all be fighting who is to attend on you. The Duchess of Pozzo d'Oro is at Hoxworthy with her father; you remember Constance Downes? And again," he continued, taking off his spectacles, and fixing an honest manly eye on General Hilton's, "there is Lady Poyntz; she would form one of the Nightingale sisterhood, my dear fellow. How you and Laura used to squabble and fight, to be sure! She is down there also——"

" Lady Poyntz ! " said Hilton, clutching his arm ; " is she *there* ? "

" Not the dowager, you know ; not Maria Huxtable— Laura Seckerton, I mean. She pitched me overboard, you know, and married Sir Robert Poyntz, who had been down there before, masquerading, as a foxhunter from Leicestershire, and got drowned, and buried, and sundry. Not that Miss Seckerton did not behave nobly, sir—but that is not to the purpose. You must come to Grimwood, and all the old set will vie with one another in taking care of their dear old Bayard."

General Hilton did not speak for nearly a minute ; and then he said, very low, but without a quaver in his voice :—

" How monstrous kind you are, Hatterleigh ! If I ever had been upset in a sentimental way, I should be so now. I am not all sure that I could have answered you a moment sooner than I did, though. I am very weak and ill, and your wonderful kindness has, I will confess, discomposed me. Will you do something for me ? "

" Is there anything I would not ? " said Lord Hatterleigh.

" I want you to go to the ' Lord Warden,' and ask if anyone is waiting for me there. Lest you should be puzzled, I must tell you that I had persuaded the captain to come in close enough to land me here. I thought that Chatham, or even London, would not do so well under the circumstances. We have all had to land here, as you see."

Lord Hatterleigh's face grew pensive, but rapidly began to brighten again.

" It is well as it is," he said. " I was beginning to get uneasy at what seemed to me an extraordinary conjunction of circumstances ; now I see it was designed. You asked me if I would go to the ' Lord Warden ' for you with an enquiry. I can answer that enquiry for you, and the answer is ' Yes.' "

Nothing more worth mentioning was said. The special

train, with the wounded soldiers, moved away, leaving General Hilton, with Lord and Lady Hatterleigh, standing on the pier. There were a few feeble cheers as the carriages moved on, and a few wasted hands were waved towards the kind and gentle general, who, in all his own agonies, had crept about from deck to deck, to see to the wants of the strange soldiers who had been committed to his care.

Then the three walked to the hotel; and Hilton soon was alone in his rooms, lying on a sofa, watching the door, waiting eagerly for each footfall on the corridor. But no footfall came, and after a time he turned from the door, and buried his face in his hands.

There was no footfall in the corridor, and he never heard the door open; but after a time he was aware of a presence in the room, and he said, " Is it you ? "

And a voice answered, " George ! "

" Maria, come to me—oh, Maria, come to me ! I have been through one hell of blood ferocity, and doubt about the righteousmess of my cause; and since then through another physical agony, of ghastly remorse, of wild triumph. Ever since I lost my arm, and the fever came on me, and brought me to what you see, there has been a devil dancing before me, and crying, ' On which side is the Dacoitee ? On which side is the Dacoitee ?—on theirs or on yours ? ' Come to me, and drive him away. Come to me, and never leave me again ! "

And so she came to him; for there was no cloud between them now. Lord Hatterleigh, coming in later, found the wild mournful look gone from his face, and the old Hilton of last year, smiling and happy, before him. " We will come to you at Grimwood after our honeymoon, Hatterleigh," he said—a promise which was fulfilled before two happy months had rolled past.

Leighton Court, Berry Morcambe (otherwise Poyntz Castle), Hoxworthy of the Downes's, and Grimwood of the Hatterleighs, and a new one—Ewbank, the residence of General and Mrs. Hilton—are very charming country-houses, somewhat too far from London perhaps, but still very charming indeed, whose history for eighteen months seemed to be worth the telling. Their present occupants are in possession of health and happiness, apparently un-clouded.

In conclusion let me say, using far more beautiful words than any which I could write :—

> " In vertue and in holy almesse dede,
>   They liven alle, and never asonder wende,
>   Till deth departeth hem this lif they lede.
>   And fareth now wel, my tale is at an ende,
>   Now Jesu Christ, that of His might may send
>   Joye after wo, governe us in His grace,
>   And kepe us alle that ben in this place."